THE DRACULA ARCHIVES

Raymond Rudorff

RAYMOND RUDORFF was born in Berlin, Germany, in 1933 of a German father and Irish mother. He was educated at the French Lycée, London, Sloane Grammar School, London, and at London University where he took a degree in Modern History. He lived for two years in France, then worked in a London publishing firm before returning to the Continent where he now lives and writes full-time. He is married to actress and novelist, Patricia Clapton.

Rudorff has been interested in stories of the supernatural since he was a schoolboy when he contributed ghost stories to the school magazine. THE DRACULA ARCHIVES is a literary 'homage' to the Gothic novel of the 19th century, that pillar of supernatural literature.

For my father
and to John Watson
also in homage to Bram Stoker

The Dracula Archives

RAYMOND RUDORFF

SPHERE BOOKS LIMITED
30/32 Gray's Inn Road, London WC1X 8JL

First published in Great Britain in 1971 by
David Bruce and Watson Limited
© Raymond Rudorff, 1971
First Sphere Books edition, 1973

TRADE
MARK

Set in Intertype Plantin

Printed in Great Britain by
Hazell Watson & Viney Ltd,
Aylesbury, Bucks

ISBN 0 7221 7525 6

Manuscript in an Unknown Hand

Let the world think me mad or eccentric—such things are of no account to me. What the doctors may call my lunacy is, in fact, only my loyalty to an obsession—one dating from the time that I first read that book which was to change the course of my life—Bram Stoker's **Dracula**, first published in 1897 and reprinted many times throughout the world ever since. From my first encounter with the awesome personage of Count Dracula, slowly, silently, insidiously, there grew in my mind the obsession whence sprang the main purpose of my life. The Count's terrifying but shadowy figure has haunted my nights and dreams ever since.

If the eventual reader of these lines should be ignorant of the contents of this "novel" (I use inverted commas advisedly), it will be enough for him to know at this point that it treats of the horrifying adventure that befell a young solicitor, Jonathan Harker, who was summoned in his professional capacity to the Transylvanian castle of Count Dracula and there discovered his client to be leading the undead existence of a vampire, dependent for his survival on the life blood of human beings. From extracts from diaries and letters, we learn how the monstrous thing came by stealth to England, determined to extend its domain and to infect innocent souls with the taint of vampirism until finally traced back to its Transylvanian lair and destroyed by the heroes of the narrative, in particular the learned Doctor Abraham Van Helsing.

From time immemorial, men have dreamed of acquiring immortality and mastery over the powers of life and death. I believe that Count Dracula nearly succeeded in his quest before being trapped in the tragic condition of the Undead. But of the ancestry and origins of the Count, and of how he came to lead the existence of a vampire, Stoker has said little, apart from a few scattered references to the past deeds of the Dracula race. The task of exploring this dark and blood-stained past has fallen to me. Rather, let me say that I **know**, with unalterable conviction, that this was a task for which I was predestined from the very beginning and which, for reasons which belong to the realm of darkness and death, has become a compulsion.

The obsession already lay deep within me long before the shattering revelation of Stoker's book. What I had simply apprehended, Stoker indicated clearly. The path he opened I intend to tread to the very end.

Yes, deranged I may be, but who can deny the persistent and methodical way I have searched amid the shadows and the dust of forgotten archives and doom-laden vaults until I was able to put together the whole story? People have mocked me for the way I haunted the British Museum and other great libraries, and for the way in which I spent my last few pounds travelling to strange places, for the way I have ignored or spurned every material necessity. I have been reproached for neglecting my appearance, my family and friends and for keeping company with men even more eccentric than myself who shared my beliefs and applauded my zeal.

All this has been nothing to me. I have sneered at the miserable complacency of Van Helsing and his friends, realising that their discoveries were only a beginning and that their task was only half accomplished. Everything I have found substantiates the theories that have been taken for the outpourings of a scholarly lunatic and only confirms the substance of the account that Stoker vainly attempted to bring to the attention of an incredulous world until finally he was obliged to present it as fiction. Of what he was unaware and which is so vital to the unravelling of the whole mystery, I have found by my own labours. I have been led on by my intuition and by the conviction that every sacrifice, every hardship and humiliation was worthwhile could I but amass the means to make the long journey to the Borgo Pass in the spirit-haunted Carpathian mountains and search the deserted chambers of that towering, ruined castle which the guide books so strangely refrain from mentioning. The summons came to me from beyond the seas and out of the darkness of the centuries. I have answered it and kept faith with that which lies beyond the tomb. Now I stand on the threshold of ultimate triumph. Here are the papers. Who can doubt me now?

The Last Confession of
Franz von Langenfels,
September 1876

The burden of frightful memories and of my guilt is beyond endurance. For months after the fearful occurrences which conscience now compels me to relate, no wretched mortal was ever pursued more relentlessly by vengeful furies and nightmarish visions than I after that hideous night when youth and joy and reason fled for ever. Try as I may I neither can nor will free my mind from the vision of that hellish scene. What I took away with me as we fled, will be buried with me where none will ever find it yet the night is still full of horror for me and each new day is a perpetual agony of dread and foreboding . . . Before ultimate madness engulfs what little sanity still remains to me or I put an end to my existence with drugs supplied by a compliant apothecary, let me confess what we did and how Karl died. May merciful God forgive us all!

Karl, Reinhold and I were students. Reader, if you know the University of Vienna, the charms of that city and the manifold pleasures it offers young men of means, you will readily understand that academic study played but little part in our activities. Every night we would meet and sally forth to carouse and seek adventure in the narrow, ancient streets of the old city. We met with poets and painters, wastrels and scoundrels. No tavern, however disreputable, was unknown to us. Among all our fellow votaries of Venus and Bacchus, we were the keenest. We drank and laughed and loved and duelled and gambled, giving no thought for the morrow as long as our families kept us well provided with *kröner*, as long as we wore clothes of the latest cut, and as long as we could avoid the wrath of the authorities.

After a while, our dissipations assumed a more sinister aspect. The three of us came to scorn every common restraint that decency imposes, so excited were we by the fatal attraction of vice. Escaping the vigilance of our tutors and the police, we spent night after night in the most extravagant revels, returning each time to our low haunts with new recruits and renewed ardour.

Eventually and inevitably, word reached our parents of our miserable profligacy, although the worst we had managed to conceal. Strict warnings and threats of expulsion ensued, our allowances were reduced drastically and forthcoming examinations cast their shadow across our heedless days and nights. With belated diligence, we applied ourselves to our books. By dint of long, gruelling weeks of study we finally passed and then celebrated our success regally, with unprecedented extravagance, since our apparent reformation had induced our parents to loosen their purse strings again. But months of revelry in the past, followed by the rigours of prolonged study and nocturnal vigils had taken their toll of our physical powers. Unwilling for the time being to sink back again into our former life of debauchery, we resisted the blandishments of our crones and decided to depart on a tour of the mountains and forests, to avail ourselves of Nature's sweet bounty and thoroughly to repose ourselves amidst scenes of quiet beauty and majestic grandeur.

After a month of wandering through the mountains and forests of Styria, we moved further afield and reached the city of Pressburg. There we spent the night at the Rote Adler hostelry, ate a hearty dinner accompanied by many of the flasks of good wine for which it is famed and then set off northwards with fresh horses we had hired. Two days later we arrived at a small village in the valley of the Waag whose course we had been following, and took rooms for the night in the one tavern that the spot offered. We were in the highest of spirits. Karl had been singing old ballads as we rode, Reinhold entertained us with a ceaseless flow of merry quips and reminiscences and I declaimed lines from the poets of whom we were most fond. The weather was magnificent and the landscape picturesque enough to delight any painter. On either side of the road there towered imposing remains of the many fortresses that had protected the region in former times from the depredations of the Turkish invader but one such ruin in particular aroused our interest. It was set high up on a bald rock near the village and although sadly dilapidated, its high walls, crumbling battlements and mighty keep had retained much of their former imposing splendour.

"I should like to go up there and explore!" said Karl with enthusiasm.

"I should like to sketch it by moonlight!" said Reinhold who had a gift for making sketches after the Romantic manner.

"I vow it is haunted" said I.

We resolved to make an excursion to the ruins on the morrow. The idea that was to cost us so tragically dear was—alas! —born that very evening. We had dined copiously and were drinking deep of the landlord's excellent vintages when Reinhold called him over to our table and asked him about the ruined castle we proposed to visit. The good fellow's countenance clouded as he replied:

"Do you not know, Sirs? Oh, but it's an evil spot!"

Our curiosity was now fully aroused.

"It is an ill-famed place," continued the landlord with much relish, "they say that it once belonged to a noblewoman—a countess. An exceedingly evil countess! A very evil lady indeed!"

"Indeed, and how was this countess of yours so evil?" I queried.

The landlord struck a very melodramatic pose and said in a stage whisper: "They say that she was a murderess. She would lure young maidens up there while her husband was away at the wars and then—"

He paused to cross himself.

"And then?" I asked.

"Heaven help me, dear Sirs, but I do believe that it is said of her that she would drink their blood and even anoint herself in it, believing that it would preserve her beauty and prolong her life."

"The Countess Bathory!" Reinhold suddenly shouted excitedly. We all turned to look at our friend whose face betrayed extreme excitement.

"Yes!" he continued, "that is her castle is it not?"

"I believe that indeed was her name," the landlord assented.

"I know the story," said Reinhold. "But I did not know that this was her castle. Yes, my friends, we shall go there tomorrow."

"Tomorrow," said the landlord, "workmen will be there. It is a historic ruin and they have been sent by the authorities to pull down part of the tower and a wall which threatens to collapse, to the danger of visitors like yourselves."

Reinhold frowned. "That does not suit me at all. Then we shall go tonight!"

"Nay sirs, you must not!" exclaimed the landlord. "They say that evil spirits haunt those ruins. It is shunned by all save a few curious travellers such as yourselves. It has been a place of madness and blood and who knows what a man might find there? Besides the way is rough and hard. I would not go for all the gold in the world though they say that some treasure is to be found there."

13

"*We* shall go there!" said Reinhold firmly. "Karl! Franz! Will you not come with me? I shall tell you there of its sombre history and if indeed there be phantoms—why then, we shall defy them! Are we agreed?"

He looked at us expectantly while the landlord raised his arms imploringly and urged us not to contemplate so foolhardy and perilous a venture. But Karl and I readily assented to the plan. We were flushed and merry with the wine. Heedless of the landlord's warnings and direful premonitions, we agreed that on the following day in the evening after the workmen had left, we should visit the ruins and explore them thoroughly. This done we called for yet more wine to drink to the venture. Then it was that another idea insidiously suggested itself to our eager minds. We would brave superstition and mock local fears and add spice to our visit and our vacation by not only visiting the castle in the evening but by spending the entire night there. For too long we had denied ourselves the excitement we craved. The sinister reputation of the castle offered us new sensations to refresh our sensibilities that had become jaded through overmuch dissipation in the past. We would bring food and wine there and tell tales of Gothic horror and similarly entertain ourselves while defying any ghosts or devilish apparitions to appear and lend substance to the tales of the local folk. Our plan aroused such intense excitement in us that all thoughts of immediate repose were banished and we spent another hour in deliberation, while enthusing over the originality of our scheme and the prospect of buried treasure to which Reinhold mysteriously alluded. A ruined castle, the memory of hideous crimes, a wicked and bloodthirsty Countess—verily, to the totality of our perverse pleasures there would now be added the exquisite element of *fear* itself.

"Which of us has not longed to experience the delicious terrors of the supernatural?" asked Reinhold. "Shall we not add to the sum of our experience by braving the night and all its supposed terrors together?"

"The idea is most poetical," mumbled Karl who was fast becoming drowsy over his bottle.

"No person of artistic sensibility would forgo such an opportunity," I agreed solemnly.

We shook hands upon the venture and retired for the night.

The following day, despite the landlord's protestations, we hired a mule, provided ourselves with food and wines and lanterns as well as implements for digging, and began our ascent of the steep track after the last of the workmen had come down from the castle, ignoring their shouted warnings to us. The journey uphill took us the better part of an hour as the sun gradually sank lower in the heavens. Upon closer view, the walls of the great castle seemed less ruined than we had first anticipated. The stern, commanding air of the great pile, the majesty of its setting upon that desolate rock, and the wild beauty of the landscape around were all an invitation to the poet or artist. No apter setting could we imagine for fearful crimes or mysterious hauntings.

The sun was still above the rim of distant hills when we came to the main gateway. Piles of massive masonry cleared by the workmen lay on the rocky ground at the foot of the walls but the main keep and part of the inner structure had retained their roofing and, in them, a number of gaping windows and dark openings attracted our notice and seemed to lure us on in exploration of its recesses. After tethering the mule in the great courtyard, we began at once to seek for some suitable spot for our vigil and nocturnal banquet. After penetrating through an arched doorway we found ourselves in a vaulted hall of fair dimensions but bereft of furniture and decorations. An open door in a far corner led to a staircase ascending to the upper apartments of the edifice. After a glance at the ceiling reassured us that there was no imminent danger of falling debris, we began to ascend the winding steps until we came to a derelict chamber where half the wall had crumbled away. There remained a large stone fireplace, surmounted with a much-worn armorial bearing.

"The arms of the Bathory," said Reinhold who seemed to have a curiously thorough knowledge of the subject.

"What do you know of them," asked Karl, much impressed.

"Wait!" said Reinhold mysteriously, "it is a story of death and terror and darkest mystery only fit to be told by the flare of midnight torches in such a deserted spot as this. Be patient for I promise to make your flesh creep and your blood freeze ere sunrise!" The wild look in his eyes and his unholy glee would have disconcerted those who did not know him as we did for we knew of his imaginative reveries and his passionate interest in the *morbid* and *horrible*.

"What, are you frightened then?" he asked, seeing our countenances.

"Not a whit," said Karl stoutly, assuming an air of bravado as we peered about us.

We descended again to the great hall and took advantage of remaining daylight to make systematic investigation of the rest of the castle. Other steps had fallen in decay but in one corner tower we came upon a thick oaken door with rusty hinges and a great lock. Unwilling to leave any part of the castle unexplored, we tried the door which at first resisted our attempts to open it until Reinhold finally shattered the lock with a piece of stone, and the wood yielded to reveal yet another staircase whch led us to the upper storey. There a strange sight awaited us. Where a long corridor should have led to a series of apartments, there had been built a brick wall as though to seal up the chambers beyond. In the middle of this wall there gaped a jagged aperture, both high and wide enough to enable a man to pass without bending his head and besides this hole there lay some dust-laden implements of ancient manufacture as though the workmen who had breached the wall had flung down and abandoned their tools upon the completion of their task.

Passing through the aperture, we were faced by yet another door, but this lay open. Beyond it were two chambers of equal size and then a third of larger dimensions and octagonal in shape, plunged in utter darkness. Lighting candles, we saw that the windows had been bricked up and that it contained a few domestic objects, pieces of furniture, the remnants of a bed, scraps of mouldering cloth, candleholders, a table and a few other objects which gave evidence of habitation at some remote date.

"Ha!" exclaimed Reinhold, "so this is where she spent her last days!"

"Who?"

"The Countess. Who else? It was her last dwelling place."

"For how long?" I asked, shuddering at the tomb-like atmosphere of the windowless prison chamber for this is what it was.

"I shall tell you later," said Reinhold, and we fell silent again. Beyond the thickness of the walls, we could faintly hear the sighing wind of evening. A curious unease pervaded my soul as I gazed at the pathetic relics contained in the octagonal chamber. There was something unutterably oppressive and disquieting about this chamber where night had reigned unbroken for centuries. I imagined its sole tenant, shut away for ever from the light of day and the world outside, dragging out her wearisome existence in the silence of the tomb. No hermit's cell could be half as ghastly and dispiriting as this and no other

16

prison cell more filled with awful memories. Despair, futility and the dreadful languor of a futile existence that can only yearn for death's release—such was the message imparted by the chamber of living death.

"Come," said Reinhold in a commanding tone as though he were the leader of our expedition, which in truth he was. On emerging from the tower, we saw that the sun had fallen below the horizon. From somewhere in the shadows of the battlements an owl hooted thus adding to the general mournfulness of the scene. We crossed the courtyard again, and fetching lanterns from the mule pack, resumed our wanderings in the gathering dusk. We made our way through a wilderness of passages and vaulted halls where every now and again some gap in the masonry allowed a glimpse of the starry heavens and the pallid moon before we stumbled into the other chambers plunged in blackest darkness. No other sounds of life were there as we wandered save the melancholy hooting of the owl, the sighing of the warm summer breeze and our own footfalls, soft on the carpet of dust that lay so thick. Everywhere there was decay and everywhere there was the dust of centuries as we roamed through that accursed castle from which life had so utterly fled two centuries or more ago. There seemed no end to the eternal subdivisions and windings of the interior but eventually we emerged thankfully into another high-ceilinged chamber, vaster even than that with which we had begun our survey. One wall was pierced with high, pointed windows of Gothic design, whose trellised but obscured panes allowed only the feeblest rays of moonlight to straggle into the interior and reveal to our gaze a vast table of massive oak, some stools and chairs, a few tattered remnants of tapestry which had still resisted time's ravages, and a number of heavy swords and lances affixed to the walls. At the end of this great chamber, there was a dilapidated wooden gallery with steps, flanked by arched doorways on either side, and by the table, two huge iron candleholders from which we hung our lanterns.

"Here shall we hold our revels and feast tonight!" cried Reinhold. "But let us see what lies beyond!"

Due to the singular geography and bizarre design of the castle, we had come upon a part which had at first escaped our attention and which seemed more extensive than we might have supposed. Beyond the door to our right, we found a low arch and a wide flight of steps leading downwards and without hesitating, we ventured for the first time into the subterranean regions of the great building. From the foot of this wide staircase, we began to penetrate the recesses of a multitude of vaulted chambers which must once have contained stores and no doubt have provided a safe haven for vassals and the local population in times of war or siege. An intolerable gloom pervaded my spirit as we slowly wandered from one cellar to the next, stepping where no other mortal had walked for centuries and where not even the sudden scurry of a rat broke the quiet of the catacomb. But despite the depressing aspect of our surroundings, Reinhold's eagerness to continue remained no less ardent as he lifted aloft his lantern and scrutinised each chamber as though in expectation of some great discovery. His eyes gleamed as we came to the far end of one of the innumerable subdivisions of the endless crypts and beheld an arched door. With feverish excitement he began to try the door but it firmly resisted all his efforts.

"We must come back later," he said, "for we shall need the tools we have brought. Patience! The night is young. Let it suffice that we have found where we must begin our search in earnest!"

Somewhat tired by the long climb to the castle and our roamings inside it, we gladly agreed to postpone further investigations until we had refreshed ourselves and taken some repose. It was in the great hall that we decided to hold our feast. After removing the dust from the table and seats, we fetched the hampers from our mule and there began the strangest dinner we had ever had. With the fine fare we had brought, and the noble wines, our spirits soon rose as we toasted each other by the light of candles we had placed in the great iron holders, and the warm glow of a lantern suspended from a hook in the wall, and we were an island of good cheer and life amid the sea of desolation and darkness that encompassed us. Our fears gradually diminished and as we commenced to drink in earnest, we would occasionally interrupt our discourse to dwell for a moment upon the originality of our venture and our brave defiance of idle superstition and derive aesthetic pleasure from the way our shadows danced like giants on the arrassed wall.

Eventually we brought out the Tokay—the first of the bottles of that peerless wine we had brought with us. With reverence we opened the flask and filled our goblets. Upon a sign from Reinhold, we rose to our feet and drank the solemn toast he proposed:

"To the Countess Bathory, mistress of the castle!"

But what of this Countess, rumoured to have been so evil? Reinhold was no longer to keep us in suspense.

"Gentlemen and boon-companions," he said gravely, setting down his goblet after quaffing deeply, "we are the first mortals —if we accept a few workmen outside—to have set foot within these walls for more than two hundred years. We know this castle to have been abandoned and shunned since the demise of the lady whose story I am now about to relate to you—so much you have already gathered. Our minds are modern and free from superstitious bigotry but to the simpletons who inhabit this locality, no spot could be more accursed and sinister, or more frequented by the Evil One and all his fellow fiends. But let us pass from hearsay and legend to what is part of history. I know not whether there be phantoms and evil spirits here but I do not exaggerate when I tell you that hell itself could have no fiend more infamous than the noble Elizabeth Bathory, sister and cousin to kings and wife of one of Hungary's noblest warriors."

He paused and drank another deep draught before continuing:

"Elizabeth was born into the noble house of Bathory. Her father boasted one of the most illustrious lineages in the country and came of a line of warriors noted for their valour and skill. Of her mother we know little though some say she was of gypsy origin. The age they lived in was one of constant strife and danger. Centuries of savage battle and the ever-present menace of the Turkish heathen combined to produce men who were as hard and inflexible as iron, fierce-tempered and ruthless, and capable of cruelties that must now seem barely credible to gentler generations such as our own. But Elizabeth's father's ancestors were crueller than most. A sinister vein of degeneracy ran through the family lineage—ever since, it is said, that one of her forbears had contracted a sinister and ill-omened alliance. Many of her more recent ancestors had their minds blasted by madness and warped by long practice of the most extravagant follies and the most hideous cruelties. Some of the Bathory succumbed to epilepsy, one claimed to be possessed by the devil, another's inordinate cruelty was only equalled by his monstrous lust which spared neither young nor old of either sex. In addition to these melancholy vices, they were prone to an excessive love of luxury and avaricious greed yet despite such taints, their courage on the battlefield raised them to positions of eminence in the Empire and won them many royal favours and privileges and so it was with Elizabeth's father who entertained great hopes for his daughter.

"We know that she was a fair child, showing great promise of future beauty. Her childhood was often a lonely one and her only close companions were a few aged servants said to know much of local lore. From them she must have imbibed many of the dark superstitions and quaint beliefs that had still a stronger grip on many souls than the Christian faith. The country was said to be peopled by monsters, dragons and werewolves. Every forest was full of sprites and hobgoblins, every village had its old women who would mutter incantations over hideous brews and conjure the powers of darkness, and more than once there were reports of how the Evil One and the old gods were worshipped on hill-tops at dead of night and venerated in the hearts of the primitive folk of the mountains.

"Elizabeth may well have learned many secrets from her rude mentors but as the years passed she grew haughty and aloof, confiding in none and dissimulating any emotions she may have felt behind an impressive countenance in which not even the eyes mirrored the state of her inner soul. Pale as parchment was her face and large and lustrous the eyes that looked out so strangely from it. She was beautiful: men admired the delicacy of her skin, the nobility of her features, her luxuriant hair and slender, elongated fingers that seemed destined for no task more arduous than the plucking of lute-stings and the caressing of the gems for which she displayed the only deep passion observed in her.

"Her strange and disturbing beauty brought many suitors to the Bathory castle. Eventually she was betrothed to another of Hungary's noble warriors, Ferencz Nadasdy, a man of many properties, who stood high in the Emperor's favour and who had led many armies against the Turks. When news of the Emperor's assent to the match was brought to Elizabeth she was in her chamber, clad in one of her many sumptous gowns, lost in admiration of herself and caressing her flowing tresses in front of her mirror. "So be it" she said on being told of the signal honour conferred upon her and no other utterance relating to the matter was ever heard to pass her lips. She remained an enigma to all, and to none more than the triumphant Nadasdy. She would spend long hours brooding by the window in her chamber and sometimes sang strange ballads learned from an aged attendant—a Bohemian peasant woman —which caused some servitors to cross themselves when they

20

heard her. At another time, the family were astonished by the inexplicable arrival of wolves in the vicinity, long before the winter snows usually sent them down from the mountain forests. As the hunt was conducted even under the castle walls, Elizabeth was seen calling down in words that none could understand to a gigantic wolf that sat on his haunches below the tower and which only fled when in imminent danger of being slain by the hunters. On other occasions, she would wander alone into nearby woods and then return, serene and unharmed, the glimmer of a smile playing around the corners of her slim, delicately modelled lips, and a smouldering glow in her dark eyes."

Reinhold fell silent, gazing into the depths of his goblet. I poured more wine and Karl opened a fresh flask. The owl had ceased hooting and all around us there reigned the most complete silence—a silence as dense and impenetrable as the darkness that reigned in the octagonal chamber we had seen.

"She became a mystery to all," Reinhold continued, "and no sphinx ever guarded its secret more jealously. The day of the wedding came and all who were present admired Elizabeth whose beauty never shone to better advantage than it did that day when she entered the chapel arrayed in a white robe of shimmering satin, bedecked by cascades of pearls and precious gems. And it was thus that she came to the castle of her lord where she was to spend most of her life—this very domain where we now reseal our friendship and defy all ghosts!"

"To the bride!" cried Karl whom the rich and mellow wine had made slightly tipsy.

"I beg you," said Reinhold, "there is still much to tell. Despite his many absences, Ferencz was a loving and attentive husband who sought only to satisfy her every whim. Precious jewels, fine pearls, velvets and brocades from Genoa and Venice, rich silks from France—all these he gave to her. To array herself in her finest gowns and gems and spend long hours lost in contemplation of her own beauty before a mirror became an ever increasing absorption with her. Meanwhile, with the Empire menaced and in turmoil, her husband's absences grew ever longer. Alone with her mother-in-law who had come to live in the castle, she would spend the long months without Ferencz either deep in meditation or, as always, before her mirror. What had been a habit now became an obsession. Whether there were guests in the castle or not, she would change her gowns five or six times a day. Hours she spent over her caskets of jewels, playing with each gem in turn, holding it up to the light to study its myriad reflections by the wan light of a wintry day or by the glow of a candle. Sometimes, she would be found as in a trance, moving her lips as though speaking to herself although no words were uttered. Then her Ferencz would return and the great halls of the castle would again blaze with torches and be filled with the merry laughter of guests and music. A son was born to her and there was even greater rejoicing. Shortly afterwards, with Ferencz again at the wars, a change was observed in Elizabeth. She became increasingly harsh with her servants and once, after she had struck a maid who had been careless with her hair, and caused blood to flow, she gazed entranced at a drop of blood that had fallen on her own unblemished skin which had not lost its dazzling whiteness since she had been an infant. For two hours, they said, she remained thus absorbed.

"Sometimes, the castle stewards would have some servant punished and supervise the flogging in the kitchen or the cellars of the castle. After a time, Elizabeth herself came to observe the spectacle and would rebuke the steward when he did not show sufficient severity in the administering of the punishment. Otherwise her main interests remained as before—in endless contemplation of her beauty, a beauty so perfect and unflawed that it seemed to defy time itself.

"Her mother-in-law was ailing and soon died. Elizabeth was now sole *châtelaine* of the castle. No sooner had Ferencz departed again than strange, new recruits to the domestic staff of the castle made their appearance. A squat and dwarfish man of peculiarly repellent aspect was appointed as her valet; a maid of advanced years and equally repulsive cast rapidly came to assume the position of a confidante. The chaplain noticed that the servants grew increasingly afraid of their mistress, that she remained for long periods closeted in her room, and that she had taken to solitary walks. Sometimes there was talk of wild cries emanating from her apartments; once she was heard to shriek words of a dialect little spoken for generations; and once the castle was pervaded by a peculiar bluish smoke with a singularly nauseous odour. Then, one day, the villagers were horrified to discover the remains of one of the Countess's kitchen maids, horribly lacerated and hastily buried in a shallow grave discovered by a passing hunter.

"Then Ferencz died and henceforth Elizabeth was sole ruler of her domain. Whatever joys matrimony may have held for her—and Ferencz had been heard to praise his wife for her equable disposition—they were now eclipsed by darker and more terrible joys. As a widow, she would now only taste the sombre pleasures of sorcery, torture and murder.

"She rarely left the castle save for brief visits to the capital where she would attend the Court. A mysterious old woman from a remote mountain region came to the castle and was rarely seen out of the Countess's company. Other maids were recruited. After two young maidens had failed to return to their homes nearby as was customary on every Sabbath day, enquiries from the anxious parents merely elicited the reply from the steward that they had died after a brief illness. A sum of money was sent to the parents and all other enquiries were rigorously discouraged. Fresh maidens were brought but few were even seen again after they had gone through the gates of the castle. It was said afterwards that they had died very suddenly although whether by violent means or from some strange malady none could tell for sure. The compliant chaplain was summoned to conduct the last rites for the unfortunate girls who were interred within the castle precincts at the dead of night. What secrets he learned he kept to himself. Certainly, Elizabeth had the power to assure his silence.

"It was bruited abroad that unholy ceremonies were being conducted in the castle and that blasphemous incantations had been heard by those who passed near the Countess's apartments. Later, the village was agog with rumours that a hunter in the nearby woods had chanced to witness a strange ritual by a lake. Attended by an old hag and a dwarf, the Countess had disrobed, recited strange words and then plunged three times in the cool waters by the light of the full moon. Other rumours multiplied concerning the crimes allegedly committed in the castle. People said that the Countess had become insanely cruel, that she and her attendants would bind young girls and pierce them with sharp pins or brand them with hot irons. The castle had become a vast torture-chamber and the Countess a blood-maniac. The number of nocturnal burials increased as more and more young girls were brought as servants for the Countess. A circle of dread terror spread ever more widely around the castle. Fathers would no longer allow their daughters to be allured into the Countess's service by promises of fine clothes and privileges. Couriers rode from the castle to bring fresh recruits from remoter regions. Often they were successful and then the fear-struck villagers would sigh and cross themselves as closed coaches would pass, bearing their human cargoes to the castle. Sometimes they would see Elizabeth ride out and wonder greatly for although she was now well past her fortieth year she had retained the fresh beauty and bloom of a virgin. They glanced fearfully at her pallid face with its deep lustrous eyes, her flaring nostrils and lips quivering with secret passions, and they would shudder.

"Elizabeth still enjoyed the Emperor's favour. Few knew of the vague rumours that circulated among her subjects in her far distant estates and never did she display the slightest sign of abnormality, either physical or mental. She returned to the castle after conferring with a master craftsman, it was later learned, who was well versed in the construction of exceedingly ingenious mechanisms not unknown in the questioning of obdurate prisoners who were reluctant to talk.

"Terror attained a paroxysm at the castle. Disappearances increased almost daily. It soon became no secret that Elizabeth had developed an insensate lust for the sight of torture and bloodshed. Others said that she had been maddened by the fear of losing her beauty and of seeing her complexion decay. Her minions scoured the land for new victims. It was related that once she had prepared a banquet for sixty beautiful virgins who were afterwards slain and drained of their blood into a great basin in which Elizabeth immersed herself after shedding her garments. Two maidens succeeding in emerging from the castle still alive and told how they and others had been brought before the Countess and tortured for hours. Another maiden reached the village more dead than alive and was found to have her lips sewn together and the marks of a branding iron on each shoulder

"As the local people voiced their protests ever louder so did Elizabeth's arrogance increase. Once, she even accompanied a melancholy funeral cortège as it proceeded with the body of the mayor's niece to the village cemetery. Maddened and emboldened by grief, the father insisted on beholding his daughter's body and despite efforts to stop him he succeeded in wrenching open the coffin to find his daughter's body apparently unhurt but bereft of every last drop of blood. Upon being communicated the discovery, the villagers could no longer contain their wrath and cried out against their mistress as she sat, stony-faced, upon her charger. It became impossible to obtain any more victims from the surrounding districts. The Countess's men met with defiant resistance and petitions were drawn up and sent to the governor at Pressburg and magistrates in the region but all to no avail, so protected was Elizabeth Bathory by her great name and rank.

"At length, other maidens of nobler birth were induced to come to the castle, being ignorant of its sinister reputation. We now know that they would be treated with exquisite courtesy and gentleness on their arrival. After being greeted by Elizabeth who would tell them how overjoyed she was to have such comely and refined new maids-in-waiting, they would be led away to be bathed and anointed and clad in the richest silks and brocades. One of the maidens would receive very special attentions and be told that she had been selected to attend at a very important ceremony. After being perfumed like a bride-to-be and lovingly combed and bedecked by skilled attendants, she would be given a flowing robe of virginal whiteness and then led into a certain chamber where the Countess would await her, surrounded by her minions. The doors would close and the rest was darkness and death.

"This time, Elizabeth had gone too far. The Count Palatine of the province was apprised of the rumours circulating and with a strong body of men at arms arrived at the castle with a warrant to search it. Elizabeth met him with equanimity and declared that all rumours about her activities were false and that the only young women who had died under her roof had done so from natural causes and some contagious malady. But despite her protests and threats to appeal to the Emperor, a thorough search was ordered. In her own chambers, there were found pentacles, and all manner of occult paraphernalia, including spell books and parchments with necromantic incantations. In the vaults of the castle, nothing but horror awaited the Count Palatine's men: secret stairways leading to underground chambers were found where starving, manacled maidens were held. Worst of all were the chambers prepared for torture and murder. Men who had been there spoke but little of what they had seen afterwards. There were certain iron cages and fiendish devices for dismemberment by slow degrees and the draining of the last drop of blood from a living body—faugh! Let it be enough that every horror imaginable to man was there discovered.

"Grim-visaged and overwhelmed with disgust, her accusers came to confront Elizabeth in her bedchamber. They found her arrayed in all her finery and jewels, sitting before her beloved mirror and stroking her cheeks softly as though to savour their unblemished purity. Their thunderous words of denunciation left her unmoved. Once more, she retreated into that strange inner world of hers into which no other might penetrate. Not a word of explanation, of remorse or self-justification did she ever utter"

Reinhold fell silent. The candles were burning low in their sockets.

"More Tokay!" cried Karl.

"Aye, more wine!" said Reinhold grimly.

"And then what became of her?" I asked.

"Despite the fact that she had sinned as no other mortal woman had sinned, and had plumbed the nethermost depths of hell in her infamy, her name and rank saved her from the executioner's sword for to have had her executed would have brought too great a shame upon her husband's family. Her accomplices were tortured and put to death but it was decreed that she should be immured for the remainder of her days in the castle that had witnessed her crimes. It must have been in that octagonal chamber that she was confined and it was part of her punishment that she be deprived of the light of day.

Only one concession was made to her: as the masons bricked up her last living quarters, she was allowed to wear her finest gown—one only—and her jewellery which was held to be so accursed by contact with her that none would take it. Her son was far away at the time and never returned to the castle. There was talk of some other child she had once borne after a visit to a mysterious nobleman said to have been her lover—but no proof of this was ever found. An aperture was left in the wall for food and drink to be passed to her and two servitors were paid well to see to her nourishment but even then they could not speak for they had lost their tongues when prisoners of the Turks. And there, in this very castle, she lived for another four years, in silence, in darkness, in irrevocable solitude, in a living tomb where there was no sound to be heard save the pacing of the servants twice a day, the sighing of the wind and the distant howling of the wolves whose natural ferocity she had so greatly surpassed with her own. She died during a violent thunderstorm which people said was the worst in their living memory."

"And then?" I queried.

"And then it is said that in her remnants of finery and still bedecked in jewels of immense value, her remains were removed from her prison after the wall had been opened and were interred in the vaults beneath us, in some hidden chamber deep in the recesses of the crypts where her victims had breathed their last. Afterwards, none would approach the castle and it was said that not even the birds would fly near such a dismal spot. A few years after the Countess's death, tales were told that her shade had appeared to haunt all who lived in the vicinity but after a time the apparitions ceased. Whether we shall see anything I do not know—but beneath our feet she lies and with her a treasure that shall make us rich for life can we but find it, as I determine we shall!"

The soft summer breeze had by now become a strong wind. Through the great windows we saw dark clouds scudding across the face of the moon. A sudden blast of wind blew through the shattered panes and extinguished our guttering candles. The elements themslves seemed to be warning us not to linger in that terror-haunted ruin! Would that we had not!

"Light the lantern again!" shouted Karl. We did so and saw by its glow the wild exultation on Reinhold's countenance.

"Drink!" he shouted, holding high his goblet. "drink to the most evil woman who ever sullied the face of the earth and to the treasure she will yield up to us!"

In our mad perversity we drank and sent our goblets crashing to the ground.

"Let her ghost appear! I am not afraid!" cried Karl as he staggered to his feet.

Reinhold laughed with wild hilarity as he picked up the lantern.

"Shall we not know the taste of fear this night?" he jeered. "You will both know the terror and the dread of the tomb, I promise you, as we pay our respects to the Countess!"

Miserable profligates that we were! Reinhold's wild words and aspect encouraged all that was most perverse in us and heightened our unholy desire to seek the ultimate in ungodly sensations. The dreadful details of his recital, the funereal aspect of our surroundings, the knowledge that somewhere beneath our feet there had been committed infamies beyond the ken of ordinary humanity, that a fiend in human form lay sepulchred and that riches beyond the wildest dreams of our cupidity were awaiting us—all this stirred our wine-maddened senses and caused us to reject the last decent impulses that may have survived in our corrupted souls. We shuddered—yes, reader, we shuddered—but mingled fear and hope of what we should find only made yet more feverish our depraved sensibilities.

No ghouls ever went on their blasphemous errand with greater enthusiasm than we as we descended with our implements to the eternal night of those subterranean vaults where a delicate soul might still have detected the last lingering echoes of cries that torments had wrung from innocent victims. Possessed by greed and morbid curiosity, we soon forced an entrance through the locked door. I shall not tire you with details of how we systematically searched our way through a bewildering succession of crypts and corridors, of how we came to another arched doorway that led us to a final passage way. It is enough that we eventually reached the nethermost kingdom of torture and death.

We were standing in a chamber of vaster dimensions than any we had previously seen underground. A multitude of strange objects, some shrouded under heavy canvas, still undecayed, met our wondering gaze. All the hideous apparatus of the Spanish Inquisition seemed contained in that hellish chamber. There were heavy iron basins suspended above long-extinct braziers, knives and pincers whose purpose was all too dreadfully apparent, blocks and posts with irons embedded in them, racks and whips, pulleys for the *strappado* and a long, rectangular table of iron with clasps for wrists and ankles. No cry of anguish could ever reach the upper regions of the castle from that torture den where the Countess had once slaked her thirst for blood as she watched maiden after maiden writhe and expire amid unspeakable agonies.

It was there that madness took possession of our souls. As though insatiable for further horrors, Reinhold dragged us from one instrument of pain to the next, gleefully exulting over each new device for the lacerating and grinding of human flesh, for the twisting and shattering of limbs and for the piercing of holes in unresistant bodies. Finally I dragged him away.

"Let us go forward," he said hoarsely, his eyes burning with the fires of dementia. Clutching a pillar for support, Karl raised the bottle he had been carrying to his lips before staggering behind us. At the far end of the chamber, there yawned a hole that might have been the pit of Hell. By our lanterns we saw that it revealed another short flight of steps. At their foot we found ourselves in an oblong chamber containing cavities in the walls as in some Roman catacomb, and in those cavities,

28

the last pathetic remains of those who must have died above, and in the centre of the beaten floor of earth, surrounded by the mouldering dead, a huge stone sarcophagus bearing the Bathory arms. It was there, amid the bones and phantoms of the slain that her gaolers had finally laid her with ironical and terrible sense of fitness. There had the slayer and the slain slept together until we had come to violate the secrets of the sepulchre.

We fell silent as we approached the tomb. There was evidence that it had once been disturbed and that the massive stone lid had once been shifted slightly before being replaced. A minute's effort and we had removed the heavy lid and sent it crashing to the ground with a great and sullen reverberation.

"Look!" commanded Reinhold.

"I dare not," I whispered, sickened by all that I had seen.

"Fools, you shall look!" cried Reinhold as he held the lantern aloft over the sarcophagus. Obediently but trembling, Karl and I peered down into its depths.

"There," exclaimed Reinhold, "does that not reward us for our efforts?"

Indescribably withered, yellow and parchment-like, her head flung back, her skeletal arms raised as though to press against the lid, clad in rotting garments that had once been rich velvets and silks, and macabrely bedecked in great bracelets and necklaces and pendants that glowed like fire, and with a terrible grimace on her skull-like countenance with its sightless sockets as though she defied us to come yet nearer, there lay the dessicated remains of the Countess Bathory! It was but the work of a moment to tear the precious jewels, the golden clasps and the heavy pendant from her corpse and wrench the dazzling rings from her withered fingers. One ring alone resisted my attempts to tear it off its finger—a large ring bearing a coat of arms I did not recognise and set in massive gold.

"Come, let us begone!" cried Karl while I struggled to remove the ring in a last convulsion of greed.

Desperate with longing for this final trophy, I took out a pocket knife and severed the ringed finger from the mummified hand and placed it in my pocket, before ascending again to the torture chamber where I found Karl and Reinhold gazing in wonderment at yet another array of treasure. What I had at first thought to be a shrouded figure revealed itself on close inspection to be an iron effigy clad in heavy robes and with a female countenance, and adorned around the neck with a heavy necklace and pendant yet richer and more sumptuous than those we had ripped away from the Countess's corpse. Yet even despite another fever of cupidity, there was something in the effigy's face that held us back as we stared entranced at its mocking features and enigmatic lips carved into a smile by the genius of some unknown sculptor.

"Perhaps this was some pagan goddess of destruction and death whom the Countess worshipped," said Reinhold. We stared at it in silence and wonderment. The walls seemed to rotate around me as I gazed at that hellish semblance of femininity. To my half-crazed mind, it seemed as though blood-red vapours were arising from the burial crypt below and transforming themselves into clutching shapes as though to drag us down into that ghoulish tomb again. Our shadows danced like demons on the rough walls while the lanterns flared in our unsteady hands. Suddenly a conviction came to me that we were no longer alone. It was not so much a *presence* that my feverish senses seemed to detect but rather the *echo* or *remembrance* of a former presence. Intangible as it was, it chilled my blood and caused my eyes to blur as though I would swoon.

Then, with a wild cry of joy, Karl lurched forward and flung his arms around the statue as he plucked at the great necklace and began to lift it. There was a dull grinding as of hidden levers and wheels. As Karl drunkenly struggled to remove the necklace, the arms of the effigy sprang up and, actuated by some ingenious machinery, enfolded themselves in a deadly clasp around Karl's waist and held him tight against the iron body.

"Ha!" he cried, "she holds me tightly!"

A moment later his vinous hilarity gave way to such a screech of agony as I have never heard before and which still shrills through my tormented mind. Before the merciful oblivion of a sudden swoon obliterated the terrible spectacle from my starting eyes, I saw, in an extremity of terror, pointed iron spikes protrude through our friend's neck and back and his life's blood ooze from each ghastly wound and flow in rivulets towards our feet as we stood petrified.

How we left that abode of horror I shall never recall. I only have the dimmest recollections of how Reinhold dragged me through unending corridors and crypts and back into the blessed cool of the night air, of how we stumbled dementedly with our mule down the rocky path and of how, after recovering our mounts from the terrified landlord, we fled in the early light of dawn.

Enquiries were made into the reason for Karl's disappearance. I disguised myself and abandoned home and family, living in concealment, wandering from town to town in mortal dread. On my finger I still carry that accursed ring for no power can move it from my finger though I have tried in vain to divest myself of it. Night after night, in fear and trembling, I have gazed at it in the privacy of a miserable lodging, cursing it for the horrors it evokes and everywhere I have been with it, I have been pursued by the Countess's vengeful shade. I have seen her in the cerements of the grave, in her robes and finery as Reinhold described her, in my dreams. I have seen her pallid face and sombre eyes and sphynx-like smile. I have seen her in my waking hours as a gliding wraith; I have heard her spirit cursing me; I have heard her whispering to me in my wretched chamber, in the dusk of evening, in the crowded streets of cities, and in the lonely countryside into which I have fled and always do her words ring in my mind—"Give me back my ring!" I know that our intrusion into the vaults of the castle and our ghastly violation of the secrets of the tomb have released her monstrous spirit from its confinement. I fear that even after I am gone, she may yet continue to plague mankind with her hauntings. Who will be the next to suffer from her devilish persecution? I dare not think . . Only this I know, the ring is accursed and it shall fall into no other's hands. I shall take it to the grave with me. Yes, reader, I am determined to make an end to this tormented existence for its misery has become past all bearing. Opiates alone have brought me some temporary release from my anguish but the means for procuring them are now exhausted. The slightest noise appals me; I cannot hear a footfall without dread nor look my fellow-beings in the face; darkness terrifies me yet daylight brings me nothing but peril.

Only death, I hope, can deliver me from this and also from that other memory of what I saw in the burial crypt. Reader, I have not told you yet of what I saw in the sarcophagus as we despoiled it. *I did not tell how, as in my ghoulish frenzy I hacked off the withered finger that bore the ring, an infernal glow as of some burning ember illumined each of the vacant sockets of that grimacing skull.*

Dark and lustrous indeed were the eyes of the Countess Elizabeth Bathory.

From the Österreichisches
Tagesblatt, September 24th, 1876

"Our correspondent reports from near Kalasz that a young student, Franz von Langenfels, has committed suicide and been buried in the vicinity after a coroner's report. The wretched young man who ended his short existence in so melancholy a manner is now known to have been eluding the police who had wished to question him with regard to the mysterious disappearance in the summer of a fellow student, Karl Esterhazy. Further investigations have been ordered etc. etc."

*Leaves from the
private journal of
Ambrose Lessing*

Ambrose Lessing's Private Journal

A singular and alarming missive from Conrad Morheim reached me today by the mail. The tone of his communication, the despair that underlay every word, the anguish suffusing the entire epistle—never did I receive a sadder invitation from my friend of old. I shall go at once of course. Would that after so long a separation, his invitation have been proffered under happier circumstances! The letter is short and I reproduce it here:

"Ambrose, shall I presume upon the long friendship that binds us if I entreat, nay beg and conjure you to come to Kalasz this very instant? Come ere it be too late! Adelaide—my beloved Adelaide—is afflicted by the strangest malady imaginable—*if indeed it be a malady*. I am at my wit's end. The physicians confess themselves baffled and can do nothing. I am alone with her and Stephen. How *alone* you will see. I shall tell you all when you come. Suffice it for now that the most hideous blight has fallen upon our lives. I await you with desperation."

Thank Heaven I have few affairs in need of urgent attention and those I can entrust to my colleague. I shall leave tomorrow morning by the railway and then take the diligence.

DECEMBER 7TH

Shortly before I left, a second letter was delivered to me from Conrad. It is longer and more explicit than the first. He began by telling me that so uncertain is he of his own reason and powers of communication due to the anxiety that oppresses him unendurably, that he thought it best to apprise me to some extent of the nature of the mysterious affliction which has so suddenly struck his beloved wife. What has happened is this: until a short time ago there had been nothing to mar the serenity of the devoted couple save the melancholy fact of their only child's mental infirmity or rather, let me say, his complete failure to develop mentally since his infancy. Yet even despite this tragedy, they have loved their child and one another amid the peace and quiet of the beautiful countryside, and lived as happily as a couple might be expected to do under the circumstances until the most peculiar transformation began to be observed in Adelaide. How suddenly this change came about, Conrad does not say. No doubt he will tell me later. All I know as I go to him is that, in but a short space of time—*Adelaide appears in her behaviour to have become another person.* She has been ill—gravely ill—and subject to strange fits and losses of both consciousness and memory. She frequently gives signs of no longer recognising either her husband or her doctor or even her child. Sometimes she will spend long hours in a kind of torpor or trance from which nothing can wake her. At other times, she seems to have become her normal self again until, by some chance word or mannerism, she evinces signs of a subtle change in her condition and very personality. Even more disturbing to poor Conrad are certain of her *utterances* which completely baffle him. But of late certain of her actions do more than merely alarm him—he hints of something horrible and unnatural in her behaviour. God knows what it can be! Tomorrow I shall arrive at Kalasz. I already dread what I may find there. I am seized by a stifling sensation of foreboding as though by some sympathetic current, Conrad's anguish has become *mine.*

KALASZ, DECEMBER 8TH

Dark clouds were lowering and a chill wind was blowing from the mountains as the calèche that Conrad had sent to the post station brought me within sight of his mansion, situated amid woods upon a slight eminence, some mile and a half from the village. I remembered the last time I had been a guest on his estate and I sighed. My driver shared my depression for as we drew near he said "aye, 'tis a thousand pities she should be taken so!" and devoutly crossed himself as though praying inwardly for his mistress's speedy recovery.

Conrad met me at the door. I could not repress a start as I beheld his countenance To say it was that of a man *haunted* would be no exaggeration. He was both paler and thinner than I had ever seen him and his eyes glowed with feverish fire in a face so emaciated that I had difficulty at first in recognising it as that of the friend with whom I had once shared so many joyous hunting trips. Indeed, as I gazed at he whom I had once known to be the happiest of men, I had difficulty containing my emotion. We stood speechless for a moment while a servant slipped noiselessly away with my baggage. At long length, my friend extended a trembling hand and with a wan smile bade me enter. "Welcome to the house of sorrow!" he said in a voice so low I could scarce detect it. With sinking heart I followed him into a high-celinged hall whence a wide staircase led to the upper apartments of the building. Conrad gestured feebly about him. "You will observe that the house is sadly neglected," he said. "The servants have fled. They could not bear the atmosphere that has reigned here ever since poor Adelaide has been ill and, besides, they are a superstitious folk here. Only good old Caspar and Matthew remain faithful to me." Seeing that I was about to question him, he raised a warning finger to his lips. "Hush! You will know all soon!" he whispered, motioning me into a capacious room. Dark draperies hung across the windows and the gloom was only partly dispelled by the feeble light of a few candles. To my surprise, I saw the Lady Adelaide reclining upon a sofa at the farthest, darkest end of the room. She rose to her feet and slowly moved towards us as we entered.

"My dear," murmured Conrad, "our old and dear friend Ambrose. I trust you will remember him? Let us hope he will bring cheer again within these walls."

I bowed low over the listless hand that was offered me. It was strange to my touch, being both cold as ice, and yet, in some peculiar way, suggestive of sudden fire. The woman who stood before me, smiling faintly and seemingly in perfect possession of all her faculties albeit wearied in her stance, was indeed but the pale shade of the beautiful laughing girl I had once known. Yet her lassitude was belied by the intense, piercing brightness of her gaze which seemed to pierce right through me as though to fathom the very depths of my soul. So large and dark and lustrous were her eyes that I found something hypnotic in their look. They seemed to absorb me utterly and suggested both a wisdom and a knowledge of one far older than herself. So strongly did they hold my attention that I forgot the darkness of the room, ignored her flowing invalid's garments, and the condition of extreme physical debility to which she had evidently been reduced There was strength and fierce will in her eyes as though all the remaining forces in her slender frame had been concentrated in that one compelling gaze. "Yes," murmured Conrad as he stood beside me, "they glow like burning coals!" Apparently ignorant of his remark which showed how well he had divined my thoughts, Adelaide graciously motioned me to a seat.

"Welcome, dear Ambrose. Conrad, will you not give our dear friend (she lingered lovingly over these last three words) some wine. He must be tired after his journey."

Her voice was as soft and melodious as ever and this, together with the fact that she undeniably recognised both Conrad and myself and seemed in a state of perfect mental lucidity, went some way towards reassuring me. Conrad went across the room, to a quaintly carved sideboard, poured two glasses of wine from a heavy beaker and handed first one to me and then the other to Adelaide with a glance of tender solicitude which went straight to my heart. As we drank the good, warming wine, Adelaide continued to speak to me, asking me of my life and activities in the years since we had last met, remembering places where we had been together and incidents connected with my friendship with Conrad with an ease of manner that was strangely at variance with what little I had heard of her sad condition. As we spoke, Conrad tenderly held her hand and fondly gazed at her with an expression that alternated between deep melancholy and sudden, fitful hope.

"Tell me, beloved, does it not gladden you to see our dear friend here again? Oh how happy I am that he is here with us!"

Adelaide smiled at his delight.

"Yes, yes! Truly I am glad and happy also!" To my great pleasure, she seized my hands in hers and said with unfeigned sincerity: "Dear Ambrose, welcome a thousand times to Kalasz! Yes, yes, you must stay with us. You must stay for as long as you may. The happiness of past days returns with your presence, does it not Conrad? They say that I have been ill but I shall fast be much better. Forgive us for this darkness—I have lately much suffered from a migraine which makes bright light intolerable for my poor eyes but I know that I shall not have to wait long for my recovery. Oh, if only those dreadful dreams would cease!" As suddenly as the face of the sun is veiled by a passing cloud, her expression turned to one of anguish but with an obvious effort she regained her composure a moment later and continued to smile at me.

A few moments later, she pleaded to be excused and retired to her chambers accompanied by Conrad, after reassuring me that she would later join us for dinner, leaving me to my reflections for a few minutes. Conrad returned shortly and together we paced around the grounds, conversing earnestly. I told my friend that already I was much reassured by what I had seen of Adelaide but he hastily cut me short. "Ambrose, you know nothing yet!" he exclaimed fiercely, clutching me by the arm. "Do you not see how she has changed. Such recoveries are not unusual—pray God that the present one lasts!—but she has too often relapsed from them into such a state that sometimes I think she were better dead! Yes, better dead!" So overwrought was he that he at once burst into bitter tears. I endeavoured to console him but Conrad's despair only increased. "You shall see, you shall see how she is! Wait until after we have dined and then you will know all! I will not apprise you of what has happened now—she may hear us—she can hear everything. Besides, there is too much to tell and I have kept a journal in which I have noted down the course of her malady—or bewitchment! Oh God, that a man should be called upon to be a spy upon the woman he loves!" There was a renewed outburst of grief while I endeavoured to comfort my stricken friend to the best of my poor ability. How dreary and dispiriting the house and grounds looked now, under a leaden and fast darkening autumn sky! The elements themselves seemed to be sharing Conrad's grief and the house, now abandoned by most of its personnel, seemed to my overwrought fancy to have taken on the semblance of a huge grey mausoleum tenanted only by phantoms of those who had once been alive and full of joy. At length I ventured to ask Conrad the whereabouts of his son who, I had noticed, neither he nor Adelaide had mentioned once in the course of our brief colloquy. He was away, with relatives, Conrad told me. The house was no place for him. Adelaide had been too weak and ill to give the afflicted child a mother's care. It was not good for Stephen to remain in such a place and fortunately, his extreme youth and mental deficiency had kept him in blissful ignorance of the calamity that had overtaken his parents. But as to the precise nature of this calamity I was kept uninformed for the moment. I could see that Adelaide had been ill and subject to fits of unconsciousness and strange dreams and that was all. Although I had been summoned with such haste and a full three hours had still to pass before we dined, Conrad was strangely reluctant to say any more on the subject and I had to contain my curiosity. It was as though he were determined that first I had to behold something with my own eyes before he would apprise me with all the details of his wife's case. And so it was that, each a prey to his own thoughts, we spent the latter part of the day sitting in

Conrad's well-stocked library, he studying some tome of medical lore, I pretending to peruse a volume of travels until a soft-footed servitor came to announce that dinner was served, and we moved to the dining room where a roaring log fire and sumptuously decked table seemed to invite us to banish all thought of gloom.

Adelaide appeared clad in a gown of rich green velvet and seemed much restored by her long repose. Less pale than before, her beauty shone to its greatest advantage and as we sat at table some semblance at least of cheer had returned to Conrad. The conversation turned to music—a pursuit of which both Conrad and Adelaide were more than ordinarily fond and it was proposed that she should play for us. After a moment's nervous hesitation, Conrad assented and we left the table to repair to the music room, which like the drawing room was heavily draped from floor to ceiling and which contained a handsome pianoforte—a present to his wife, Conrad told me, which he had brought from Vienna. Smiling and radiant, Adelaide began to play some of the latest waltzes and mazurkas while we settled ourselves comfortably and resolved to forget all cares for the moment at least.

After rendering some of the most delicate airs for a while, Adelaide began to play fierce melodies. Some sudden passion had seized her: her eyes blazed with an unearthly fire, she grew pale again and swayed slightly but despite a momentary unease, she hit the keys with redoubled vigour and embarked on a new series of melodies, each wilder than the last. Strange images came to my mind as one vibrant chord followed another. It was the music of great tempests in the mountains, the roaring of the sea, of age old, frenzied dances such as those witches once performed on Walpurgis night on barren mountain tops, of tumultuous passions that knew no restraint—louder and louder rang the music through the house until the window panes trembled and rattled in their frames. Paler and paler grew Adelaide; wilder and more tempestuous each melody until, with a frenzied shriek, Conrad leapt to his feet and shouted "Stop! In heaven's name cease!" Quivering with an intense anxiety he advanced towards the pianoforte while Adelaide rose to her feet, confronting him with furious eyes.

"Adelaide! I implore you, desist! You will tax yourself too much!"

Dramatic indeed was the change that had come over her countenance! The sweet and gentle girl was no more: instead we beheld a livid mask that suddenly contorted in a spasm of

41

intense anger as, in a voice so harsh and cold that it chilled me to the heart to hear it, she uttered "I obey only my master!" A terrible tremor shook her frame, she moved forward a few paces and then fell unconscious at Conrad's feet.

With a sob that wrenched my heart, Conrad picked her up and then staggered under the burden as though he would swoon. Together we carried her up the stairs to her bed-chamber and there gently laid her upon her couch. Aghast and horror-struck we stared at each other until Conrad motioned to me to leave him. A few minutes later he joined me in the library.

"You see!" he whispered. He staggered and would have fallen had I not caught him and led him to a chair. After I had ministered to him with some *eau de vie*, he opened his eyes and groaned.

"Oh my poor friend!" was all that I could bring myself to say as he stared vacantly around him as though grief had bereft him of his senses. With an enormous effort, Conrad rose and feebly made his way across the room where he took a small, leather bound volume from a shelf.

"Read it!" he commanded, sinking weakly back into his seat. "It will tell you all. It is a journal I am in the habit of keeping. Read it from the entry of October 5th. Before then, all was well—" His voice broke into a sob and he buried his face in his hands. Wondering, I began to read. When I had finished, the candles had burned low in the room and Conrad had sunk deep into the sleep of profound exhaustion. I gazed at his unconscious form with deep pity and with something more besides in my heart. I had begun the perusal of the singular journal he had handed me with sentiments of profound dismay and melancholy. Now, added to these two was the far more terrible one of horror.

(At this point, several pages of later date have been inserted into Ambrose Lessing's journal. By way of explanation for this addition, the following prefatory lines have been written in his own hand:

In view of the terrible events that later occurred, I deem it best to present at this juncture the relevant passages which I have copied from Conrad's journal. They are chronologically apt here and are, indeed, the only valid account of those events that led to the tragedy.

Leaves from Conrad Morheim's Journal, truly transcribed by Ambrose Lessing

OCTOBER 5TH, 1876

My poor, beloved Adelaide is ill although what the nature of this malady may be neither the doctor nor myself are able to surmise with any exactitude. He has, however, asked me to observe with all attention any further symptoms that may occur and all changes in her condition. This I shall endeavour to do faithfully. It is all the more important as—so he tells me—he is unable to detect anything physically amiss with Adelaide beyond a certain lassitude which may be only a passing condition. The first hints that anything was amiss with her date from about a week ago. I remember that she awoke one morning complaining of a severe headache, some strange and frightening dream she could no longer recall, and a dim recollection of a sensation akin to that of being stifled or in some way pressed down by a great weight. After resting that day she was much recovered by the evening and had fully regained those good spirits which are her wont. Two days later, she awoke again complaining of similar dreams and sense of suffocation in her sleep. The local physician (a good fellow but otherwise much inferior in medical science to Doctor Axel) prescribed her some cordial and pills but otherwise can do nothing. Today, something of greater gravity occurred. Upon awakening I noticed that Adelaide too was awake—her eyes were opened wide but upon being gently called by me, she gave neither any sign of hearing nor of movement, nor could I detect any comprehension or intelligence in her eyes which remained curiously vacant and glassy. I observed her thus with increasing alarm for some quarter of an hour and, despairing of arousing her from this state of wide-eyed insensibility, rang for Marta when my beloved suddenly regained full consciousness and sat up in bed. Upon my questioning her, she laughed merrily and merely said that she must have been sleeping with her eyes open, however improbable that might seem! "You looked as though you were in some waking dream," I observed to her. Hardly had I uttered the words than I seemed to detect a shadow of a doubt

43

darken her face. "Oh my dear!" she replied, "if I had a dream at all, then it was the very sweetest, most delightful dream I ever had. I wish I could remember it! I was so very very happy and somewhere very far away although I know not where!" I gently reminded her that when I had seen her lying thus, her eyes staring and oblivious of my presence, she had indeed seemed to be 'somewhere very far away'. After arising and attiring herself, Adelaide seemed unusually wan and listless. In the afternoon, after she had retired to the drawing room to attend to a piece of embroidery in which she is currently engaged, I found her asleep in her chair, her work having fallen to the floor. As my soft calling failed to awaken her, I took her arm gently but she remained deep in slumber for several minutes. Finally, she opened her eyes and stared at me with a look of complete incomprehension which was as alarming as it was unexpected. Her lips moved as though she would say something but no sounds came issuing forth from her lips. She arose and made unsteadily towards the door whereupon I sought to restrain her. Turning round, she said "oh, but you are hindering me. Leave me, I do not know you!" Struck dumb by amazement, I watched her move to the door, open it, gaze out for an instant, then exclaim "oh, but this is not the place." She turned horribly pale and fell to the ground in a deep swoon from which she only recovered an hour later, when she endeavoured to utter words in a tone too low to allow comprehension. I am much disturbed and have sent word to the doctor again.

OCTOBER 7TH

Yesterday passed uneventfully. The doctor came and went, after explaining that Adelaide had doubtless been prone to much dreaming lately, probably as a result of some internal disorder caused by something in her diet. He prescribed a light diet for the next few days and left us to spend a peaceful afternoon in the drawing room.

OCTOBER 9TH

Adelaide has complained of more dreams at night and of an increasing feeling of oppression as she sleeps.

Last night I awoke suddenly to find that Adelaide was standing at the window. I tiptoed after her and took her by the arm. By the dim light of the waning moon I could see that her features were strained and tense. Insensible to my touch, she stared through the window with strange intensity, despite my pleas to her to return to bed at once. When I tried to pull her gently, she swung round and angrily said "no! I shall wait. I *must* wait!" What next she uttered I can scarcely bring myself to believe, yet if it be true, then I know not what strange dream or obsession is holding my poor wife in her thrall. She had torn herself away from my grasp and was resuming her strange vigil by the window when I heard her murmur: "no, it cannot be tonight! It cannot be tonight!" After uttering these few words which fill me with perplexity, she allowed herself to be led back to the bed, as meek and obedient as though she had been a little child. In the morning, I asked her the meaning of her words and actions but she smiled innocently and uncomprehendingly at me and assured me that I must have dreamed the episode since she had not the slightest recollection of it. Poor Adelaide! That her behaviour that night—when she gave every sign of full consciousness—should have been so blotted from her memory I find deeply disturbing. I have never known her to somnambulate before. I must discuss it with the doctor ere it becomes a fixed habit with her for who knows where those strange dreams may lead her?

Today was one of those brilliant, golden-hued autumnal days which by their very serenity make us regret the summer's passing all the more. Together with little Stephen, Adelaide and I went forth to take a promenade of longer duration than is customary at this time of year. We walked slowly through the woods, admiring nature's colouring and the landscape and were approaching a pretty little church that stands near a hamlet when Adelaide uttered a low cry. As I enquired the reason for this cry, Adelaide motioned me away and began to run towards the courtyard, there looking around her with wild staring eyes as she dashed from tombstone to tombstone in the verdant little cemetery where the local people sleep their last. As I caught up with her again, she swayed, turned deathly pale and would have fallen had I not caught her. "Come," I said, "we must go back. You are indisposed," but she would not move and instead stared as though hallucinated at the grave before her— the recent grave of a poor young man, Franz von Langenfels, who had lately been interred there after a death which some people rumoured to be suicide, and who had been living in the vicinity for some time. A few moments later, Adelaide's eyes shut and her teeth began chattering as though she had been afflicted by a sudden ague. When she again opened her eyes, she stared at me as though I were a total stranger. Her lips moved in an inaudible whisper and then she burst into floods of tears. This attack passed as suddenly as it had occurred for she then raised herself, gazed at me with eyes still unaware of my identity and said in a calm, low tone: "it is not time yet. I will know when it is time." She relapsed into a sullen silence but suffered herself to be led back to the house while Stephen followed behind, uttering gentle gurglings that did little to distract me from my gloomy thoughts. Try as I may, I cannot banish the dread thought that Adelaide's—my sweet Adelaide's —reason is unhinged. God, let it not be so!

OCTOBER 15TH

I have called the physicians. Doctor Horvarth will come from the city. The doctor here can do little. The ailment—if it be such—baffles him and to his credit he makes no secret of the fact. All we can do is to watch over her and hope. Since that strange scene in the churchyard, whence I led her to our bedchamber, she has given me no sign of recognition, and shown a total lack of interest in her surroundings. Even worse, when Stephen came in the room she looked at him with no more interest than if she had seen a stone or a piece of lifeless wood. Marta, who is quite distracted, tends to her and sees that she takes nourishment. Otherwise, Adelaide is dead to me, dead to her son, dead to the world.

OCTOBER 17TH

Thank Heaven! The doctor has come! Yesterday morning, Adelaide was found in a profound sleep from which it was quite impossible to awaken her, despite our every effort. At first, I thought in an extremity of despair that life had fled for ever from her rigid frame. How can I describe her condition beyond saying that she might have been made of marble? I was about to yield to the ultimate grief when the doctor restrained me. "See," he said, feeling her pulse attentively, "she still lives!" It was true: her heart still beat though faintly and although undetectable to the untrained eye, there was still breath in her body. Today something even more peculiar has happened. As Doctor Horvarth and I tiptoed into the chamber, her eyes were open! They stared upward at the ceiling with a gaze so fixed and glazed that they might have belonged to a statue. Doctor Horvarth showed himself much moved and with an expression of profound sympathy bade me leave him alone with the patient. An hour later he emerged and in tones of the utmost gravity imparted to me the melancholy news that Adelaide was—is—in a state defined as cataleptic hysteria which is still a condition little understood by our present medical science. He made some notes, prescribed some remedies to be administered upon her regaining consciousness (he has assured me that this will come to pass), bade me be of good heart, and left after promising to return in a few days as soon as his many commitments allow, and leaving instructions for our good Doctor Muller.

OCTOBER 20TH

Adelaide has emerged from her death-like torpor, much weakened. Doctor Horvarth has come again and earnestly explained how in such cases, patients are known to be at first subject to intermittent fainting fits of short duration before losing all apparent signs of animation in a prolonged death-like trance. All this is terrible enough but there are some further peculiarities in this case at which he hints but which he is curiously unwilling to specify. He is disturbed—I can see that —and his own bewilderment only adds to the crushing burden of my sorrow. *Why* should this tragedy have struck us—at her whom I love about life itself, whose existence was to me the supreme reason for Life, the justification of the entire universe with all its joys and sorrows, its terrors and delights? Adelaide's state is worse than even that of her unconsciousness. She has become as an alien here—in her own home, in the presence of her husband and son. Of recognition for her surroundings she gives no sign. I speak to her and she answers me not, yet she can now rise, walk a few paces, eat and drink a

47

little, and then lie down and sleep again. There is vacancy in her look, she cannot communicate, she has become an automaton.

Copy of a letter to Doctor Horvarth.

You will scarcely believe what I have to tell you. To be quite fair I would not believe what I have to tell you myself were it not that our good friend Doctor Muller has seen and confirmed all. Two nights ago it was Marta's turn to sleep next to Adelaide's chamber. Sometime after the devoted servant had retired, she found herself quite incapable of sleeping on account of an old and painful ailment which is prone to recur as winter approaches. She lay awake for some time until, prompted by what we might best define as woman's intuition, she decided to visit Adelaide's chamber once again to assure herself that all was well with her mistress. As she later told me, the conviction suddenly seized her that Adelaide's condition had changed in some dramatic way. Impelled by this premonition, she quietly rose and went to Adelaide's door and was on the point of opening it when she heard—so she swears by all that is holy— two women's voices speaking within the chamber. *The first was that of the stranger and it was low, and soft though marked by a tone of urgency but what words were being uttered Marta cannot say. The other voice, faint and pleading, was that of Adelaide. Thoroughly alarmed and mystified, the good woman opened the door and rushed in. There was no sign of the female visitant. Adelaide was lying in bed, eyes wide open and muttering wildly in an alien tongue for several moments before relapsing into unconsciousness. I was called but there was nothing we could do and when morning finally came Adelaide opened her eyes again and showed herself to be still in her alien state. The following night, Doctor Muller and I resolved to keep watch by Adelaide's bedside. As evening drew on, her eyes flickered, her eyelids drooped and she slumbered soundly. As the hours passed it seemed that our vigil would be an uneventful one and then, towards two of the morning, an alarming alteration was observed in my beloved's condition. Her body began to writhe beneath the bedclothes, her face became flushed, her breathing heavy and laboured. Doctor Muller at once felt her pulse and found it highly irregular in its beating. Again and again she writhed as though some terrible battle*

48

were being waged within her and uttered intermittent low cries as if in pain. The doctor was reaching for some laudanum with which he had come provided when Adelaide suddenly half rose, as though to start from the bed and then fell back with a sigh upon her pillow. And now comes the strangest part of all: her lips moved again as though about to give utterance and she opened wide her eyes that were, for the first time in days, filled with lucid intelligence and comprehension! Our hearts leaped with hope for here at last was a sign that Adelaide had fully recovered her mental faculties but we were soon cruelly disappointed. She stared hard at us for several long minutes while the doctor endeavoured to question her but she never uttered a word. Finally, after being shaken by another terrible spasm, she cast at us a glance of indescribable malice—a look such as I never again wish to behold on any human countenance on account of its terrible, intense, blood-chilling malignity—before sighing deeply and sinking back into sleep. The remainder of the night passed quietly. The night following, Doctor Muller insisted that we should divide the night into two watches, as sentries do, forbidding me to sacrifice a second night's sleep on the grounds that I was utterly exhausted which was only too true. My vigil was undisturbed by any untoward incident and the doctor relieved me an hour past the midnight. Next morning, he had a strange report for me. Towards four in the morning, he had been unable to restrain himself from dozing off in fits and snatches despite every effort of his will. Then, while he was in that intermediate state between full slumber and half-wakefulness, he heard two female voices conversing. He was fully awake in an instant and swears that no other person either entered or left the room. As he bent over the patient, her eyes opened and again seemed filled with intelligent perception before closing again in a resumed slumber.

We are completely at a loss to account for these weird nocturnal conversations between my wife and this apparently invisible intruder. No one has seen any strangers hereabouts. I have searched the house. For a female visitor to have penetrated into the house and so speedily have made her exit after being detected in conversation with Adelaide is manifestly impossible. And yet, there was someone else in the chamber with her. Of that we are sure. I pray that you may soon throw light upon this mystery which, together with the sorrow of dear Adelaide's alienation threatens to destroy what reason I still possess. I pray you please come again as soon as you may.

Physically, Adelaide is much recovered of late. For this much we can be thankful but in all other respects she is still afflicted by that terrible malady which cuts her off from all recognition of those nearest to her and from all memories of her former life and present environment. What can we do? I have had word from Doctor Horvath who tells me he is going to Vienna. The case greatly interests him and he hopes through consultation of certain medical records and discussion with his learned colleagues to find some means of effecting a complete cure. There she is now, passing the window as I write, like a wraith, a mocking reflection of her former self, now lost in a world she comprehends not. Oh my poor beloved!

OCTOBER 28TH

Will this nightmare never cease? It is beyond endurance—each new day dawns more wretched than the last and each night brings with it fear of yet greater horrors. Yes, I too have heard the voices. Worn out with mental suffering and the anguish that only they who love as desperately as I do can understand, I stationed myself in Adelaide's chamber last night. Doctor Muller has been called away for a day or so and poor old Marta has tearfully confessed to me that not for anything will she spend a night in the mistress's chamber. How peacefully Adelaide slept as I contemplated her from my chair! How I longed that she might awake as the person she *is*, the one I love and who loves me! My misery is yet further increased by the absence of little Stephen whom I have had to send to the loving protection of his uncle and aunt, since it is not good for him to see his mother's state which, thankfully, he cannot apprehend. Towards two o'clock, I looked up from the volume I was endeavouring to read and noticed with a start of horror that Adelaide was a prey to another of those seizures that had so bewildered us. This time the writhings were more violent, almost as though she were wrestling bodily with an invisible fiend. Her eyes opened, she threw me a glance of uttermost despair and then shrieked my name as though imploring assistance. Nothing more heartrending can be imagined. My joy that at last she had recognised me was turned to ashes by the convulsive agony of her soul as it battled against I know not what fiendish force within her extenuated frame whose frenzied contortions I was powerless to end. Demented and tormented by my sense of helplessness, I witnessed every phase of the bitter struggle until at last peace returned to my dear's tortured body and she slumbered again. I pray that Doctor Horvath will be here again soon. I know—yes I am confident—it is my unalterable conviction that my darling's soul and mind is still present in her body. Some devilish force, perhaps some alien spirit, is imprisoning it but that the flame of her own soul still burns within her, be it but a spark, *I know*.

OCTOBER 29TH

Another dreary day has passed. Adelaide arose with a sigh, moved about the chamber, touching objects and furniture uncertainly, gazed at me with lacklustre eyes and then asked in a distant voice whether I would leave her to dress. I sent Marta up to her but after a few minutes the good woman came down the stairs in floods of tears, vowing that she could no longer bear the painful sight of her mistress so demented. Shortly afterwards, Adelaide slowly progressed down the stairs, through the hall, into the music room and there sat in the same high backed oaken seat that had been her favourite in happier days and remained there brooding (on what) for hours, oblivious to my entreaties that she take nourishment. Eventually, after food was brought to her she toyed listlessly with her tray of victuals, then mounted the stairs again as though in her sleep and so returned to her couch. This time, I prevailed upon her to swallow a strong sleeping draught which Doctor Muller had left prepared if it be needed. Thank heaven, this time there was no repetition of the fearful incidents of other nights, although at times I did detect some change in her breathing and complexion.

OCTOBER 30TH

Today, Doctor Hovarth returned with a colleague, a sharp faced, sallow little man with piercing eyes, whom he introduced as Herr Vogt. As we passed through the hall we met Adelaide, fully attired, as she listlessly made for the music room and there resumed her strange brooding, oblivious of our presence. We retired to the library where the doctor apprised me of what he had lately learned in the course of his investigations.

"What we are faced with," he said, "is nothing more than a peculiar form of hysteria which manifests itself as a *doubling* of the sufferer's personality. I should explain more fully; let us suppose that a person suffers from some sudden shock—often one produced by the most ordinary and natural causes such as an accident, a sudden fall, or else by the after effects of some debilitating malady, or even from onsets of a hereditary proneness to temporary unconsciousness followed by periods of amnesia. So—under certain conditions, what we shall call the primary personality of the patient is affected. He or she loses sense of time and awareness of present surroundings. The memory—let us say it is lost. It strays back into the past. Memories of former years, or even memories of other people's lives, even memories of something read in a book, will come into the patient's mind and so dominate it that the physical and mental constitution will be dominated. We have now this false personality, this compound of former memories and impressions, taking the place of the real, primary personality and dominating it. How long it will do so I cannot say but be assured, good Sir, that with my worthy colleague, Herr Vogt, we have, I think the means to set free your wife's true personality."

"But there was no shock of which you speak, or debilitating malady that could account for my wife's affliction," I objected.

Doctor Horvarth was not a whit dismayed by my denial. "Then we must look deeper, my friend. It is in her heredity, it must be—no? Such cases have been observed before. Believe me, the seizures suffered by your wife are due to no more than the revival in her memory of past scenes and incidents."

"And the other voice?"

Doctor Horvarth smiled: "that is not uncommon in some cases. It is your wife dreaming aloud, believing that she is someone else. A relative, a parent perhaps, or some very dear friend. The world of sleep and dreams is a mysterious one. Now thanks to Herr Vogt, I think we shall effect a simple cure —simple, that is, to those who accept the science of mesmerism for what it is—a useful addition from nature's armoury in our fight against maladies of the mind. Oh, do not be frightened, Sir, I do not mean that your wife is infirm of mind—how shall we say?—there is merely *confusion* in her faculties. I trust we may restore her to you as she was. Herr Vogt!"

Herr Vogt leaped to his feet with alacrity. "If my good Sir would care to observe the proceedings I shall be honoured," he said.

We went to the music room, finding Adelaide still seated and gazing into vacancy. After leading us to the far end of the room and bidding us on no account to make any sound or remark, Herr Vogt drew up a chair and sat close to Adelaide, directly facing her. I have read a little of this practice of mesmerism and of some of the remarkable experiments performed with it in the medical faculties of Budapesth and Vienna, and was not surprised when Herr Vogt began to make certain passes with his hands before Adelaide's face, speaking softly to her all the while. Her eyelids drooped then closed; she seemed to sleep.

"Adelaide," said Herr Vogt, "Adelaide! Do you hear me?"

Her bosom heaved, her face flushed and she began to breathe stertorously.

"Adelaide," he repeated in a tone of command.

A terrible shriek rang out, freezing my blood. Adelaide rose from her seat, uttered a choking cry, staggered forward a few paces and then fell swooning to the ground. We rushed forward in an agony of alarm and picked her up. As we laid her on a sofa, she opened her eyes and gazed at me softly. Unutterable joy filled my heart as I heard her speak my name and look about her wonderingly, saying: "Oh, my darling, I have been feeling so strange and must have slept. Who are these gentlemen? And why are you all looking at me so strangely, Have I been unwell?" Choking with tears of relief and ineffable gratitude, I fell on my knees and covered her sweet face with kisses while Herr Vogt discreetly retired and Doctor Horvarth cleared his throat noisily and said gruffly: "So! With modern science all is simple, did I not say? There is your wife, safe and sound!"

NOVEMBER 7TH

Yes, Doctor Horvarth said he could bring my wife back to me and so he has done. He and his peculiar colleague have brought her back through the valley of Death or the valley of Hades— I know not which. The terrible battle that was fought within her is over. Yet I am not satisfied. I am convinced that during her trance-like state and those terrible convulsive seizures, she was *possessed*—possessed, I say, in a manner that men of the Church understand better than our self-styled modern men of science. Yes, I do verily believe that for a time her sweet soul and mind were engaged in a terrible, bitter struggle with some other mind, or spirit or *essence* which relentlessly strove to take

53

possession of her. The peculiar shriek she uttered as Herr Vogt began his process of mesmerisation was not *hers*. The *other* voice that spoke in the bedchamber was not—nor ever could have been—*hers*. Of that conviction, I am certain. The enemy has departed but the struggle has left its marks. How and why it departed is beyond conjecture. Had it succeeded in totally taking possession of my dearest, I do not believe any doctor or mesmerist could have driven it out. Such a task could only have been performed by a qualified priest and is known to Christians as *exorcism*.

LATER

Strange, how I dwell upon the thought that some alien, sentient being had seized upon Adelaide for its prey! Had it done so successfully, then the writhing fiend that Doctor Muller and I saw for but an instant on that dreadful night would have manifested itself continuously. Despite the explanations given me by Horvarth, I am not satisfied. Something has been happening to Adelaide of which we know nothing. That cataleptic rigidity, that somnambulistic demeanour, that total amnesia and alienation from myself and her surroundings—what did they all mean— Adelaide can remember nothing of any of this yet her fortitude and the rocklike constancy of her deep religious faith saved her from the total destruction of the soul. Poor darling, as I cast one last, long, lingering look at her before she retired (peace and rest are essential for her. Until fully restored, she must sleep twelve hours a day at least) I realised again what a terrible toll this experience has taken of her.

NOVEMBER 10TH

To the intense joy that followed my despair of recently there now succeeds a deep unease. I had thought my beloved recovered and so in all appearance she is. And yet, in some way I cannot fathom or define, I detect in her a subtle transformation. She is still—she is again, shall I say?—the Adelaide of former days, but still she is *different*. I have the feeling that although she conceals it from me, she has certain recollections of what has occurred. My husband's intuition tells me that there are now certain thoughts and feelings in her that were not there before. At times, when she looks fondly at me, I do surmise a certain shadow of unease in her countenance, almost as

54

though she inwardly is afraid that I may detect something
that lies deep within her as a result of her affliction. There is a
wisdom in her eyes that was not there before and at times a
hint of mysterious wistfulness, a suggestion of longing for
something *which is not*.

NOVEMBER 12TH

I am right. Outwardly she is as loving and attentive as any man
could wish for his wife to be, but she has grown more thoughtful and at times a veil of reserve seems to fall between us so
that I can no longer as before follow every succession of senti-
ment and emotion in her eyes and face. Where she was trans-
parent as a rocky mountain pool, now she is opaque.

NOVEMBER 15TH

She is more prone to reveries than before. She laughs less; her
mien is more contemplative. There is also another mystery: I
came upon her this afternoon, gazing far into the distance from
an open window, with an expression of intense longing. She
had been writing a letter to a relative, and on her *sécrétaire* I
espied some curiously written sheets of paper with characters
in a strange language, written by her own hand. "Why?" I
cried in surprise, "what is this, my dear?" She flew from the
window and in a state of the greatest agitation snatched the
leaves from me. "Why did you come in like this?" she demanded with a tone of anger I had never heard before from
her. "You know how nervous I am these days." Despite my
attempts to calm her, she pushed me away, muttering that they
were only letters. I pretend to accept her explanation and left
the room, all my former misgivings renewed. As I paused by
the door, I observed that she was furtively watching me in a
manner quite unprecedented and which I can only qualify as
sly. There is a secret between us—I know it. Furthermore, I
do not like the way she has been looking at Stephen lately as
though he and she were participants to some secret knowledge.
I do not like the way she has been whispering to him and above
all, I do not like the way his eyes seem to gleam with hitherto
lacking intelligence as she speaks to him and caresses his head.
Something is stirring within that afflicted mind and it is Adelaide who is responsible. At other times, Stephen is the same as
always—a growing lad with a mind atrophied since birth.

NOVEMBER 17TH

The artless innocence in Adelaide that so delighted me is now a thing of the past. Every day, it becomes more apparent to me that she is concealing things from me—whether they be her thoughts or some actions I have not detected. At the same time, she remains weak and listless, spending long periods playing melancholy airs upon the pianoforte, or erding the grounds and scanning the distant prospect like one waiting a visitor from afar. I let her out of my sight as little as possible. Meanwhile two servants have been oddly agitated and informed me that they can no longer stay in our service. I entreated them to let me know the cause of this but they were reluctant to say more than they wished to seek employment in a spot less remote.

NOVEMBER 20TH

I have been sleeping more heavily than is my usual wont of late. I wonder if I too am unwell. Adelaide is even paler and more listless and refuses even to attend the services at the village church any longer, pleading fatigue and stating that she henceforth prefers to remain in the privacy of her room for her devotions. I told the good priest who was much distressed by the news. Doctor Muller came again and after confirming that Adelaide is still in a very weak state, though mentally quite restored, prescribed me some strong cordial for my own lassitude which he ascribes to the terrible strain and anxiety of these recent times. Stephen is well with his uncle and aunt but they do not advise that he returns here until Adelaide is stronger which is a sad blow to me.

NOVEMBER 22ND

Despite the cordial, I am still feeling singularly weary and awake in the morning with a head aching as if it would burst. I saw Doctor Muller again (poor man. How we overtax him!) and he told me a singular rumour which is circulating in the village. It is that a woman, young in years and clad in white, has been seen wandering at night in the vicinity of our house and in the nearby woods. "I know nothing of this," I said whereupon the old doctor fixed his gaze intently on me and quietly asked me did I have any reason to suspect that Adelaide was sleepwalking again? I assured him I did not think so and that that nightmare was passed at least—or so I hoped! Still unsatisfied, he gravely suggested that I stay near Adelaide even though in her present still debilitated condition she preferred the privacy of her own bedchamber. He stopped me as I was about to leave, and in a solemn voice declared: "I think it is only fair to mention to you that from reports this nocturnal figure is not unlike your wife." Good God! Is the horror starting anew? If it is, then all hope is indeed lost.

NOVEMBER 23RD

Adelaide was adamant that I do not keep watch in her room. "Do you think then that I am walking in my sleep? These are fools' tales spread by superstitious folk!" Amazed, I asked her how she had come to hear of these reports of a nocturnal wanderer. For a moment, all composure left her—her visage blanched to an even greater pallor, she flinched as though struck by a blow, and then, with a supreme effort, mastering her emotions, asked me what other reason I could have for my request. Now I am sure that it is indeed her. I shall keep watch this night.

NOVEMBER 24TH, MORNING

Some invincible weariness prevented me from keeping my vigil. Scarcely had I retired to the library after Adelaide had retired than a leaden drowsiness overcame me. The first rays of the morning sun woke me from the slumber of one who had been drugged. I had fallen on to a settee and there slept the night. My headache is painful. Even more painful, however, is the suspicion that she has been administering to me nightly some potion or sleeping pill. Henceforth, I must be on my guard.

EVENING

She has the cunning of a fox. My wife, my love, my life, has now become a dissembler and as I realise the awful truth I fall headlong into deeper gulfs of despair. I even wish—yes, I do wish it—that she had died rather than become what she is now. She *is* transformed and dissimulates the fact with marvellous artfulness. What it is that she is concealing is slowly but surely destroying her. She refuses to be visited again by Doctor Muller but I insist. This afternoon when she came to me she was as merry, sweet and loving as ever. For a few sweet moments I felt that she was the gentle, frank, adorable creature I had married. She is often so: every day I see in her the Adelaide of *before* and then the bitterness of suspicion and disillusion overwhelm me anew and with increasing alarm I note the change in her appearance, her sagging vitality, her waxen pallor, her extreme languor. Even walking seems too much of an effort for her. We had proceeded in the grounds for some hundred paces or so when she hung on my arm and begged me to desist. Afterwards, as she reclined limp and motionless on a chaise longue, it seemed to me that all that was left to her of life reigned solely in her glowing, unfathomable eyes whose peculiar brilliant intensity of late compensate for the rest of her condition.

I have learned how she administers the drug to me. Every night for the past few weeks, after she has retired, it is my habit to go to the library and there take a glass of brandy as I sit and read for an hour or so. Tonight, seeing how wan and weary she appeared before our dinner, and observing that she swayed lightly as she came down to the drawing room, I hurriedly rang for Caspar and asked him to fetch the brandy with a glass for his mistress. As he reappeared, Adelaide refused the restorative with surprising vehemence, pleading that strong liquors were quite unbearable to her and would only worsen her condition. None the less, on a signal from me, Caspar set the decanter and glass down upon a nearby table, and after I had apparently accepted her refusal and offered her a glass of wine which she accepted, I observed in a mirror that overhangs a sideboard how her eyes fixed with peculiar intensity upon the brandy. Her look—that look I had learnt to detect—spoke volumes to me. No verbal admission she might have made could have been franker than the commingled excitement and alarm with which she regarded that decanter. Guilt was never more evident, for all her newly acquired powers of dissimulation. With studied calm, I told her that I would wait until after we had dined before taking my customary glass of the brandy in the library and try as she might, she was not wholly successful in masking the merest hint of exultation and relief. Tonight, I know I shall not sleep.

NOVEMBER 25TH, MORNING

A chill wind blew around the house as I emerged after Adelaide

58

had retired. There was winter in the air and promise of early snow. Clouds had hung low over the earth the whole of that drear day, and the darkness of the night was wellnigh impenetrable. Wrapped in my greatcoat, I patiently prepared myself to wait as I stationed myself in the little wooden lodge that stands by the gate, leading out to the road that descends to the village on one hand and rises to the forest on the other. As hour succeeded hour, marked by the distant chiming of the church bell, I grew desperately chill although I fortified myself with some other *eau de vie* taken from a safer source, and all but forgot my surroundings and even the purpose of my watch, so all-consuming were my melancholy and bitter thoughts. At length my patience was rewarded. There was a crackling on the path: I concealed yet further beneath the cloak that covered my shoulders the lantern I had brought and held my breath. Closer and closer came the footsteps. They paused for a moment outside my hiding place, so near that I knew I had only to stir slightly and outstretch my arm and I would touch *her*. I heard a soft cry and then the nocturnal wanderer turned in its tracks and began to hurry back towards the house. Some sense had warned her that I lay in wait to follow her. There was no longer any need for my concealment. Uncovering the lantern, I dashed in pursuit after her and caught her by the arm. Holding high the lantern, I inspected her features. For an instant, they contorted into a terrible snarl (*snarl* indeed is the only word that suffices to describe her expression at that moment). For a terrible, fleeting moment I was gazing not at my beloved wife's gently moulded features but at the face of a demon possessed of the ferocity of a wild beast when cornered, and then, with a lightning-like transition, her countenance changed and assumed an expression of utmost bewilderment as in a beseeching tone such as a small child might use, she faintly asked me: "Oh Conrad, where am I? What are you doing? Why do you stare so strangely at me? What am I doing here? Oh, I am so cold!" She clung to me as she spoke and then sank to her knees, shivering with the damp autumnal cold of the night. My heart heavier than ever, I picked her up and carried her gently back to the house, up the stairs to her chamber and there laid her on her couch. Sorrow and dread rendered me speechless as I tended her. My hand trembles as I write. God give me strength to see this ordeal through! I know—and knowing it as I do, I can hardly bring myself to write it—yes, I know that even as I apprehended her, she was neither in a trance nor wandering purposelessly as the somnambule will do. No, she was fully in possession of her faculties, fully awake and perceptive and bound on some premeditated errand whose object I cannot surmise but which can only have been prompted by some evil power.

EVENING

Adelaide has lain in her room all day. I summoned Doctor Muller and together we examined her as she slept. "See!" I cried in anguish, "see how pale and wasted she is! She might be dead. Her soul is absent and her body has become dreadfully emaciated. What fearful malady is this that so consumes her?" I told him all and added that although she had shown such a singular determination to leave the house at night, in other respects she behaved as though she had lost the will to *live*. We were both baffled. After long observing her, all the doctor could tell me, after much hesitation, was "My friend, from what you tell me, and from what I have seen, it is as though she were pining. Of physical ailment there is no sign. Yes, you are right, something is slowly consuming her." He laid a sympathetic hand on my arm. "My dear friend, prepare yourself for melancholy news. I am a humble country physician and know only the plain facts of this life but unsuperstitious as I am, I cannot but feel that something—do not ask what—is robbing her of all will to live, drawing from her the vital current that sustains human existence. Against such an affliction, medicine can do little."

"But she has never intimated to me that she wearies of this life. Why, until recently and even now, at times, she has indicated that to live and love and be loved by me even and to cherish our child is her dearest wish and intention. What then could have weakened such a natural determination. I tell you —laugh at me if you will—she is possessed. I swear it!"

Doctor Muller looked thoughtful. "Such a weakening of bodily vitality has already been observed although under dissimilar circumstances. It is a peculiar story. I shall tell it to you when we descend." We left the chamber and made our way to the library where the doctor began his narrative. "Some years ago, in a part of Carinthia, there was born to a family of great antiquity a son who from an early age manifested the greatest and most precocious intelligence, but whose physical constitution, like those of his forebears, was exceedingly delicate.

His brothers and sisters were all of a more robust build and showed greater resistance to the various ailments to which young children are so often prone. Not he, however. As he approached manhood, he fell into a melancholy state of increasing physical decline although his powers of intelligence waxed even greater. Greatly alarmed, his parents had his faithful nurse sleep in his room at night that she might keep watch over him and attend instantly to any need he might evince. In a short time, the boy showed signs of recovery. Blood came back to his cheeks, his step was more alert, his endurance increased. Simultaneously, the nurse had been complaining of diminished vitality. Where her charge returned to health, she began to waste for no apparent reason. No sooner had she been removed from her post of attendance, than she recovered. Shortly afterwards, the boy showed the same symptoms of decline that had previously been manifest. Another servant was appointed to attend him day and night. Once again the boy returned to health, and the servant complained of increasing lassitude—as though the life in him was being subtly drawn out of his body. In the end, no servant would go near him, the family were terrified, and even his brothers and sisters avoided him. All agreed that when they were in his presence, they felt curiously faint and unwell while *he* showed every sign of increasing vigour".

"And then?" I queried. "Another attendant was hired but in vain. The same thing happened. Finally, in despair, his loving mother insisted on treating him herself despite the objections raised by the rest of the family. After a short time she died. Then all avoided the boy as though he were the pestilence. It seemed that he possessed the peculiar power of draining the vitality of others into his own constitution as a sponge will absorb water. He was kept in isolation in the house; victuals were provided for him but neither his father, his brothers and sisters nor any servitor would suffer to remain for more than a few moments in his presence. In a few weeks he was dead."

"But who or what could be so draining my beloved Adelaide of life's essence?" I objected. At that moment, Caspar entered to tell me that the priest had called, being anxious to enquire after Adelaide. I repeated what had happened and Doctor Muller told him the story. The priest was particularly alarmed by the lengths to which Adelaide had gone in order to leave the house undeteced by night and asked to see her at once. We found her awake and cheerful.

"My daughter," said the priest gently, "can you tell us whether you have been having strange dreams or visions at night? Your husband tells me that of late you have been found walking in your sleep." Adelaide smiled sweetly at him and denied all knowledge of any such behaviour with such accents of sincerity that although *I knew* of the deception she was practising, I could not find it in my heart to disbelieve her at the time she spoke. As he spoke gently to her, the kindly old man leaned over her and seemed to gaze with deep concentration at her white throat, gently lifting aside her streaming, heavy locks of hair that coursed lustrously over the counterpane. As I too bent forward, I heard the priest softly whisper —as though to himself—"no, it is not that, the Lord be praised!" before straightening up again and turning to us.

"My friends, I pray you leave us while we pray a little," A few moments later he descended from her room and, drawing me aside, told me gently that he would be back in an hour. He returned after the doctor had left, bearing a little casket which, among other things, contained Holy Water and wafers of the Consecrated Host. "I would not have you tell the doctor," he said smilingly, "he will think I am a credulous old man, yet I have an inkling that perhaps my medicine will be more powerful than any he can devise, since it is that of God and not of man." Shortly after he had gone into her room, he called for me and showed me how peacefully Adelaide was sleeping. "Now I think your wife will no longer leave you," he said. I pray that it may be true!

NOVEMBER 28TH

Where Doctors Muller and Horvarth have failed, Father Johannes may have succeeded. The change in Adelaide's condition has been remarkable. In a few days she will be able to leave the sick chamber and little Stephen will return home.

DECEMBER 5TH

What power is this that has Adelaide in its thrall? No sooner did she return to our matrimonial chamber than the horror recommenced. I caught her last night descending the stairs. The same hideous visage—followed by the same sweet uncomprehending look of amazement. Father Johannes has failed. We have all failed. I shall go mad, here alone: I cannot maintain a nightly vigil—I am weak until death—and yet I must watch her. In my extremity, I can only call upon my dearest oldest friend. I shall write to Ambrose at once.

DECEMBER 9TH

After completing my perusal of Conrad's diary, the immense sadness of which touched me unutterably, I gently roused him and suggested it was high time that we retired. His gratitude at my coming here is quite pathetic and at the same time my presence gives him new heart. I assured him that come what may, I will stay by his side and see, whether by my help, we can together solve this mystery which threatens to end in death for Adelaide and madness for Conrad. The remainder of the night passed quietly. Although I did not tell Conrad today, I did not sleep but instead lay awake with my door slightly ajar so that if Adelaide had left his side I would have been in a position to observe it, since our rooms are near and to get to the staircase she would have to pass mine.

As usual, Conrad had to play the dreadful comedy of seeming to ignore the untoward incident of the night before. Adelaide was all gentleness and sweetness and even invited me to take her for a short stroll around the grounds—a proposition to which I readily assented. As we walked, she told me how she loved Conrad and how greatly she missed her dearest child although it would soon return home. Stopping suddenly, she took my hands in hers and staring hard at me said: "Conrad thinks that I am sick, does he not? Tell me, does he express fears for my reason? I know he thinks I act so strangely yet I know nothing. I am so happy, truly so very happy here!" Her tone moved me strangely. Even while she spoke, there was a hint of yearning in her eyes as though she spoke to reassure me while inwardly thinking of some other matter.

Ambrose Lessing's Journal

DECEMBER 10TH

It is true. Adelaide is possessed by some secret power or longing. Today she asked me how long I would stay and when I told her that I hoped I would be here as long as Conrad and she desired my company, she was unable to dissemble a sudden look of dismay for all her feigned joy at my answer. Worse—she is becoming increasingly restless at night. Conrad privately informed me that he awoke towards the hour of dawn to find Adelaide murmuring "soon! soon!"

Another incident: the priest, a venerable and saintly man came today (it is Sunday) to conduct prayers as Adelaide is too enfeebled to go to the church. Upon his saying: "Come, let us pray to Our Lord" a terrible change overcame Adelaide's countenance, and with a look of deep contempt at him, she muttered in a low voice: "My Lord is not your Lord!" before swooning again. Father Johannes is much distressed and spent some time afterwards in earnest converse with Conrad. What they said I do not know. When the priest had gone, he drew me into the library and in low, earnest tones said: "I cannot bear this any longer. To whom Adelaide alludes I know not but I am resolved to find out. Anything is better than this wretchedness. Father Johannes has sprinkled holy water in our room and blessed it but he has done this before in the chamber wherein she slept and it availed not. She would not go in the room—she pleads that she is not weary although she always rests at this time. I believe it is true that some dreadful demon has her in its thrall. There is only one thing that we can—nay, must—do and that is find it and destroy it. Will you help me?" I readily assented. It is agreed that tonight we shall keep watch and follow her if she leave the house. We know that she will do so soon. She is becoming distracted in her manner—her pretence at normality is rapidly becoming less and less convincing. She would not take luncheon with us but stayed listlessly playing in the music room. Her eyes dart here and there, like an animal trapped, it is obvious that she is in a state of desperation.

From hour to hour she has weakened. But there was surprising vehemence in the way she pleaded to be allowed to spend the night downstairs on the couch in the drawing room. After we had exchanged a look of complicity, Conrad agreed. We have prepared our ruse well. Caspar came in with a note which he handed to Conrad. It urgently summoned Conrad to the village. One of the workers on the estate, an old and loyal retainer of many years' service, was dying and wished to proffer his last respects to his beloved master. There was an unholy flash of triumph in Adelaide's eyes as Conrad broke the news to her and told her that he was duty-bound to go. What she did not know was that Conrad and I had devised the note together some hours before. He has now left and awaits me outside. I am alone in the house with her. The remaining servants have retired. It has been snowing gently and the sky is clear and starry. As I left Adelaide, reclining on her couch, she seized my hands again and passionately begged me to remain with Conrad lest anything happen to her. "I dare not tell him for it would break his heart, I know," she said, "but I am not long for this life." I pleaded with her to banish such morbid thoughts but she repeated "Oh, I know that *this* life will soon be over."— "*This* life?" I echoed, struck by the manner in which she had lingered over the demonstrative pronoun. She averted her eyes and lay back with a sigh as I left the room. I went upstairs and, fully clothed, climbed into my bed and waited. An hour passed and then I heard a stealthy tread on the stairs, along the corridor and outside the door. There was a pause. I shut my eyes and pretended to sleep. An instant later, there was a soft turning of the handle and the door opened slightly. It shut again and the footsteps retreated. I am ready. Soon she will go out and we will follow her.

DECEMBER 11TH

I must be very careful and try to recollect everything exactly as it happened last night despite my exhaustion and horror.

No sooner did I hear Adelaide descending the stairs than I sprang to the window, opened it quietly and began to descend the rope ladder that Conrad and I placed there hours previously. Conrad was there, in the bushes, below the window.

He gripped my hand convulsively in an extremity of emotion and would have cried out had I not clapped my hand over his mouth. Before us we beheld the slender form of Adelaide as she moved towards the entrance gate. There was a click, as of a key being inserted, and it swung open. The moon was half full and by its icy radiance we saw her slowly proceed to the left of the gate, up the road towards the forest. Moving with infinite caution, we followed her as silently as shadows for we wore dark clothes and soft soled boots and had both had training as hunters, for we had grown up in regions where game is plentiful and the secrets of stalking are learned early in boyhood.

Now and again, she stopped as though suspecting we might be behind her, but each time she resumed her onward progress while we hid in the shadow of the great trees that came down to the wayside. Although it was already winter, an unnatural stillness reigned—broken only by the intermittent howling of a wolf in the mountains. As we rounded a bend in the rising road we came to a sudden halt. She had paused, barely fifty yards in front of us at the point where two little paths branch off from the side of the road. As we cowered in the shade of an overhanging rock, we observed her turn first one way and then another as though unsure which path to follow. A moment later, she sank on her knees, in an attitude suggestive of exhaustion or despair—we knew not which. There she remained as though she would never stir again. There was a profound silence. The distant wolf had ceased howling and even the wind that had sighed through the tree-tops had subsided. Conrad gripped my arm fiercely and I knew by the trembling of his tensed body that he was on the point of dashing forward towards her but I pulled him back as he was about to arise from his crouching position. The night wore on and still she never moved.

Then, after several long minutes had dragged by, she stood up again and began to walk along the lower of the two paths which, from previous stays here, I remembered led to a tiny hamlet and chapel, now largely deserted in favour of the village downhill. We resumed our pursuit, each wrapped in the most painful thoughts. Onwards she went, noticeably quickening her pace until the little chapel came into view, and glided like a wraith towards the cemetery. A moment later she had disappeared behind the wall. Casting caution to the winds we ran forward and into the cemetery and there, on a grave, lay Adelaide, convulsively scratching at the earth like a wild animal. She arose and shrieked as we bore down on her and struggled like a fiend in Conrad's grasp until at last she quietened and no sound was heard save the convulsive sobs that racked her frame. We brought her back, obedient as a child. She is still lying on her couch, wild-eyed and dishevelled. She has not uttered a word. Conrad still sits beside her. He has summoned the doctor. There is nothing else that we can do.

DECEMBER 13TH

Adelaide's condition has improved. She has spoken again, with every semblance of normality but the secretiveness is still in her eyes. Tomorrow I must leave but I shall be ready to return at a day's notice, should Conrad need me. I do not like to leave him alone with her like this but I must. He will not leave her out of his sight for a moment.

CONRAD MORHEIM TO AMBROSE LESSING
DECEMBER 29TH

Ambrose,

She is dying. The doctors say there is no hope for her. In a day or so she will be no more. Yet—although it breaks my heart to say it—it is better so. I have married a ghoul! I know now why she was so intent on going to that little cemetery by night. It was to desecrate the privacy of the grave! Yes, she is a ghoul, an insane lunatic, a scavenger! Two days ago she eluded my vigilance again. The following day there were reports of the horrible violation of a grave in that village. Someone had dug up the coffin of a poor young fellow who had shot himself in despair and whose body was allowed to lie in consecrated ground through the kindliness and forgiveness of a priest and his remains showed every sign of having been disturbed by an impious hand. This has been a great scandal naturally. Worse, I found traces of fresh earth in her room, and blisters on her hands when I went to her in the morning. She had succeeded in drugging me again—I fell asleep in the study and it was then that she must have accomplished her nefarious task. She was dying and scarce able to speak. Eventually, she whispered brokenly to me that she knew she had only a few hours, a day or two at most to live, and begged me to bring Stephen to her. I would not, I will not. It is bad enough that he is so mentally

67

deficient. I will not bring him to his mother who is worse—a blasphemous lunatic and grave-robber. At last, seeing that I was immovable, she implored me to go to a drawer and take out a little casket. In it I found a curious and finely wrought ancient ring. It is an heirloom, she says, and she begs me to see that it is given to Stephen when he is older—should he live to his majority. I agreed and she was calm again. I can hardly bear to see her. As for the frightful thing that she has done, I cannot bring myself to utter a word concerning it. She will only deny all knowledge of it. The purpose of her crime remains and will remain a mystery for ever. Why have I been stricken thus—is it not enough that our son has been born an imbecile? Ambrose, Ambrose? why has this terrible thing happened to us? What demon has possessed her?

JANUARY 1ST, 1877

On this drear and melancholy day, under a leaden sky and to the mournful accompaniment of the wind as it sang its dirge in the distant forest, Conrad and I, a few relatives and mourners, watched the priest perform his sad duty and the remains of she that was Adelaide being lowered in a flower-laden casket into her final resting place. As we turned away, my arm supporting poor Conrad who could scarcely stand, so broken was he by grief, I saw, out of the corner of my eye, the priest placing something in the grave with a gesture so swift as though he sought to avoid observation. A moment later he had joined us. "She will lie at peace," he said gravely. A sob from my friend was his only answer. "Yes," repeated the good priest, "she has suffered much but now she will be at peace. God's mercy is infinite."

Tomorrow I must leave Conrad again alone with his sorrow and memories. For the time being, Stephen stays at Ravensburg.

Dear faithful friend,

No words can ever express the gratitude I bear you for the noble, selfless way in which you bore with me in my ordeal. You sustained me in my hour of need. When, in my black sorrow, I was so sorely tempted to end this existence which has become so hideous to me, you gently reminded me of my parent's duty to little Stephen. You were right yet for the moment I cannot have him near me. Do not ask me why. It is better that he should stay where he is. It is strange but I feel that Adelaide is still here. Her loving soul seems to hover around me. Once indeed I imagined that I saw her walking in the grounds but I know that such a vision can only be the product of my over-wrought mind. I sleep with difficulty and when I do so, am more than ordinarily subject to wild dreams. Tell me your news. I long to see you again soon.

Journal of Ambrose Lessing

FEBRUARY 20TH

Word has come that Conrad is dead. I go at once to Kalasz.

FEBRUARY 22ND

Conrad died by his own hand before ever seeing his son again. Why he should have done this I do not know, except that grief must have unhinged his mind. The circumstances of his death were related to me by Marta and Caspar. He had summoned them one evening to thank them for their years of devoted service and informed them that as he would be leaving shortly, never to return, he had placed considerable sums of money at their disposal as a reward for their long loyalty and service. A few days later a shot was heard. He was found dead with a pistol in his hand in the library.

Caspar had just given me a sealed packet which his master had instructed to be handed to me if he should die. It is, I see, a diary of his last days.

A TRUE AND EXACT COPY OF THE LAST DIARY KEPT BY CONRAD MORHEIM

JANUARY 15TH

Can it be that I too am in the grip of some incipient mania that will lead me irrevocably beyond the borders of sanity? So insistent do these dreams become that I barely know when I have left the world of wakefulness for that of dreams or vice versa. What manner of mental contagion is this that first afflicted her and which now threatens to unseat my own reason? Why do I haunt her grave as though I expect to hear her speak to me from it?

JANUARY 18TH

I was wandering again. Strange that while my mind errs beyond the bourne of sleep, this body of mine imprisoned in the other world of solid reality should obey the imperatives of my dream existence! I was obeying her call last night, joyfully proceeding to where she lies when my arm was seized, a thousand confused images fled from my mind, and, in a lightning-quick transition from one state to the other, I awoke to behold Caspar holding me with a look of tender, grieving solicitude. "Master, where are you going?" he asked me. Where indeed? What was I doing at the bottom of the stairs, fully clad, after I had retired a full two hours previously?

JANUARY 23RD

Of late I have been so sluggish, so drained of energy, that I have been unable to set pen to paper. Each day I sit in the library for long hours, brooding endlessly. The servants move like shadows around me. They look at me strangely as though they suspect that I too shall become insane. I know that they are whispering about me but I care not.

JANUARY 25TH

Yes, they think I am mad. The doctor came today. Did I summon him or did they? I no longer remember. It matters not. To his persistent questioning I merely replied that my dreams were full of Adelaide. "But she is dead. I pray you do not dwell too much on thoughts of your loss, my friend," he said, no doubt meaning to be kind. "Fool!" I cried, in a fit of furious temper, "she still lives within me. Would you deprive me of that?" He calmed me and prescribed more sedatives—always more sedatives. I promised I would take them faithfully. I grow cunning—*I shall not* but let him be easy in his mind. He had discharged his duty. I shall discharge *mine*.

JANUARY 26TH

I must go to her. She came again to me—she was standing on the far side of some gulf—darkness veiled her from me but her voice spoke in my ear and she told me I must go to her. Yes, but how?

JANUARY 27TH

Her call is even more insistent. She needs my help. Her beseechings still ring in my mind. I awoke and sprang out of bed.

There is a pistol in my room, well concealed. Doctor Muller does not know *that*. I had picked it up and crying aloud "yes, my dearest, I shall come to you now!" I had placed the muzzle to my temple when again she spoke to me, bidding me desist. No, that is not the way. Not death—not yet. There is some other way. I shall be patient. I shall find the way.

FEBRUARY 2ND

I have been in a state of feverish coma these last few days. They tell me the fever has abated. They have left me. Now that I am alone I must confess all in these pages. No nightmare was ever more frightful, no reality was ever more soulrending than that I experienced that delirious night. Would that some final merciful blast of madness sweep down upon me and blot for ever the hideous recollection of what I did that night from my tormented consciousness!

But let me be calm if I can. I tremble uncontrollably. The pen drops from my fingers. I pick it up again and it quivers in my hand like an animate object. Perhaps it is. What *is* animate and what is not? I no longer know. *She* called me again, faintly and despairingly. "If you come not, I die for ever," she cried. So there is a greater death beyond death—did not the priest say that beyond death there is Life eternal? Terrified lest her already receding image—nightly becoming dimmer—should for ever pass from me, I dreamed that I answered her. Obedient to her summons and joyful in my obedience I arose and after donning my garments hurriedly, crept forth from the sleeping house with infinite stealth. It was cold, I recollect, bitterly cold. I shivered terribly as I went through the gate—Ha! they thought to lock it little knowing that one other key I have kept concealed, for do what they may, they shall not imprison me! Firm of step, heeding not the pitch darkness of the night nor the nearby howling of the ravenous wolves, I went down the road to the village unafraid and joyful in expectation of reunion with my beloved. No, I was not afraid and as though guided by some marvellous instinct I faltered not once as I hurried onwards, her cries still ringing in my ears. I passed as quietly as the fox into the cemetery, swiftly and surely I found my way to the side of her grave, led always by her summons. There was a spade nearby, doubtless left by the gravedigger. *She* led me to it. Like a furious maniac possessing the strength of several I dug deep through the mantle of snow into the

frozen earth. I dug like a madman, endowed with truly pre-
ternatural strength. I dug deeper and dimly recollect that as I
dug, I picked certain objects from out of the pit that yawned
under my feet. No fatigue slackened my efforts; I toiled in a
frenzy, in a dream of madness. like one possessed, her voice
growing ever louder until there was a piercing cry of triumph,
a flash before my eyes, a fleeting vision of her features, her
eyes open, a terrible smile of joy and fiend-like exultation
mingled, and then—blackness. . . I awoke cold almost unto
death, three-quarters covered by the snow that fell thick and
fast. I could barely stir my limbs and had it not been for an
immense effort of will, I would have lain there and succumbed
to the cold. Would that I had! A terrible lucidity replaced the
previous wild disorder in my mind. Aghast, I realised what I
had been doing. In a paraxysm of ghoulish frenzy, impelled
by I know not what unhallowed prompting of necrophiliac
lust, I had dug down to her coffin! Spurred on by horror and
remorse, I flung back the cold earth and shuddered as each
clot resounded hollowly on the wooden casket below. I must
have dug for at least two hours. There is little doubt but that
my frenzied activity saved me from the cold, while the wind
shrieked and tore around me. At length I could feel—I could
not see—that the pit had been filled in again. Casting away the
spade, I staggered away and after an eternity of stumbling
found my way out of that cursed cemetery and back on to the
road and painfully battled back to the house. Caspar found me
as I collapsed inside the hall and with tender sorrow stamped
upon his features led me to my room, asking me where I had
been and wondering at my sorry state, my torn clothes, my sore
and blistered hands, my wild expression. I fell into a deep
coma. Shadows moved around my bed. I heard the doctor
speaking yet knew not what he said. I returned to consciousness and learned that after Caspar had led me to my couch I
had dismissed him, returned to my bed and there been discovered on the morrow, a prey to a raging fever. When I returned to consciousness, I found Doctor Muller looking at me
gravely. He smiled with relief after feeling my forehead and
said "we thought you would die. Thank God, the fever has
ended. They found you fully dressed, you know. You had
evidently gone outside and wandered in the grounds." A terrible fear seized me. Did they but discover where I had been
and they would have me locked away! I looked at the window.
"It has been snowing day and night since you fell ill," the

doctor told me. "A terrible blizzard. One of the worst in living memory. The village is quite snowed under." The elements have come to my aid. With such snow my footprints must have been effaced and as for the grave—will traces of its desecration be found after the snows have melted? I shudder to think.

FEBRUARY 4TH

They say I am much better. I have been sleeping soundly and—strange to relate!—not once has Adelaide appeared to torment me in my dreams. I mourn still, the sorrow in my heart can never be effaced but something that was tormenting my soul has gone. In some way, I feel that my nocturnal expedition to the grave brought peace to her soul. As for myself, it is obvious that grief-crazed as I was, I sought to hold her form again in my arms in my demented state. Thank heaven, I regained my senses in time! The storm has passed. Henceforth I must lead a new life here, with my little Stephen.

FEBRUARY 7TH

I was madder than I thought. This morning, by chance, I remembered the place of concealment which contained the spare key I used to let myself out that night and discovered something else there too. Wonderingly, I held the still earth-stained crucifix in my hand and—and . . . Such were the sacred objects that Father Johannes must have placed in the grave after her body had been lowered into it. What compulsion led me to steal them so? I dare not confess to him. Let me replace them when I may. This further evidence of my madness has upset me grievously. I went to church and attempted to pray but some gloomy premonition distracted my thoughts. If only I could unburden myself to the good priest! He will understand and forgive. But courage fails me. I know that the snow will soon melt and that the disturbed earth over Adelaide's grave will reveal the presence of a desecrating hand and still I cannot, dare not speak.

FEBRUARY 12TH

Doctor Muller joined me for dinner. The strangest thing has happened, he tells me. In a village some miles from here, and not far from Ravensburg, there have been reports of a ghost. Worse, a peasant was found on the point of death, savagely bitten in the throat as though by a wolf. But upon regaining consciousness for a short time before finally expiring, the poor man swore that it was no wolf that attacked him but a woman who sprang at him from behind a tree, her eyes blazing, her face contorted with devilish ferocity. "They are superstitious there," I remarked, concealing my unease. "Yes, such superstitions are not unknown in these parts and derive from age old beliefs, yet such a thing has not been reported for at least a century," Doctor Muller replied.

FEBRUARY 13TH

A copy of the *Correspondent* dating from two days ago has come to my hand. It carries a report from the village of C***** some forty miles from here where another incident, similar to that related by the doctor occurred. The writer mentions increasing agitation among all the folk in the region.

LATER

Father Johannes called this afternoon. Usually of a cheerful disposition and of an energy that belies his years, he was strangely gloomy and preoccupied. Upon my asking him the reason for this, he informed me that he had received sad news from a colleague of his, a priest who had studied with him at the seminary, and who had just informed him of similar melancholy occurrences to those mentioned by the doctor and the newspaper. The people in his parish are in a constant state of alarm. A girl and a farmer have been savagely attacked and in addition, a member of the household of Ravensburg had reported the apparition of a white-robed female figure in the vicinity of the *Schloss*. "They say that the devil is among them," he said. He made as if to say something more then restrained himself. He is anxious, terribly anxious. If only I could speak to him!

FEBRUARY 14TH

It is done. I have unburdened myself at last to the good Father. I did well to do so. Together we have discovered a horror as yet undreamed of—a dread suspicion that reason and instinct urged me to dismiss from my mind has been proved only too

75

dreadfully confirmed. We leave tomorrow. There will be no sleep for me tonight. I do not think I shall ever sleep again.

This is what happened: no longer able to withstand the intolerable burden of my secret, I made my way down to the church. The snows had melted in the course of the night. I found Father Johannes standing with a look of painful sorrow by the grave of my beloved. "My son," he told me with infinite gentleness, "if you have faith then let it fortify you for I have dreadful news to tell you." He pointed at the grave where the churned earth spoke all too eloquently of having been disturbed. "Behold, some impious soul has attempted to disturb her remains." He fell silent and observed my face keenly. His look of gentle reproach was too much for me. I fell to my knees with a sob and began to confess all. He raised me and led me to the vestry after I had spoken only a few words. "Such a confession requires the utmost privacy," he told me. Seeing my condition, he offered me a glass of wine and then sat opposite me, until I was ready to speak to him again. He followed every word of my narrative with the keenest interest, sometimes asking me to repeat a phrase again, sometimes asking a question whose relevance to my tale I could not quite detect, and all the while his sad, wise, old eyes never left my face. I told him how *she* had come to me in my dreams, of her insistent summons, of my nocturnal wanderings, and of that climactic night when finally I had wandered out of the house and come to dig up her grave. "And then you say your sleep was no more troubled by visions of your dead wife?"—"From the moment I regained consciousness beside her grave, she had never again appeared to me in my dreams and no more have I heard her calling me," I said. I took the crucifix and Host from my pocket and handed them to him. He sighed deeply. "It is as I thought," he said anxiously. "You are *quite* sure that you never saw her again?" —"Yes." After another long pause, Father Johannes murmured: "The vampire travels fast. It has other things to accomplish for its hellish ends."

I looked at him thunderstruck. I had read in old books—who has not?—of the dreadful superstition of the vampire which lives in the bodies of the dead and causes them to arise from the grave and thereafter prey upon the living, but when I looked into the priest's earnest face I knew that what I had previously dismissed as idle tales and fanciful legends comparable with those that speak of witches, warlocks, werewolves and the like was indeed no fancy but a terrible, if rare, reality.

"Have you fortitude, have you courage?" he asked me. "Can you endure one last test? Will faith give you strength?"—I nodded. "Then we must proceed this evening, when it is quiet, to one final verification. If what I believe is true, then I will ask you to accompany me on a journey, this very night. Are you ready?" I assented.

As dusk fell, we stood by the grave while the gravedigger uncovered the coffin. Father Johannes had merely said to him that he was afraid some robber had attempted to despoil the remains of my wife thinking that some precious jewellery had been buried with her. Happily, the gravedigger was a simple fellow and asked no questions. When we sighted the coffin, Father Johannes motioned the digger away, telling him he merely wanted to bless the coffin and ensure that it had not been disturbed. "Wait here," he commanded me as I was about to descend into the grave with him. "It is enough that I see." With a strength and dexterity unusual in so old a man he unscrewed the heavy lid, moved it slightly, peered within and then shut it. "It is so," he said, emerging from the grave again. "She has risen." A short while later, we were in a carriage, riding furiously in the direction of Ravensburg. Tonight, we are in the hostelry at Pressheim. We resume our journey in a few hours.

FEBRUARY 16TH

We were met at Ravensburg by the priest, Father Sebastian, who showed great relief at our arrival. He told us that a young maiden had been haunted that very night by an apparition. The entire population were terrified. The authorities had been notified but so far had been able to do nothing. No one would venture out that night. Every door would be barred and marked with a cross. All dreaded the dusk that would shortly fall. With special insistence, Father Johannes asked his colleague whether there had been any reports of a grave having been desecrated in the neighbourhood and emptied of its contents? "The vampires, they that are dead and yet not dead, must rest in the day. For what unholy reason I know not, but they must lie in consecrated ground. I do not doubt but that she who *was* your wife—do not start so, she is not *now*—is even now lying concealed somewhere near here"—"Then let us search at once!" I cried in an agony of suspense. "Wait. First let us see if she will appear tonight." No evening meal was ever stranger than that I shared with the two good priests in that village and no vigil was ever tenser than that we performed after night had fallen and the last terrified inhabitant had bolted his door and shut every window tight: "This is the house of the maiden who complained of the apparition," whispered Father Johannes as we crossed the village square and made for our hiding place, a great shed where carriages were kept for farm produce. Hours passed and yet we saw naught. "Patience, my son," whispered Father Johannes, observing my restiveness, "it is not yet midnight." Shortly after that hour had come, he pressed my arm gently. Striving to see through the darkness, I fancied I heard a faint, remote voice calling softly. "Janiska!" Through the gloom, I could vaguely glimpse a whitish figure. I remembered that awful night when Ambrose and I had followed Adelaide through the forest on that fatal night and shuddered. Father Johannes squeezed my shoulder and gently pushed me forward. "You must go!" he whispered. "God's protection is close behind you! Now go, if you would help us rid the earth of this curse!"

Faltering, I emerged from the shed and began to walk across the wide square. It seemed as if an eternity had elapsed before I reached the other side and then—strange to relate—all fear fell away from me. Instead, a feeling of delicious expectancy stole into my soul. Why, there she was—my dearly loved Adelaide, as beautiful and radiant as she had been in life, standing before me. In that instant, it seemed to me utterly natural and expected that I should behold her like this. I was possessed by a curious happiness like that of a lover meeting his mistress at a preordained rendezvous. I forgot my previous wretchedness and the two priests who waited and watched in the shelter of the carriage shed. I only had thoughts for her. She extended her arms towards me and uttered a glad cry in a voice so sweet that it resounded like music in my soul. "Conrad, you have come to me! Come nearer, come nearer, my darling!" Entranced, I advanced still further. Despite the darkness that enveloped us, her face glowed as bright as the spectral moon, her eyes were like coals. "Come, my darling, come with me! Together we will serve our master. He is waiting for us. We shall find him soon. Help me find him. It will not be long now!" I came ever closer, yearning for the kiss that she would give me, for the feel of her arms around my neck, and had nearly reached her when there was the sound of dash-

78

ing feet, a cry of "In the Lord's Name!" and Father Johannes interposed himself between myself and her, brandishing a cross. With a fearful shriek and a visage contorted with hatred, she backed away, hissing furiously. "Back, back, in God's name!" cried the priest. With a last look of yearning love at me and with a glance of fiendish resentment at the man of God, she retreated ever more rapidly towards the nearby church. "Back! In God's name, I command you!" There was a last snarl, a flash of white, and she was gone. We were by the edge of the churchyard cemetery and were standing there unsure of our next move when Father Sebastian came up to us and tapped me on the arm. "I have it!" He whispered. "I know she is in there!" We waited for another half hour but there was no further sign of the apparition. Father Sebastian went in the church and re-emerged after a few minutes bearing a stoup of Holy Water. Together we made the entire circuit of the church and cemetery, sprinkling the water as we talked. Afterwards, Father Sebastian told us that he remembered that only a few days ago, as he was leaving the church to visit one of his sick parishioners, he had seen a strange lady bent in front of one of the tombs, the mausoleum of a local family, apparently engaged in prayer. Being in haste and unwilling to disturb her devotions, he had hurried on without going to speak to her. She wore a veil and he did not see her face.

Morning came. We had not slept a wink. "Now comes the most terrible trial of all," said Father Johannes, "but when it is finished your sweet wife will be back in God's grace and at peace." Father Sebastian conducted a short mass in a side chapel and then we emerged, Father Johannes carrying something in a black bag. The door of the little mausoleum was open. The lock had been snapped easily for it was of great age and much rusty. Inside, three coffins rested on shelves on either side. In a corner I shudderingly recognised the pitiful remains of one who had once lain entombed, and whose bones had been roughly thrown down by some godless hand. "This is the coffin," said Father Sebastian. Together we laid it on the ground and lifted the lid gently, the screws having rusted to dust.

Let me finish quickly—it is an agony to write these lines. In that violated coffin there did indeed lie a woman in all her strange beauty, her eyes open, her cheeks glowing with the flush of life, her lips ruby, her dark hair flowing about her shoulders, her entire body immersed to a depth of an inch or

79

so in blood—but it was not *her*. "This is some other woman," I shrieked, "it is not my Adelaide! There is a resemblance, there is a similarity of features, yet I swear it is not her! This is not my wife!" I forced myself to look again. Yes, there was more than a vague resemblance, she might have been a sister, but it was not *her*. I *knew* it was not her but the uncanny likeness filled me with such horror that I nearly fainted. "Then, if it is not her, my son, you will find it easier to strike," said Father Johannes, opening the bag and handing me a pointed wooden stake and mallet. "*You* must strike. Father Sebastian and I are old and weak. Besides it was you who raised her!" As though in a dream I placed the stake over her breast as instructed, I gazed one last glance at the living corpse who so strangely echoed my wife's lineaments, and then, in a black haze, I struck the stake with all my might.

I hear her shriek now. I see the writhing of that infamous *thing* in its coffin, I feel the spattering of that awful jet of blood against my face, I recall how for a short instant before consciousness left me I again beheld the peaceful countenance of Adelaide in the coffin after I had done my dreadful work. But worse was to come, I do not wish to remember how we had to sever her head or what we did with the pitiful remains . . . I do not wish to remember . . .

FEBRUARY 18TH

Stephen remains at Ravensburg. It is not fitting that he should stay here any more. I wish for solitude, for darkness and oblivion. Only one way remains to me to achieve that which I crave. It is a mortal sin, I know, but God will forgive me if he can. Stephen will never know. The priests promised that of that frightful scene in the mausoleum, of Adelaide's final state, no one at Ravensburg will ever hear a word. It remains a secret and I beg my dear friend Ambrose to respect it. I have but one last request: let him and Father Johannes drive a stake through *my* heart and cut off my head when they bury me. I have heard that suicides may walk again under certain circumstances. The agony of *this* existence has been enough for me.

By the Same
Unknown Hand

In view of the tragic fates of Conrad Morheim and his wife Adelaide, some remarks relative to their past history and origins are in order. Conrad Morheim was descended from a long line of warriors and administrators, had served the Empire as a soldier and civil servant and left public life to retire to his estates shortly after his marriage. His wife Adelaide Helsdorff came from an equally ancient family which, through a series of wars and pestilences not uncommon in that troubled part of Europe, had gradually been reduced to a single lineage, the collateral branches having, for various reasons, become extinct. Adelaide's father, although living in reduced circumstances, had succeeded in maintaining a certain position in local society but had few intimate friends and through persistent ill-health lived largely as a recluse, especially after the death of his wife. The match between Conrad and Adelaide occasioned some surprise for it had been expected that Conrad would have contracted a brilliant alliance with one of the wealthier families through his attendance at Court where he enjoyed high favour. Adelaide had little to commend her save a singular sweetness of disposition and a certain beauty which, while not outstanding, sufficed in her suitor's eyes to make her outshine all the beauties of aristocratic society. Unfortunately, the young girl laboured under another graver disadvantage in the eyes of Conrad's family and friends for she was of exceedingly delicate health and it was known that few in her family had ever succeeded in attaining man's full allotted span of years. In addition, certain rumours and disquieting stories had circulated in the past concerning her ancestor's origins and it was even said that they had changed their name on account of some dark crime which had once made their house shunned and feared. Despite all this, Conrad brushed aside his family's objections, quarrelling violently with most of

them as they remonstrated, declared himself passionately in love with the young girl and married her after
a courtship that only lasted a few weeks. Even though
he subsequently severed all contacts with his parents
and several relatives, Conrad's marriage was an idyllic one and when at last their union was blessed by a
son and heir named Stephen their happiness knew
no bounds. Then tragedy struck at the couple. Soon,
the child began to show alarming signs of mental
abnormality and backwardness, until it was sadly obvious to his parents that he was as deficient in intelligence and perceptive powers as his mother's line had
been in physical health and endurance. Despite the
constant care of physicians, the child seemed incapable of ever learning the powers of speech and communication that begin to display themselves in normal
children in the first two or three years of their life.
Physically, Stephen grew normally in every respect
but it was clear that while he might mature to manhood bodily, he was so mentally retarded that his intelligence, if it could be called that, would never be
more than that of an idiot. As the years passed, the
realisation that there was no hope of any cure for her
son's affliction proved too much for the unhappy
mother. Relatives and acquaintances spoke darkly of
the child's abnormality being the result of a union that
had been ill-advised from the start and although they
never uttered any words of reproach to her, Adelaide
must have been aware of their ill-concealed resentment of the fact that she had been responsible for
producing an heir so incapable of ever adding to the
lustre of the distinguished house of Morheim. No effort was spared to bring the child to some semblance
of normality but by the time he had reached his tenth
year, his mind remained that of an infant aged two
years at the most. It was while Adelaide's health suffered a rapid and alarming decline and she was dis-
playing all the symptoms described by Conrad and
Lessing, that the boy was removed to the care of a
distant relative, Colonel Tekely, who alone of all the
relatives, had always showed sympathy and understanding to the couple and encouraged them in their

hopes for an eventual change in young Stephen's condition.

After Adelaide's death and Conrad's suicide, it was agreed that the Colonel should remain the boy's guardian after various testamentary provisions had been executed and lawyers consulted. The question of the estates to which Stephen would eventually become heir at his majority was left unresolved until such time as it became definitely established that the boy was irrevocably beyond any hope of a cure.

Shortly after Stephen had gone to stay with the kindly Colonel and his wife in their pleasant property amid the rolling hills and vineyards of Ravensburg, and a few days after Adelaide's death, his mental condition showed signs of a change as dramatic as it was unexpected. The circumstances of this recovery are related in the Colonel's correspondence at the time.

Exchange of letters between Colonel Gabriel Tekely and Doctor Mathias Spitz; with notes on the correspondence

LETTER FROM COLONEL GABRIEL TEKELY TO DOCTOR MATHIAS
SPITZ, FEBRUARY 2ND, 1877

Dear Doctor.

Perhaps we may yet achieve that of which we pray. These last two days there has been evidence of some further betterment in Stephen's state which has given new hope (at last!) to Matilda and myself. We have sent word to poor Conrad but grief and a desire for solitude make him unwilling to see his son as yet. It is most peculiar and I could almost swear that since Adelaide's decease, Conrad holds the child in some aversion. I trust that he will eventually come to his senses. Meanwhile, it is much better that Stephen remain here than in that house of woe.

His babblings and broken utterances seem more coherent. Today he was able to utter at least a dozen words in logical succession, evincing a serious and considered attempt to express some intelligently conceived thought. There is a new light in his countenance, a spark in his eye that was never there before. Now when we speak to him, instead of his attention wandering as it did before, he gazes solemnly at us as though he were striving, with some immense inner effort of the will, to apprehend the meaning of every word. I knew ever since he came here, that there was some sentient intelligence locked away in his poor head. I now feel sure that we can free it from its dreadful prison. Do not ask me how I know. We have failed in the past but did you yourself not bid us hope? I will of course keep you informed of any new developments.

Meanwhile, it may amuse you to know that the folk here are as superstition-ridden as ever. A girl a few miles away was apparently found wandering in the woods at night despite the cold and claims to have seen a female demon or ghost or some such nonsense. If she were not completely unlettered I would say that her maiden's fancy had been set aflame by one of those supernatural romances which my niece tells me are so much in vogue at the time. But no tale of the marvellous can ever be half as strange as this betterment in Stephen's faculties if it but continues. Your friend.

Dear friend,

Yes, we are not mistaken. There is a betterment. Stephen awoke today and to our unutterable joy murmured several words. Naught of importance—only that he had "bad pain in head" and was thirsty but at least a beginning! His gestures and gait are more confident. He is beginning to co-ordinate his movements and that dreadful emptiness in his eyes has gone. I am sure he can understand me when I speak to him. Matilda is praying fervently with redoubled vigour for his eventual complete recovery. I prefer to speak to Stephen. I asked him whether he understood my words and to nod if he did so. The poor little fellow did not answer but sat gazing at me wide-eyed but then, as I turned to go, he suddenly came up to me and caught me by the hand. You know that such gestures of affection have never been normal to him. I was inexpressibly moved.

By the by, there is quite an epidemic of these rumours of hauntings and apparitions. The cause is this: a quite dreadful murder has been discovered. A poor farmer's labourer returning from some tryst with his sweetheart was found dead—horribly mutilated about the throat. No doubt some jealous rival is responsible. What is peculiarly horrible about this affair is that the murderer endeavoured to make his crime appear the work of a wolf to avert suspicion from himself. This melancholy occurrence has further inflamed the fears of the local people. They say, if reports are correct, that the wretched fellow's death was not due to any human or animal agency but to witchcraft. Well, well, you know as well as I do that we live in a strange and romantic land where the centuries may pass but still the natives believe in gnomes, spirits and forest sprites.

Your hopeful friend.

P.S. Matilda sends you her warmest greetings. Will you not stay with us soon? I assure you I extend the invitation quite as much from our desire to see you as a friend as from our wish that you examine Stephen again and tell us whether our hopes are illusory. I think they are not.

Dear friend,

Those long spells of torpor to which Stephen was so continuously subject now seem to be a thing of the past. There is an alertness in his manner. He strives to speak, and although he can only manage a few disjointed words, the will is there. Come soon.

There have been more reports of an apparition in the neighbourhood. The servants are now infected by the rumours and, indeed, one of the maids swears that she beheld a female form near the château last night . . .

(the rest of the letter is of no importance here and need not be reproduced).

RAVENSBURG, FEBRUARY 13TH. COLONEL TEKELY TO DOCTOR SPITZ.

Dear friend,

An odd little incident occurred today. So manifest was the improvement in Stephen that we decided that he should accompany Matilda to the village church. I, as well you know, believe that Church is for women and God for men, as the Spaniards say, finding my old soldier's simple faith quite sufficient to meet my spiritual needs without the intercession of the local clergy, many of whom I find scarcely less superstitious in their own way than the local peasantry. However, on this occasion I decided that I too would go to attend the service and show my face to the villagers. To be brief, I went down with them in the carriage and paid my respects to the priest who was greatly pleased to see that little Stephen is no longer the pathetic idiot-child the villagers held him to be (as you may guess, pride in his improvement was another motive in my wishing to display him in public). On emerging from the church, we walked some paces along the road, greeting various acquaintances that we passed when a carriage appeared in the distance, being driven at a furious pace. It came to a sudden halt near us, the door opened, and an elegantly dressed and heavily veiled lady, whose gait indicated youth, stepped out and went up to Stephen who had run forward to see the horses. She was dressed in black and through her veil I could vaguely discern her pale features and two dark lustrous eyes. After saluting us gravely and with majestic dignity, the strange traveller extended her hand to Stephen crying "Oh what a pretty darling! Come here, little one!" with such grace and such a melodious tone that Matilda and I were quite touched. Completely unafraid (formerly he would either ignore strangers or flee from them), Stephen went towards her upon which she laid one gloved hand on his shoulder, bent down and kissed him and, with her face close to him, whispered a few words none of us caught. She then straightened up, said "he is a delightful child. I wish you good-day" and mounted in her carriage which was driven by a surly-looking rider whose traits and costume proclaimed him to be one of those gypsies of Szgany who are to be found in the mountain valleys to the east of our province. They then drove off at the same breakneck rate. She was evidently a lady of the nobility journeying through the district but to what family she belongs I do not know as the carriage was without armorial bearings or indications of any kind. Anyway, Stephen has met his first admirer. Does he but attain a complete state of intelligence with time, and he will have many, I do not doubt it. He is a handsome lad.

We are delighted that you are coming. I trust that you will find Château Ravensburg a brighter place than when you last left. . . .

NOTE FROM DOCTOR MATHIAS SPITZ'S JOURNAL,
FEBRUARY 15TH

The Colonel and Matilda are quite right. There certainly has been an immense improvement in the child. Many of the abnormalities formerly observed in him have disappeared. His mental faculties, so long dormant, are now beginning to manifest themselves. I recommended that a teacher, well experienced in the coaching of difficult or backward children, be provided for him if all continues to go well. With application and judicious coaching, I am sure that he will eventually learn to speak normally and even learn the use of letters. The cause for his retarded condition remains ever a mystery but as yet these are things of which medical science still knows little. The human brain, especially that of a child in tender years, is a delicate instrument.

The rumours among the peasants which my friend related to me seem to have spread even to the château. Today, two more reports of a female apparition in the night and stranger still— when little Stephen came down this morning and I asked him whether he had slept well (he has been looking a little tired these last two days) he shook his head and said "no sleep. Lady". "What lady?" I asked him, gently intrigued. He seemed to think hard for a moment, rubbed his eyes, and then repeated the word 'lady'. "Come now, what lady do you mean? Was it Auntie Matilda?" Again, Stephen shook his head. "Not Auntie, Lady." "And who was she—this lady?" I asked, very slowly and distinctively, coaxing the child and deciding to humour him along. "Lady. M-m-m . . ." I bent over him to better observe him as his lips struggled to frame the syllables of some word that began with *M*. "Of course," said the Colonel, his face brightening after looking long puzzled, "he has been dreaming of his poor Mama. Obviously since he has improved in his mind memories of his poor Mama have come back to him. It is only natural." "You do not think there is any truth in these stories of apparitions of some mysterious female spectre?" asked Matilda anxiously. "Oh come now!" said the Colonel gruffly, "these are old wives' tales. The credulity of the local people knows no bounds and the slightest pretext is enough for them to start whispering their nonsense and falling prey again to the fears that plagued their ancestors."—"Perhaps our young man has fallen in love with the beautiful lady of whom you wrote," I suggested jestingly to the Colonel. "Ha! He has discernment. I'll vow he leaves few pretty heads unturned when he grows to manhood," said the Colonel proudly. Of course it is his mother. I begin to see the key to the mystery of the boy's affliction. Such cases are by no means unknown. A sudden shock, in infancy, some inherited weakness maybe—amnesia, inability to grow mentally, some atrophy of the intellectual faculties . . . Some slight shock or unexpected stimulus, who knows?—has been sufficient to redress the balance of his mind and unlock his imprisoned intelligence. I begin to see it all.

A dreadful shock to us all. That poor Conrad, little Stephen's father, has taken his own life, distracted by grief and oblivious to the good news we sent him concerning Stephen's improvement—it is a dreadful thing. Stephen is now an orphan but the Colonel swears that henceforth he will bring him up as if he were his own son. I know that he will do everything for the lad and that his presence will alleviate much of that sorrow at having lost his two sons in the recent terrible war. There seems to be death everywhere around us now. I heard that the wife of Baron Sandor died the other day after a short wasting sickness.

Interesting to note that there are no further stories of apparitions in the neighbourhood.

I am much heartened by Stephen's progress which grows daily. I am sure he will finally reach full normality. What a mystery is the human mind. In all honesty I do not think that any of us can take full credit for this recovery. Some greater power in nature has done that.

By the Same Unknown Hand

A few months after his recovery which daily became more complete, Stephen's eleventh birthday was celebrated by his rejoicing foster parents. Teachers were brought to give the boy all the instruction which should have been his since his early years and results were soon promising beyond expectation. In six months, he could speak normally. By the age of twelve he could read and write fluently; by the age of thirteen he could converse in French and German (the Colonel being of Saxon origin as so many in that part of the country) and was already well advanced in mathematics. So swift was his learning ability and progress that he soon outstripped his teachers' capacity to provide him instruction and more qualified mentors had to be sought for him. With every year that passed there came an immense increase in his intellectual and academic capacities. His mind showed unbounded agility, his memory proved to be enormously retentive and his ability to absorb great quantities of information was truly astounding. From first being a mental invalid, he became a prodigy. Simultaneously, he showed increasing signs of a gravity of one far beyond his years. Childish sports soon lost whatever little appeal they may once have had for him. The company of other children seemed to bore him and it was observed that when in their presence he would display a certain irritation and impatience as though, through the loss of his first ten years, he could no longer afford to waste time in pursuits usual to the young. It was remarked that as time went on he showed an increasing tendency to be imperious and reserved in his manner—except to his guardian and Matilda for whom he had nothing but respect and fondness. He also showed a marked inclination for solitude and reading. When not at his studies, he would go for long, lonely walks over the estate and the nearby forest, venturing even further towards the mountains, and riding for long hours without ever tiring, or he would devour the books in the Colonel's capacious library as though he could never satisfy his passion for knowledge, particularly in the fields of natural science, history and geography. By the time he reached the age of fifteen, his temperament displayed none of the natural exuberance of youth but only the intense, serious purposefulness of one destined to make a mark in the world. It was soon obvious that he had a scholar's bent and that his intellect would take him far if he were able to pursue his studies to the highest academic level. Accordingly, in order that he might be fully prepared for university, Colonel Tekely hired the services of a new private tutor and companion with the highest qualifications—a young Englishman who had been engaged in preparing a monumental thesis at Budapesth university, named Andrew Fuller, and who had been highly recommended to him through his friend Doctor Spitz by his professor.

It was at this time that Colonel Tekely began to show himself somewhat worried as to Stephen's absorption in studies to the exclusion of all other pursuits. Both he and Matilda agreed that the boy spent too much time on his own. The voracity of his reading was such that at times they became curiously uneasy—especially as some of the matter Stephen picked from the shelves of the Colonel's library was of a nature more suited for a mature and experienced scholar of certain philosophical and metaphysical disciplines than for an impressionable lad of thirteen, no matter how brilliant his mind. As the Colonel wrote to his friend, the doctor "let him be brought back to the normal, everyday life of a boy! There are some strange tales and histories among my books that I do not like to see him peruse for fear they inflame his still tender imagination. He tends to talk to himself and shuts himself alone for hours, neglecting his food until sternly reminded of the importance of a healthy body." As for the kind of tutor the Colonel had in mind, he specified that although Stephen obviously stood in need of an instructor with greater academic equipment than any who had so far been provided, "at the same time he needs a friend and a companion not too far removed from his own age. I do not want any of those dry-as-dust, bookish fellows who usually perform the office of a tutor in these parts. Rather, let us have someone who is as much at home in the country as in the schoolroom or library. An Englishman, such as he of whom you speak, would do perfectly. They are a sensible and well-balanced race in which keenness of intellect and scholastic prowess rarely become fossilised through pedantry, and they are also great lovers of nature and exercise in the open. Besides, to be a fully accomplished gentleman, Stephen needs practice in the language and must speak it perfectly." Accordingly, the proposition was laid before Andrew Fuller who accepted after being told that he would still have enough spare time of his own for him to complete writing his thesis and that the surroundings of the château were picturesque in the extreme and offered many delightful excursions. Of his pupil, he was told that he was of a healthy constitution despite the fragile health of his early years, and had been free from all serious ailments, that he was intelligent in the extreme, precocious even, amenable and pleasant mannered, but overmuch given to reading and solitude. There were a few other traits in his temperament which the Colonel did not mention, either because neither he nor his wife had observed them or, if they had, because they attached little importance to them. That Stephen had spent his first ten years of life in a mental void they did not see fit to inform Fuller.

Upon meeting his charge, Fuller's first impression was that the boy was far older in appearance than his years warranted. In view of his physical aspect and manner, he was sincerely amazed to learn that Stephen was, in fact, only a few months past his fifteenth birthday, and later confessed that he would not have been surprised if Stephen had been at least eighteen years old. His description of Stephen at that time is highly interesting. He found him thin yet wiry, slightly pale and possessing the delicately formed features that speak of true aristocratic birth. His mouth was remarkable for its thin but determined lips, his hands were strong with fingers "lean and tapering like those of a musician". Most of all, Fuller was struck by Stephen's eyes. They were "neither wholly grey nor wholly green although as the light changed so did one or the other colour take predominance but their glance was the most piercing, the most intense, the most *disturbing* (no, the word is not too strong) that I had ever experienced". In addition, what first seemed to Fuller an almost feminine languor in Stephen's movements was belied by an impression of intense inner liveliness, a kind of 'electric' quivering and restless energy which was part physical and part mental. It was with something of a start, Fuller later said, that he realised that what he had instinctively felt in the boy was some kind of compelling power or *force* which dominated those around him. This encounter seems to have caused Fuller a slight unease which was heightened by the way Stephen scrutinised him in return for "everything in his glance and demeanour suggests one who is descended from a race whose every look is a warning or a command, whose every word rings with confident authority".

In a short time, Fuller forgot his initial disquiet as he investigated the entire range of Stephen's studies till that date and began to plan his daily curriculum. History and languages, particularly those of that part of Europe together with its geography, were his favourite subjects, and already he could speak French, German and Magyar fluently. In Latin he was as proficient as any university student but in English grammar and syntax he still had much progress to make. But he was a more than willing pupil, his enthusiasm verged on passion, and with his splendid memory, his ready grasp of even the most complex propositions, and his pleasant manner, he could not have been a more satisfactory pupil.

But in many respects, Stephen remained an enigma to his tutor. In several of his letters to his friends and parents, Fuller repeatedly mentioned his impression that there was a slightly sinister trait in the boy, perhaps due to some atavistic streak of ferocity, inherited from his forebears of whom he knew practically nothing but whose bloodstained deeds seemed to occasion Stephen considerable pleasure. "They are a wild race still," Fuller wrote, "and in view of the almost uninterrupted series of wars and invasions which ravaged their nation, it is not so very surprising if still today they display a more than average tendency towards violence and aggression. Some of the family histories in this region are truly hair-raising. They fascinate Stephen to an unusual degree. I fear that in certain ways, his passion for past history is tinged by the morbid." In another letter, Fuller described one instance of his pupil's preoccupation with the violent past:

"As we went for a short walk I admired the architecture of the château, much to Stephen's amusement 'Oh, all this is nothing,' he said, 'look how restored it is. I love best the places that are really ancient. The castle where I was born—that was a fine place! I would like to go back there and dream again of the many great deeds performed in it, the battles it witnessed, the sieges it sustained and all the blood of valiant men that was shed there.'—Surely you do not admire the fact that so much blood was shed, do you?' I asked. 'Like so many other historic sites, its history seems to have almost exclusively been one of killing and strife.' To this Stephen smiled scornfully and replied: 'Blood does not frighten us. We are warriors and used to death. We fought the Turks, the Magyars, the Austrians,

Slovaks and Wallachs. Every inch of our land is drenched in their blood and from that earth there sprang new generations to avenge their forefathers and cause yet greater rivers of blood to flow!'

"I was taken aback by this unexpected show of blood-thirstiness. Stephen's eyes were glowing and his cheeks flushed as he spoke. He pointed at the jagged ruins that crowned a distant eminence set against the mighty backdrop of the mountains and rising out of a sea of trees like some great galleon, and said: 'See, that was where Prince Arvad held back the Turks and later defied all the Emperor's forces. For seventy days he fought then died like a lion, surrounded by the corpses of twenty-five knights. I should like to fight so—not with bullets and cannons but with an axe and a sword, severing veins and limbs and letting my enemies' blood run fast and free. Oh, I would love to see an old-fashioned battle!'

"He spoke with a tone of ghastly vehemence. What stern, cruel men his ancestors must have been! It was not so much ordinary boyish enthusiasm for the martial life, the sound of the fife and drum, and all the splendour of military panoply with which we poor mortals seek to disguise war's grim reality, which fascinate him. More than the feats of courage and endurance with which the history books are filled here, it is the actual thought of bloodshed and slaughter for their own sake that enthralls him. A strange boy indeed! I know very well that a vein of ferocity is reputed to run through successive generations of his race and that the history of every great family in these parts is filled with instances of the most atrocious cruelty and violence yet even so, this morbid relish of Stephen's leaves me uneasy. It suggests that there is a dark side to Stephen's nature of which I know little."

Another characteristic which Fuller detected in his pupil and which aroused his curiosity was the boy's reserve touching his own feelings and ambitions. He was extraordinarily self-sufficient, showed not the slightest desire for friends of his own age and time and time again gave Fuller the impression that his own thoughts mattered more to him than anything—apart from instruction—which others could communicate to him, and that he was in some manner the possessor of secrets that none would ever know. He never confided in either Fuller or his foster parents as most children do upon occasion. He *gave* nothing, Fuller noted, only *took* and nothing did he take more eagerly than the instruction so generously supplied him as though the absorption of knowledge were as essential to him as food and drink. What purpose he entertained in life, to what use he eventually would put his education he never told Fuller and yet, in all this gathering of knowledge and in particular in his passion to know as much as possible about the past there was undeniably some specific purpose. Even the Colonel could sense that there was some secret here and that Stephen was inwardly entertaining plans for the future. Like Fuller, he had to confess after a time that he could not understand the boy, and that communication with him, except upon the most superficial level, was rapidly becoming well-nigh impossible. Yet Stephen continued to show strong affection towards the couple who had nurtured him with such devotion even while refusing to open his heart to them. As Fuller wrote: "Stephen converses easily with the Colonel yet each time I cannot help feeling that there is little real understanding between them. It is as if each, by mutual and unspoken consent, had withdrawn from the other, recognising the other to be as a stranger, alien in temperament, interests, and vocation. Of course they are dissimilar—Stephen is not a son—but there is something else— a reticence on Stephen's side which grows more marked daily. I experience it myself. Sometimes Stephen will chat happily about something I have told him or which he has read but of himself, of his inmost feelings, his dreams and hopes and ambitions, he will say nothing. I feel—yes, I am convinced— that although there is much of *passion* lying within him, there is little of ordinary human emotion. The fire that burns in his soul is a cold one."

As the months went by, Fuller found himself subject to bouts of acute mental exhaustion after teaching his pupil. In a letter to his professor at Budapesth, Fuller declared that Stephen was making fast progress in English grammar, was able to read even the most difficult texts in Latin and Greek, and applied himself with diligence and enthusiasm to every subject set before him. Indeed, his zeal for learning was so great that both Fuller and the Colonel had the utmost difficulty in restraining the boy from working late into the evenings and neglecting all other activities. In the meantime, Fuller was finding it increasingly difficult to concentrate upon his own work. His mind would wander as he sat at his desk in the study the Colonel had provided for him, he found it hard to tear his thoughts away from his pupil and to immerse himself in his own manuscript, the fruit of years of brilliant study. He complained that his mental energy seemed entirely consumed in giving instruction to the boy while interest in his own academic enterprise was frequently diminishing. Stephen seemed to be absorbing his own mind and dominating his every thought. In this curiously despondent letter, he ended by saying; "I know too well now what it means to be 'wrapt in someone else'. I may well be taking my duties too seriously. Surely a tutor and companion must have some life, some interests independent from those of his charge. So I tell myself and then in my mind's eye I see again that young face looking straight at me, those intense, luminous eyes that seem to read my every thought. Do I but indulge in some slight jest to break the tension that arises on such occasions, and he will look at me as though he were in some strange way my superior and senior, endowed with an unearthly prescience, a wisdom of great antiquity and a mental vision far beyond my own."

Two other incidents during the period that Andrew Fuller stayed at the château disturbed him deeply. The first occurred during a hunting expedition led by the Colonel who was a keen shot and a magnificent stalker. There had been reports of a wolf being sighted in the vicinity. As it was winter and by no means uncommon for a hunger-maddened wolf occasionally to stray near the village in search of prey, a hunt was organised and the Colonel offered a prize for the first man to spot the beast. Stephen and Andrew accompanied the hunters. Many peasants of the district had been recruited as beaters but although an area of many acres was combed, the hour of dusk drew near without the wolf being sighted. Despite Fuller's alarmed objections, Stephen suddenly insisted on leaving the main party to wander into one of the densest parts of the forest. After a few minutes, Fuller lost sight of the youth completely. He called him in vain and, panic-stricken, was frantically scouring the area when, in the rapidly falling dusk, he came upon Stephen standing by a tree staring intently at a huge, bristling wolf that faced him from a distance of a mere ten paces. He raised his rifle to shoot, praying that he would not miss when Stephen peremptorily told him to desist. "Look," he cried exultantly, "he will not attack me!" It was true; although the beast growled at Fuller's approach, it remained still, gazing at Stephen as though rooted to the spot by the boy's hypnotic gaze. "No, I shall not kill it!" said Stephen softly, "let it die by some other hand. Go!" Before Fuller's astonished eyes, the wolf turned and disappeared through the trees. Stephen leaned back, pale and seemingly exhausted, against a tree, his eyes shut. After Fuller had agitatedly asked him if he were well, he smiled strangely and merely said: "You see, if the will is strong enough, what is there that will not obey?" A few minutes later, there was a loud report and the Colonel reappeared, followed by some of the beaters, carrying the dead body of the beast. No mention of the incident was ever made by Stephen or his tutor.

The second occurrence that both mystified and perturbed Fuller was during a walk with his pupil some time later. Stephen had been in a profoundly thoughtful mood all that day, and was little inclined to chatter as he usually did during their excursions. After about an hour had elapsed, Fuller asked Stephen what he was thinking. "I was thinking of a nobleman who once lived here," the boy replied, "he is in that book I found the other day. They say he was cruel and wild, yet what a noble ambition he entertained. To rule over life and death itself—what nobler aim is there?"

As Fuller wrote: "So strange were Stephen's words that I could hardly believe that I had heard them. Speechless, I stared at the boy who now had a faraway look in his eyes. He seemed as though in a trance for his eyes were vacant, his arms fell limply by his sides, and his footsteps faltered to a halt. 'Yes,' he continued after a pause of some duration, 'to command life and death and even beyond death is a noble destiny!' He suddenly pointed at some distant spot. 'Look there!' he commanded me. Automatically I looked in the direction he was indicating. In the dim distance, under a low and leaden hued sky, there rose the ruins of one of the many mighty fortresses whose jagged battlements and crumbling towers still attest to those lawless times when Christian and Turk struggled for mastery over the land. 'See!' cried Stephen fiercely, as he tightly grasped my arm, 'see how little there now stands of the seat of the Gernsteins whose name once struck terror into so many hearts and who knew no other will and law save their own. To think that death has ended their dominion after so many battles, so much killing, so much power and triumph! How they must have longed they could fight death and conquer that too! Now their great line is ended for ever!'—'No man can fight death,' I replied wisely, 'we are all born to live and then pass away in God's time when He calls us. No power on earth can avert the coming of *that* day.' Stephen's eyes flashed angrily. '*They* could not avert it yet others have struggled.

With knowledge and the will, they might have conquered that too! Oh, I hate death! Must I die too, Andrew? My mother died young did she not—and my poor father? I will not die! I shall not. What is life if there be death! Death too must die then! They say we die young in our family—yet I will not die!' I stared at him anxiously. Never before had I heard him speak of his dead parents and his strange words filled me with uneasiness as I tried to drag him away. 'Yes,' continued Stephen, still staring into the fast thickening gloom, 'they had not the will nor the knowledge!' Darkness swept down and hid the ruins from our sight. 'Come,' I said, 'it is dark and we must return.' He looked at me brightly and with a sense of relief I observed that his countenance was once more that of an ordinary, normal youth. As we briskly made our way back, it seemed to me that the words I had heard came from my fancy alone. They had given the impression of being strangely distant in their origin as though they had not been of recent utterance, had not even been those of Stephen but rather the echoes of words spoken long ago by some dim figure in another age who may once have stood brooding in that same spot. By the time we had returned to the château, I had practically convinced myself that I had imagined Stephen's outburst. Even now, I cannot help feeling that every now and again, I fall into a kind of daydream in his presence. Perhaps it is by some inexplicable process of mental contagion that I share his musings and am drawn into memories of that turbulent past which appears so recent despite the lapse of centuries and has such power to dominate a youthful and impressionable mind. No wonder superstition and legend are so deep-rooted in this wild country. But I digress—the Colonel was anxiously awaiting us in the hall as we entered. Gravely he told us that his beloved Matilda was seriously ill. Stephen's distress on hearing the news was as sincere as that of any boy who loves a foster parent."

*   *   *

Matilda lingered on for a few weeks then passed away peacefully. Fuller remained with the sorely stricken Colonel and Stephen until the time established for his stay had elapsed. It was not without a sense of relief that he departed for, although he would not say exactly for what reason, certain other characteristics in Stephen's temperament had disturbed him more than he could say. In any event, he had taught Stephen all he

could, and henceforth it was obvious that for such a pre-
cociously brilliant pupil, only the advanced learning of a
university could suffice. Fuller stayed a few months longer at
Budapesth, there completed his thesis to the entire satisfaction
of his professor and then returned to England. Occasionally,
at intervals of a few months, he received letters from his former pupil, and once, a few years later, briefly met Stephen in
the library of the Academy at Vienna where he had gone for a
few weeks' research, and noticed a peculiarly large and ancient
ring bearing an armorial device and set in gold on Stephen's
right hand—an heirloom, he was told. A few months later, he
received another letter that bore the postmark of Nuremberg
and which asked Andrew whether he could consult a book quite
unobtainable outside the British Museum, and make a short
note from a certain page. The book was Lessius's *De vitae et
mortuae misteriis* in Thomas Porter's English version, printed
at Amsterdam in 1612. The volume contained an addendum,
not to be found in earlier editions and confirmed Fuller's
belief that Stephen's interests were directed towards the strange
and esoteric for it gave particulars of a nobleman whose ancestress had been accused of murderous and occult practices. One
passage especially caught Fuller's eye and lingered in his
memory long after he had perused the volume and made the
note that Stephen had requested:

> *Perilous indeede be the Secrets of the Tomb. Let no Man
> in his Presumption endeavour to wrest from Death that
> from which Death shall not deliver him. Let no Man
> seek beyond Death's veil lest that which lieth beyond come
> seeke for him.*

*   *   *

Stephen's intellectual progress showed no signs of slackening
after Fuller had left. Despite the solitude that he would have
to endure, Colonel Tekely acceded to Stephen's request that
he be allowed to leave the château and continue his studies at
the University. By the age of eighteen, Stephen was a full time
student at the faculty of Budapesth and was showing the same
zeal and ability that had so impressed Fuller. He frequently
returned to the château at Ravensburg during his first two
years at the university, but although his company did much to
alleviate the monotony and loneliness of the Colonel's last
years, visiting neighbours could not help noticing that the old

man was growing increasingly uneasy in the young man's presence and curiously loath to ask him about the course of his academic pursuits. In the third year, Stephen only visited the château once. This time there was a heated altercation between the old soldier and his charge. Stephen had been asking for yet another considerable increase in his allowance which had already been supplemented many times. The reason was that he had much travelling to do—particularly to various distant towns and that the books he required for his work were now so numerous and expensive that his means were no longer adequate for their purchase. For some reason not wholly connected with the sum of money involved, Stephen's request caused Colonel Tekely great vexation. Shouts were heard from behind the closed door of the study where they were conversing, and one servant reported that in a tone of fury and despair, the old man had actually shouted: "Never, while I live! It shall not be by my aid! Wait then, if you must have it. Soon you will have means enough—and perhaps wisdom not to need it so!"

A few days later, Stephen returned to the university, apparently empty handed. That his demand for more funds had been in vain seemed confirmed by his subsequent behaviour. Previously, Stephen had been known to all his fellow students as one of an extremely reticent, retiring disposition. Although affable enough, he had constantly maintained all his relations with others at the most superficial level and even when one or two spirits were bold enough, and prompted by admiration for his immense ability, to make overtures of friendship, there was something in his manner which, while not exactly repelling them, caused them to desist. Discouraged, his fellows regarded him as a thoroughly 'odd fellow' and left him to his own devices, while continuing to talk wonderingly of his insatiable appetite for work, his long walks around the city at night, his frequent absences and the bibliophilic passion which led him to haunt every antiquarian book-shop in the old quarters near the university. The subjects which particularly engaged his attention mainly related to central and eastern European history, languages and traditions but his appearance had also been noted in sections of the university library dealing with more arcane matters, and in another library containing a wealth of genealogical material relating to many of the oldest families in the Austro-Hungarian Empire. Suddenly and to the amazement of his fellow-students, there was a complete change in Stephen's manner. Instead of being reserved and taciturn, he became positively merry and companionable. In what must have been a reaction against years of concentrated study and seclusion, Stephen began to be seen in the wine-cafés and the beer cellars of the city, joining in the student revels held there nightly with unfeigned zest. Several of his companions had sweethearts in the city and although more than one girl spoke glowingly of his handsomeness and his undeniable and previously unsuspected charm, his interest in their company remained non-existent although he never offended them by showit. One student for whose company he showed a special inclination was the young D****, the scion of a wealthy Moravian family whose financial resources were lavishly provided by his adoring and compliant parents. A few malicious tongues had whispered that the reason for Stephen's sudden affability was his need for funds and indeed, it was only a matter of a short time before D**** was flattered by his admired friend's request for a loan of some considerable amount which he unhesitatingly advanced, secure in the knowledge that when Stephen had reached his majority he would be more than able to repay the sum, even if it were increased a hundredfold. Shortly after receiving the money, Stephen disappeared, much to the annoyance of his professors, and the anxiety of D**** who began to wonder whether he had been exploited as one or two jealous students had claimed. A few days later, while Stephen was still absent, a report was published in a newspaper that a nocturnal marauder had almost been apprehended while in the act of desecrating a tomb in the country cemetery of K**** in the eastern provinces, and that although he had escaped, a night-watchman had managed to wound him with a pistol shot. When Stephen returned, two days later, pale and limping slightly in the left foot, his companions lost no time in jestingly accusing him of having been the author of this ghoulish act, only receiving a jest and a smile in reply. The following day, D**** provided his companions with a far more romantic explanation for Stephen's absence. Being Stephen's closest friend (that is as close to a friend as anyone could be, in view of Stephen's temperament), he had occasionally been admitted as a rare privilege into the intimacy of his chambers and this time, he had noticed on a portion of the wall not entirely covered by quaint old prints and maps, a small portrait painted in oils and luxuriously framed in heavy gilt. The subject was a young woman, dressed in an antique style, but of such a compelling beauty that it was no wonder Stephen had shown so little interest in such fair charmers as the city had to offer its students. Upon gazing at the portrait, unsure whether it were one of some antiquity or the representation of a living person, D**** had been startled by the way in which Stephen had abruptly reddened with vexation and snatched it off the wall, placing it face downwards in a drawer and adamantly refusing to allow any further glimpse of it, or to discuss the identity of the beautiful sitter. Highly impressed, D**** lost no time in telling his crones that Stephen had some secret love outside the city which doubtless accounted for his absences. As for his temporary lameness—what could that be but the result of some duel, either fought for the lady's favours or received from the hands of an outraged husband or rival? Their respect for Stephen knew no bounds and when, after a few weeks, he again approached D**** for a further loan, the latter readily and joyfully agreed, as though the request constituted an honour for him. No sooner had the money been handed over than Stephen again disappeared for the city, bound on some mysterious errand which, D**** affirmed, was not unconnected with the beautiful lady of the portrait. Unfortunately, a dim view was taken of such romantic escapades by the university authorities and when Stephen came back he found himself facing the exasperated wrath of his tutor and professors who solemnly warned him that no further behaviour of this kind would be tolerated, that his foster parent would have to be informed and that only his previous academic attainments saved him from instant expulsion. To make matters worse, D**** embarrassedly confided to Stephen that his adoring family's compliance to his financial needs had come to a sudden, dramatic end, after they had learned of his frivolous expenditure on matters little related with his studies, and that he stood in desperate need of quick repayment of at least part of his loan.

No sum, above that provided for the barest physical necessities was forthcoming from Colonel Tekely whose silence showed how much he disapproved of Stephen's conduct as reported to him.

In desperation, Stephen turned to the one ready way to repair his finances. He began to play cards for money with some of the less reputable elements at the faculty and after an initial period of instruction by the no less desperate D**** began to show himself as adept at gaming as at study, winning sums that grew progressively larger. After one particular bout, played into the early hours of the morning, when he had won several thousand florins from the young Baron C****, a noted wastrel known as much for his wealth as his profligacy, the inevitable happened: Stephen was accused of cheating. His abnormal luck, the succession of his winning games, and his uncanny knack for predicting the cards dealt to his opponent, all seemed to confirm Baron C****'s loudly proclaimed suspicions. As in so many other parts of Europe at that time, there could be only one issue to such a charge and that was a duel. D****, as expected, acted as Stephen's second, and the encounter was secretly planned for the following dawn in the nearby woods, the choice of weapons being swords.

The circumstances of the duel were curious. Baron C**** was wounded slightly in the arm after a few passes and afterwards claimed that his arm had felt abnormally heavy as he held his sword, and that he had been unable to concentrate after the intense gaze of his opponent had held his eyes and made him feel strangely giddy and unable to hold his ground. The matter was hushed up afterwards and considered at an end, Stephen's honour being vindicated, but thereafter no one would play cards with him any more, so that both he and D**** had to subsist on greatly reduced means. A week later, a final warning was issued to Stephen whose work had sadly declined of late. He shut himself up in his chambers for several days, refused to see any of his former companions, and then emerged to hand his astonished tutor an exceedingly brilliant and thorough study of the relationship between certain local lore in the southern provinces and Bogomil traditions followed by an amazingly detailed and perceptive appendix which completely proved what Hofberg had only dared to suggest with regard to the parallels between certain Szekely and Ruthenian traditions. The work is still consulted by scholars in the university library and was declared to be quite extraordinary for one of Stephen's age and experience by the professors of the faculty. As for his past absences, they were more than half convinced that they were due to Stephen's initiative in gathering material himself on the spot.

After his academic triumph, Stephen no long showed the slightest desire to renew his acquaintanceship with his former companions and once more became the recluse of his first two years at university, although he still showed cordiality to his creditor, D****, and assured him that full repayment of the remainder of the loan outstanding would not be long in coming. He no longer caroused in the taverns or gave his professors any cause for reproach but instead shut himself up for entire days in his rooms when he was not at work in the libraries, only going out at night. But as previously, he again became the object of rumours. It was said that he had been in certain low quarters of the city where few students ventured, in the company of a strangely ill-favoured individual who from his garb and speech came from some remote mountain region. Once even, the man had been seen at Stephen's house, delivering a sealed packet to the housekeeper for her lodger. At another time, Stephen had been seen climbing into a carriage with his new companion and riding to a village a few miles outside the city late in the evening. A week later, as D**** had finally prevailed upon Stephen to take a short walk with him, the man came up to them, from a nearby tavern, and spoke to Stephen briefly in a tongue never before heard in that locality. All Stephen would say was that the man's name was Vihar and that he occasionally performed some small, useful services for him, and that he came from a village a great many miles away. On yet another occasion, as two students passed by Stephen's lodgings and looked upwards curiously at the lighted window where Stephen's silhouette could be seen as he bent over his desk for hours at an end, they thought to recognise the profile of the strange man who appeared to be deep in earnest conversation with their erstwhile companion.

Several months passed. The vacation had come and gone. Stephen had returned to Ravensburg with a trunk load of books and spent most of his time in isolation, only joining Colonel Tekely for meals. The household remarked sadly that there now seemed to remain little of the former affection that had existed between them, and that the Colonel appeared positively unhappy during the period of the young man's presence. The only other incident of note at the time was that a rough looking fellow had been seen prowling in the vicinity of the château and had, upon being questioned, insisted that he had something to communicate to the 'young master'. Stephen descended to the village, spent a few minutes with the man, in a quiet back room in the local inn, and then returned to the château, with his interlocutor riding away in the opposite direction.

Soon after returning to Budapesth, Stephen was summoned back to Ravensburg. Word was brought to him that the Colonel was dying and had only a few days to live. When he arrived,

Colonel Tekely was rapidly sinking. The last encounter between the old man on his death-bed and Stephen was witnessed by both the doctor and the local priest and remained firmly imprinted in their memories for many years afterwards. The scene had been both moving and horribly disturbing. Stephen had shown himself deeply affected by the sight of his foster parent and had expressed remorse for the distress his conduct had sometimes given the Colonel, and proclaimed his heart-felt gratitude for the many benefits he had received since being brought to live at the château. The dying man had regained sufficient consciousness to recognise and hear him. At length, with one last tremendous effort of the will, the old man raised himself slightly from his pillow, and fixing Stephen with such a stare that seemed as if all that remained to him of vitality was concentrated in his burning eyes, said in a tremulous voice yet one filled with the utmost urgency: "Do not do it, Stephen! Beware if you value your soul! Beware!" Exhausted, he sank back again after a last despairing glance at Stephen who remained calm and impassive by the foot of the bed. As Tekely closed his eyes, his lips were seen to move still whereupon Stephen, the doctor and the priest all bent low over the bed to catch whatever last words he might utter before his soul departed. After a heart-rending struggle in which he seemed to be trying to retain the last breath of life in his wasted frame, the sufferer's lips strove to frame the syllables of his last message and in a barely audible whisper uttered as one final warning the words: "Beware, Stephen. Leave the dead alone" before expiring. After paying his last respects to the corpse, Stephen went out of the room without a word, leaving the doctor and the priest wondering at what they had heard. Immediately after the funeral which was held two days later, Stephen left the château for the last time.

*   *   *

Back at the university, Stephen resumed his studies, applying himself even more zealously than before and showing an even greater desire for seclusion. But although he fulfilled every demand of the courses he was following, it remained apparent to his professors that his real interests lay elsewhere. It was noted that several times he requested books and manuscripts from the library which led him along different paths from any he had followed before and which had little if any relation with subjects being taught at the faculty. At the same time, he wrote several letters containing genealogical queries concerning long extinct families to various keepers of records and archives throughout the country, and was showing definite signs of frustration as each time his investigations ended in failure. Finally, Stephen attained his majority and left the university to be apprised of his inheritance by the lawyers responsible for executing the testamentary provisions of his father and foster-parent.

A considerable sum of money had been left him from both sources, which, together with revenues accruing from various estates that became his, assured him a prosperous future. The remains of the mansion where he had been born were his, as was a large estate and the ruins of an old fortress many miles to the east, a still habitable castle surrounded by vineyards, and extensive farmland but what particularly excited his attention were an old sea ring, bearing an armorial device of great antiquity and a small sheaf of papers which had been found among his mother's possessions after her death together with instructions that they should not be delivered to him until he had reached the age of twenty-one. The papers, it must be confessed, had already been inspected by one of the family lawyers upon the request of Stephen's father shortly before his tragic death and showed certain peculiar features. In the first place, although they had been written in Adelaide's hand, the formation of the letters was strangely archaic, showing a style of hand-writing that had not been used for at least two centuries. Secondly the language used was a Magyar dialect of sorts with which Adelaide had not been in the least familiar, and which similarly contained so many archaisms and eccentricities of syntax that even one well versed in modern Magyar would have found them almost undecipherable. Nevertheless, Stephen was observed to betray signs of great excitement as the papers were taken out of their casket and handed over to him with the remark that although they seemed completely incomprehensible and were probably copies of some old manuscript, his mother had been most insistent in her accompanying note that he should have them. After returning to Budapesth, Stephen abruptly told his professors that he was leaving the university at once, packed his belongings, sending most of them to the care of the old retainers who still lived in his parents' house, drew a large amount of money from the banking house which administered his new wealth, and disappeared for several months.

It was later known that he had travelled extensively, throughout central Europe and even to London. Several times over a period of a year, he had visited libraries and archives in old town halls, and on more than one occasion had requested help with the study of the script and language of the manuscripts but each time it was made clear to the scholars and librarians that he approached, that Stephen was highly reluctant to allow the papers to remain in their hands for anything more than a few minutes, or to let them attempt copies of any portion of the writings despite the fact that he was told that his unwillingness made it well nigh impossible to help him. Eventually, after a careful comparison between the papers and some old letters found in a collection in Prague, Stephen ceased his travels and, accompanied by the strange Vihar whom he had hired as a manservant before leaving Budapesth, came to settle down at Torberg, an ancient château of sinister reputation in the past and which had come to him as part of his inheritance from his father. There, he established himself for the winter, dividing his time between the administration of his estates and further study. His relations with his neighbours who included several old families who had lived in the region for generations were cordial but never close and, after Stephen had politely but firmly declined several invitations, it was accepted without rancour that he was something of an eccentric and a bookworm, more at ease in his library than in society. Despite the disappointment of several mothers with daughters of marriageable age, his obvious wish for privacy was respected if not understood and all who had dealings with him in business matters spoke of him with high regard. Similarly, his behaviour towards his tenants and workers was exemplary and no complaints were ever uttered although some did remark on the presence of two or three uncouth and strange looking peasants who spoke little known dialects and seemed to perform errands for their master. The following spring, Stephen undertook several journeys into the mountains for periods of a week or ten days at a time. It was while returning from one such expedition that, to the general amazement of the whole countryside, he met and passionately fell in love with the beautiful Elizabeth Sandor.

Correspondence between Elizabeth Sandor and Marguerite Fenshawe

Dearest Meg,

Thank you and thank you again for your dear, sweet letter. I am doubly happy today for I have also had a letter from Ernest. Oh I am so happy! I wish I could tell you how much and share my joy with you. I am so glad that you are happy and that everything is arranged between you and Andrew. He is a wonderful man, kind and noble and courageous and if it had not been for him I should never have met Ernest—but there, enough of these girlish effusions! Suffice it to say that you have my every blessing and that after Ernest (and of course Papa) you are the dearest person to me in the whole world. Oh, won't you come soon and visit us here? Papa too would like it so. Even better, why not come after you are married? There could be no better place in the world for a honeymoon. But let me give you my news! Papa has consented—oh, I always knew he would! Who could not approve of Ernest? Yes, Meg, he gives us his blessing and what is more, Ernest is coming here to stay as soon as his vacation starts at the college where he is now teaching. We shall announce our engagement here to all the world at my twenty-first birthday party and then he must go back to England for many long, long weeks before we get married. It will be a short engagement as you see, but as we shall be separated for most of the time it will still seem as years. How strange to think of you in England now. Apart from you and Ernest, I wonder at times which country I love the most. It is really quite puzzling at times, being half-English and half-Hungarian. Sometimes, I feel that this beautiful wild, savage country is my only home—I am part of every rugged mountain peak and crag and forest and stream and then I long for the gentler landscapes of Surrey and Hampshire. People there are not rough and fierce as they are here and life is so deliciously cosy and well-ordered. And London—how I miss it with its great buildings, its teeming streets, noble squares and elegant shops! Yes, I concede that Vienna is lovely and that

Budapesth is very fine and antique but I can't help agreeing with the poet who said that London is 'the flower of cities all'. Here, our only capital is Klausenberg and though the people are pleasant enough it would make you smile to see how behind the times they are, and how provincial. Even Hermannstadt is more imposing, if less quaint, and Budapesth might be another world as far as the people there are concerned. As for the fashions! Well I won't bore you with my lamentations on them but please do send me the latest plates won't you? Katia will do her best if I give her proper instructions. After all, it would never do for me to appear dowdy in front of Ernest! He is far too handsome and intelligent and discerning to deserve a frumpish country maid. There—you see how I cannot write a line without mentioning him. Forgive me, dearest, let me tear myself away from him now and try to tell you something more about our home here and our simpler manner of life.

The house is not like one of those frowning Gothic piles or those great sinister fortresses that seem to crown just about every rock and hill near here and in which you imagine me to dwell. It is quite as comfortable as any English country home and built somewhat in the French style. We have few servants in comparison with other houses but they are still quite sufficient for the modest train of life we lead. The main body of the estate with the vineyards is down the road towards the village where most of the population speak a German dialect of sorts since they are mainly of Saxon origin like so many others in this part of the Austrian Empire, but we also see many gypsies nearby, all of them picturesquely clad in their sheepskin coats, tall bonnets and fringed leggings. I enclose a little sketch for you. You see I have made some progress here. Miss Wheatley would be proud of her pupil if only she could see some of the water colours I have done lately. There is a dramatic quality in the landscape that greatly inspires me here. I am sure it must also affect some of the more sensitive local people too for there is not a wood, not a portion of the great forest and the mountain slopes that does not have its traditions, its tales of past wonders and strange beings who dwell amid the trees and who are said to come out and affright the solitary traveller. Other villages further from here speak the Ruthenian dialect and still further there live many Szekelys—a strange people who say that they are descended from the original Huns who invaded Europe from the East when Rome fell. They are a curious and superstitious lot and not much liked by their neighbours on account of their uncouth ways I suppose. Still, they are all a part of that immense variety of races and folk traditions that makes this country so fascinating for the explorer and traveller and as you know, we Sandors are descended from some exceedingly ancient stock who seem to have come to Transylvania in the dawn of history. Papa likes nothing better than to browse in the old history books and to remember what a long history we all have here. Many of the stories he can tell are quite frightening and confirm me in my suspicion that all those old nobles were just as savage and uncouth as the people they lived amongst. To think that the last Sandor is myself! After so many great warriors and knights, the house is now represented by my feeble, girlish self. Collecting wild flowers and painting seems hardly a typical Sandor passe-temps, does it? I know that Papa has never stopped grieving that he never had a son because of poor Mama's untimely death although he would never show it for all the world. Poor Papa! How glad I am that I can give him some happiness at least. We go out quite a lot together. There is always something to be done on the estate and I take my responsibilities towards our people very seriously and daily gain something from Papa's wise instruction. Otherwise, our life here is spent very quietly. We see a few of our neighbours of course and there are hunting parties and occasional dinners and every now and again a trip to the city and that is all. Recently, we have had a new neighbour, a very brilliant young man I believe, who has inherited some land nearby and an old manor but so far we have not seen him. I believe his foster parents are recently deceased and that he comes of a family that was struck by some horrible tragedy —a fire or a terrible malady—I am not sure which. Nobody can tell us much about him except that he lives in seclusion and is very bookish and given to study and travel. Now with this tantalising morsel of information I must close. As always, all my fondest love to you and dear Andrew. I await your next letter with impatience.

Your loving Elizabeth.

ELIZABETH SANDOR TO ERNEST ARMSTRONG, JUNE 5TH

Dearest,

Your sweet and loving letter has made me very humble and very very happy. You are truly the noblest, kindest, most considerate and wonderful man that any girl could hope for and

*if at times I stop to wonder 'does he really love me?' it is
only because your love—our love—seems to me such a miracle,
such a blessing that I almost feel I am dreaming, and that I
am about to wake up and find it was all an illusion. Please don't
laugh at me, will you? I am still not used to such a blessing and
your absence sometimes makes me afraid that it was all a
figment of my girlish fancy until another of your letters comes
to reassure me and tell me that it was not a dream, and that
soon, soon you will be here with us and this long waiting will
be over. Papa often speaks of you and I know that he is both
proud and happy to have such a distinguished future son-in-
law. Yes, Ernest, he already speaks of you as though you were
the son he never had and I know he thinks that I could have
made no better choice although, as you know, from the first
moment we met there was never any question of choice—only
a triumphant, happy certainty. But although he is happy in this,
I have seen in Papa an increasing gravity of late. He has not
been particularly well and although I tell myself it is only an
idle fear yet I cannot help being afraid at times that all is not
well with him. The physician came only recently and although
when I asked him he was as cheery and optimistic as ever, I
thought I could detect a slight reserve in his manner as though
he were concealing something from me. Papa is not ill but he
looks older and his manner at times is that (I must be brave and
admit it to you) of one who sees his life as one that has largely
run its course. Yesterday, after dinner, he was in a very solemn
although affectionate mood and he spoke to me a long time
about you, saying that nothing had made him happier than to
grant his consent to our engagement and that after seeing us
wed and my future assured, he could die happy. Yes, Ernest, I
am afraid he spoke of dying, although gently and lightly so as
not to alarm or distress me overmuch. Perhaps it is because I
shall inherit everything and because he so longs to see me protected and loved and counselled by you, and he is afraid of
leaving me alone and defenceless should any sudden calamity
take him away from me. He spoke to me of the responsibilities
and duties of being an heiress, of the various testamentary dis-
positions he had made and of those whose counsel and aid
will always be available to us both, and of the problems of
administering our home here when we are absent in England.
Apparently we have some properties far away from here, in
wild and remote regions where no Sandor has lived for centuries and he was peculiarly insistent that they remain in our*

holding, as they have done for so long. I do not know why he made such a point of this but he laid great stress on the necessity to ensure that these estates continue intact no matter what contingencies may arise in the future. I was deeply impressed by his speech and greatly moved by the way in which he alluded to you. "Yes," he said, "there are many responsibilities in being a Sandor and an heiress and he, I know, will help you fulfil them more than any other man alive". He repeated this several times before falling into one of those reveries to which he has been increasingly prone of late. Then he arose and laying a hand on my shoulder, drew me to him and then kissed me in such a way that I was moved to tears for in his demonstration of affection I am certain I detected a kind of gentle, loving farewell with an underlying hint of acute apprehension. Oh Ernest my dearest, how I long for you to be here now—can you come sooner? Forgive me for pleading with you but if you knew only how desolate and dreary each awakening is without your sweet presence here . . . Baron Terzberg was here recently with his daughter and both send you greetings. Otherwise, I have seen no one. Our new neighbour remains invisible. He is it seems a strange man and people say here that he is of a very studious and retiring disposition. I think he must be a little alarming but this is probably only because of the mystery surrounding him and his invisibility. I like to think that he is one of those romantic heroes of opera with some secret in his life, or is it that he has been sadly disappointed in love and now wishes to bury himsef away here, far from the world . . .

Elizabeth Sandor's Diary

JUNE 17TH

A strange day. It began with another letter from Meg but none from Ernest. I must confess it to myself: I cannot help feeling a little jealous of dear Meg though it be ignoble of me. She has her Andrew near her and may see him every day. I long for Ernest dreadfully and also yearn for someone—anyone—to break the monotony of these last few days. How alone we are now! Papa has not been feeling well and shows little desire for any company. Even I seem to tire him and the house is mournfully silent. But there occurred such a strange incident today. Even now, I do not know for sure whether it really happened or whether it was a creation of my idle fancy, perhaps a result of overmuch brooding and isolation. On the whole, I suspect it was a young and romantic minded girl's daydream even though I am seldom given to such flights of fancy, either awake or sleeping.

I went out after luncheon to pick some wild flowers which I then went to place upon Mama's grave and then, the weather being so fine, resolved to walk back the long way, by the little path that ascends the hill from the village and proceeds through the woods before eventually leading back home. As I slowly made my way back, I lost myself completely in a lovesick reverie and soon found that I had strayed from the main path to the other smaller track that leads higher, to a little plateau commanding a fine view of the landscape for many miles around. It was a sublimely beautiful day—one of those days in which the whole world seems at peace while nature basks in the golden glow of a late summer's afternoon and it was with scarce surprise that I realised that by some volition of their own my feet had led me to a favourite spot I have often chosen for my musings, a pretty little vantage point I long to show to Ernest, sheltered by tall trees and carpeted by the prettiest wild flowers and herbage. After admiring the graceful and harmonious beauty of the scene and regretting that I had not brought my sketch book with me, I sat down on a small flat boulder in the midst of the small clearing, overlooking the undulating hills and the mass of forest. No more idyllic, peaceful spot for solitary contemplation can be imagined and it was there, while the still shadows of the slender trees lengthened on the uneven ground and the wind sighed through the firs above that my thoughts dwelt in succession on the solitary tomb where the remains of my poor mother rest, on my early bereavement, on my dear Ernest, so far away in space and yet so close in my heart and mind, of all that Papa had been saying to me lately and of the gentle melancholy which seems to be taking possession of him. I thought of death and life, of hope, joy and sorrow and of that love which, I so firmly believe will conquer all in this world and the next and as I sat there thus meditating there floated mistily into my mind as if in a dream images from my childhood, my growing up, my years in England, my meeting with Ernest and my return to this romantic land of my ancestors here—this land which will also belong to Ernest in a short time. My thoughts gave way to a pleasant drowsiness mingled with feelings that oscillated tantalisingly between vague regrets and delicious anticipation—in short, all the emotions of a lovesick maiden waiting for her lover. How long I lingered there I cannot remember but it must have been quite a long time for when I looked up again to contemplate the majestic scene before me, the shadows of the forest were stealing towards me and the sun was low over the mountain-filled horizon. Suddenly as I looked towards the trees, I fancied that I detected a dark figure behind the dense foliage of the undergrowth and there came to me the conviction that I had been under close scrutiny by this mysterious stranger for no little time. I stared hard until my eyes blurred and then, as though overcome again by invincible somnolence, closed them again. There was the sound of approaching footsteps, I opened my eyes and there, barely five paces away, there stood a stranger of singularly striking appearance, who uttered a courteous greeting and continued scanning me with the utmost intensity. He was young, perhaps in his thirtieth year, dark, slender, dressed in the height of elegance and obviously a person of considerable birth and breeding. His long hair was brushed back to reveal a high and noble brow and his pale, delicately formed features and aquiline nose betrayed a temperament of iron resolution while his luminous eyes shone with a particular fire which would have frightened and disconcerted me had it not been that the element of surprise in this unexpected encounter had banished any fear. Almost rudely he stared at me and I soon realised that his surprise at least equalled my own, but in a moment, that astonishment that echoed my own was replaced by another, even more disturbing look which I could only interpret of one of inner triumph although he quickly mastered himself, and asked did I live in the great house nearby? I answered that I did and enquired in my turn whether he was the person we had so recently acquired for a neighbour. His only answer was another intense stare and the remark that 'I would soon know him'. His lips moved and then trembled as if he would speak but could not bring himelf to utter, his face flushed, his eyes averted mine quickly, and then, as suddenly as he had come, he hurried away. In a few moments I had completely lost sight of his figure amidst the dense mass of trees. Completely baffled, I remained standing still for a few minutes and then hurried back home, no longer quite sure whether I had seen a phantom or not, so strangely dream-like was the encounter. Even now, I cannot tell for sure if he really was a flesh-and-blood person or some creature of my imagination who had come to interrupt my solemn musings. I fancied, I half believed, that he had said something else to me—I know not what—but although the precise import of his words escaped me, his sonorous voice long lingered in my mind like some half-remembered melody heard in a dim and distant past. I hear it even now.

JUNE 19TH

Another wonderful letter from Ernest but—alas—he cannot leave yet awhile. His work and duty detain him and though he longs as I do for our speedy reunion, he cannot depart upon the previously appointed date and so our separation must be pro-longed by a few more dreary, joyless days than we had thought. Pray God there be no other impediment after this!

I now know that the mysterious apparition of two days ago was neither a ghost nor a dream but indeed a person of un-questionable corporeal solidity. To my boundless surprise, as I came down from my room, I heard Papa conversing with someone in the drawing-room. For a moment or so, I stood breathless in the hall as I heard the voice of the visitor. A minute later, Papa and my mysterious stranger came out. Papa introduced him to me as Stephen Morheim, our new neighbour, and after I had managed to contain my initial feel-ing of surprise, greeted him civilly enough. He, in turn, greeted me ceremoniously with an exquisitely old-fashioned gracefulness and proceeded to explain that he had taken the liberty of calling upon us as a matter of social courtesy as is customary in these parts. As on the first occasion of our meeting, his presence produced the strangest impression upon me. I knew that I had seen him before at once, but even more peculiar than the effect he had first had on me was a feeling that, in some undefinable way, he resembled one I could no longer recollect but who must have crossed the course of my early life a long time ago. Papa invited him to stay for lunch but he courteously declined, explaining that he had a great deal of work that urgently needed immediate attention, although expressing the hope that he would shortly have the pleasure of seeing us again. After he had left, Papa told me that Mr Morheim was indeed a rather 'strange character' as we had surmised albeit an exceedingly intelligent and charming man whom it would be a pleasure and a privilege to know better. Exactly what studies or work Mr Morheim is engaged in, Papa cannot say with any precision since our visitor seems to have been very vague upon that point, merely referring to his need for peace and quiet in the countryside, and the necessity to study a mass of historical material he has brought back with him after many prolonged visits to universities and libraries. He is probably a writer of some sort—perhaps a poet or playwright as well since he seems to show an artistic temperament which would account for his odd behaviour upon first meeting me since artists, we are told, often behave in a way that we more humdrum people find odd. Yes, I definitely think that he has an artistic bent. Anyway, let me confess it: he has piqued my curiosity and I should like to know more about him. I fancy all sorts of mysteries in his life.

JUNE 28TH

Mr Morheim has been to lunch with us again. I can see that Papa is deeply impressed with him and I must be grateful to our guest for having in some measure dispelled the cloud of gloom that has been clinging around the house ever since Papa has been feeling unwell. Mr Morheim has revived his desire for company and conversation and certainly, he provides both in excellent measure. I still cannot fathom him: he intrigues and baffles me and I know that I in turn intrigue him. I wonder why he must spend so many of his days in isolation. He could play a dashing role in society were he inclined for such frivolous pursuits and there can be no doubt that he would turn many a fair head. Both Papa and I are quite engrossed by the question of his origins but he will speak little of his family, save that he no longer has parents and few relatives. One reason Papa has for his curiosity is that he fancies Mr Morheim is in some way related to us. He finds something familiar in the cast of his features and his manner and so, for that matter do I. It is the strangest thing but when I look at him, I am never without that inner feeling that I should recognise him from the past, or at least see in him a resemblance to someone else I knew. And yet, who should this be? I have led on the whole a sheltered life like any other young girl in my situation; I have travelled it is true and lived in England but even so, no one whose acquaintance I ever made, no matter how briefly, bears any resemblance to him in the slightest respect. When Papa does address questions to him of as personal a nature as polite-ness will allow, he seems to have a gift for leading the con-versation into other channels with such dexterity that the original subject of the discourse is soon forgotten. We know that he comes from a region many miles from here, to the east, and that he has studied at the universities of Budapesth and Vienna, that he speaks several languages with great fluency, is a proficient horseman and an experienced traveller and that is about all. No, it really won't do! Since he is near us and so intrigues us, we must learn more about him. I am sure that it pleases him to remain something of an enigma to us. Once or twice as I attempted a very leading question, I saw a kind of sardonic humour in his eyes as he parried my queries with the cunning of one expert in this kind of verbal fencing. Now I must cease troubling my mind with him and concentrate on my letter to Ernest. 'Concentrate'—what a funny thing to write! How very odd of me! Surely, to write a letter to the love of my life needs no concentration or mental exertion, and is no labour. Nothing can be more natural and easier than to pour out my love and my hopes on paper to my darling, absent future husband. Poor Papa is really getting so very absent-minded these days. When I told him today of Ernest's last letter, he looked positively blank for a moment until I rather impatiently reminded him that he had given his glad consent to our betrothal and that he was shortly destined to be a father-in-law. "And so then you must leave me," he replied sadly, persisting in this assertion even though I assured him that Ernest and I would ever be near him and that he would never be neglected by us, as he seems to fear. All he could say was:

"It does not matter. I am not long for this earth now, I know it." How dreadful it is to see Papa in this frame of mind! I cannot forget his words, nor the solemn look of resignation that came over his face as he uttered them: they have given my thoughts a melancholy tinge as though our love is henceforth to be overcast by the shadow of impending death. It must not be and yet I cannot help but see how weak Papa has been looking recently. He must rest more—the doctor insists that in his present state, both physical and mental exertion are bad for him. Even Mr Morheim's visit seems to have tired him but he will insist on seeing him again. It is as though he were fascinated by the man. I know he has been invited here again soon. There—my thoughts are wandering again. Enough for the day—I dismiss him from my mind. All thoughts are now for Ernest.

JULY 5TH

Mr Morheim has been here all day and only just departed. He has the most peculiar driver-cum-manservant—a swarthy fellow, all lean and sinister with a vulpine expression and eyes that glitter with malignant cunning. The servants do not like him and some even seem to fear him but this is probably because he is of such a different stock. I think he is a Szekely, and here the Saxons have hated them for centuries. Well, if they are all like him, then I cannot say that I am surprised.

We all had lunch together—that is to say Mr Morheim and Papa and I. Mr Morheim was in a particularly brilliant mood and his conversation was never more charming and mellifluous and although he and Papa talked much of erudite subjects dear to them both, he did not ignore me entirely but displayed such courtesy and consideration towards me that I could not help feeling more than a little flattered by his intentions. Looking at him, I could not help admiring his air of intellectual defiance and proud superiority as he argued some abtruse point with Papa. There is too an admirable intelligence and vigour which characterise his every utterance. He is one who has thought deeply and when he speaks it is with the authority of one who knows exactly what he is talking about and who is secure in the knowledge that we know it too. After the meal they retired together to Papa's study. Mr Morheim had asked for Papa's help in some part of his studies and Papa was only too pleased to be of service to him, and to offer him the freedom of the library of which he is so touchingly proud. They remained closeted together for a long time while I went for a short promenade and then returned to my room for a little quiet reading and thinking. I picked up dear Ernest's letter and read it again and again. But try as I did, I had difficulty in apprehending its sense, although every line was pervaded by his fervent love for me. Words became confused and blurred: I found myself reading a phrase over and over, as though it were in some foreign language I did not wholly understand. My thoughts strayed, I became absent-minded, my head ached, I felt curiously drowsy, the letter fell from my hand as I surrendered to a deliciously inviting languor, both of the body and the spirit. I must have fallen asleep for when I came to my senses and guiltily picked up the letter from the floor it was early evening. I have written to Ernest—I now pen these few lines before going upstairs.

LATER

Two incidents—one most distressing, the other inexplicable. When I came down, Mr Morheim had already departed. Papa was standing in the hall, looking horribly drawn and pale. As he saw me, he made as if to go forward to me and then faltered and would have fallen had I not rushed to him and held him up. "It is nothing, nothing at all. A momentary unease," said Papa, who showed every sign of exhaustion. Alarmed, I summoned Katia and together we took Papa to the drawing room and there made him lie down while I fetched him a glass of brandy. Katia scolded him gently and told him not to spend so much time in idle discussions with men who were 'too clever by half'. "Why," she said, "it's small wonder you should be taken so if you spend your afternoons arguing. What a noise you made! I really thought that you two were about to come to blows!"—"Blows? Arguing? Whatever do you mean," asked Papa, much bewildered, "I recollect no such arguing!" —"To be sure you were arguing," insisted Katia, "I could not help hearing it." Papa drew a weary hand across his brow and looked perplexed. "Argue!" he said, "We were talking at length but there was no arguing, no altercation such as you speak of, I am sure." "But what was it that you were discussing?" I asked uneasily. "Why child, I am not sure that I remember exactly," said Papa, looking quite befuddled, "only that at one time we were discussing the interpretation of a passage in Gervasius' collection of Magyar lore—a quaint work of scholarship, I must say."

"Well, anyway, enough of these tiring discussions for the next few days," I said firmly, "you must rest completely or I shall tell the doctor." Papa was more tired than I had ever seen him—it was pitiful to see how the energy had been sapped out of him. I blame Mr Morheim. It is his fault. I shall seize the first opportunity, should he come again as Papa insists, to tell him so.

Papa then recovered sufficiently to come down to dinner. He was much preoccupied while he ate, and when I asked him the reason he told me: "I cannot for the life of me find a book I was looking for. I know exactly where it was on the shelf yet when I went just now it was no longer there. I have been searching everywhere for it. It was there yesterday and I know that I did not take it down."—Perhaps Mr Morheim was looking at it and left it in some corner, omitting to replace it," I suggested. "No, I am sure he did not," said Papa. "But perhaps you left the library for a moment and did not see him look at it?"—"That is true. I did leave it for a moment but what does that mean?"—"Perhaps Mr Morheim has absconded with the book?" I suggested brightly. Papa frowned terribly at me: "Mr Stephen Morheim is a man of honour and integrity for whom I have the highest respect," he said furiously, "you will withdraw that remark. I will not have a daughter of mine casting such an ill-deserved slur on our guest!" I meekly retracted the remark and when Papa's anger had subsided asked him what the book in question was, that he should set such store by it. "It is—oh, it is nothing. A curious old work—mostly fancy and legend. Not a very pleasant book, I am afraid. But it is of no importance. I shall look again for it tomorrow."

Unworthy the thought may be, but still I cannot help suspecting that Mr Morheim may have taken the liberty of 'borrowing' the book. I am sure some of these ardent bookworms lose their scruples in their enthusiasm. May he return it soon. Or perhaps Papa did lend it to him and then forget it—he is more and more absent-minded lately. I prefer to adopt the latter theory. I should be sorry to think Mr Morheim guilty of such a lapse of good conduct—he is far too aristocratic and gentlemanly to stoop to such a thing. There I go again—every day now it is "Mr Morheim this and Mr Morheim that". Not only is he invading our household but he is invading my thoughts and that is far worse. They belong to Ernest.

I awoke today feeling quite irritated, I retire tonight feeling quite bemused. A strange, a very strange day. Papa was much better. Together we attended service in the little village church. What were my feelings when, for the first time, I saw Mr Morheim present among the congregation! He nodded his head gravely in sign of greeting as we entered. I was exceedingly surprised to see him there, since I had gathered from his conversation and remarks at table that conventional religious faith was quite alien to one of his temperament. Indeed, I could even detect a scarcely veiled hostility in his tone when he briefly alluded to the Christian church and its dogmas. Perhaps he is an agnostic. I do not believe him to be an atheist, or an out-and-out materialist since on at least two occasions, his enigmatic intimations seemed to suggest that he holds certain theories on the human soul and its power to survive the dissolution of the body. I stole several furtive looks at him during the service and although he observed every detail of the ritual with perfect decorum, I am sure that he was never praying at any moment, even if his lips did move mechanically. Twice, to my confusion, he caught my eyes and once he smiled. When we came out of the church, he exchanged civil greetings with the priest and then came up to us, saying he was sorry to hear about Papa's recent indisposition and enquiring after his health. Papa immediately begged him to accompany us to luncheon after which Mr Morheim asked whether he might have the honour of accompanying me for a ride since Papa expressed his intention to take a rest, as the doctor had ordered. Papa willingly consented and I said I would be only too happy to have a companion.

For the first half hour as we rode, Stephen was mostly silent, seeming determined to pursue his mysterious ruminations. It was the first time I had been wholly alone with him, if I except that strange first meeting. I felt a kind of awe in his presence and wondered for the hundredth time why he should have felt such a compulsive need for solitude in this part of the countryside and what mysteries there had been in his past life. As we came through the village, I dismounted at the cemetery and went to Mama's grave. "She died so young then?" asked Stephen gravely. "Yes, I was only a little child at the time. She became ill—very weak and listless—and even though she seemed to recover for a time, the doctors could do nothing for her and she quietly slipped out of this life without suffering, I believe."—"Do you know why she should have become so strangely ill?" he enquired. "No, no one could say. I think myself it may have been some unfortunate inherited infirmity." Stephen inclined his head as we stood by the grave and I saw a momentary cloud shadow his handsome features. I saw the priest approaching from a distance. "Come," said Stephen, "I am not in a mood for his talk. See how he looks in his black garb—like some bird of ill omen!" There was a vehemence in his tone which astonished me, but I could not bring myself to ask the reason for Stephen's apparent hostility to the priest. I fell silent again as we rode far into the countryside and along a path through the dense patch of forest that my childish imagination had once peopled with so many strange and fairy-like beings. My previous unease in Stephen's company dissipated and soon we were talking quite naturally. He told me of his youth, in the care of loving foster parents, of how he had been an orphan, of his past loneliness, and of the many cities he had seen in his travels with a wealth of detail and a colour that brought them alive in my mind as I listened, until I felt that I too had been there. Eventually we came to a halt and after scrutinising me keenly, Stephen asked me of my fiancé. I told him of Ernest, and of how a chance acquaintance (now a friend and dear Meg's betrothed) had brought us to meet in England, and how I was waiting for Ernest to come to stay with us. "And you do love him?" enquired Stephen, subjecting me once again to an intense scrutiny, so compelling, so intense, that for a moment I was assailed by a peculiar feeling of giddiness and closed my eyes. I must have swayed in the saddle for a moment later, I could feel his strong hand on mine. "There," he said, "I thought you would fall." He took his hand away but still I could feel its touch on mine. Then, looking hard at me as though he could read my face as though it were an open book, he asked again "Do you love him?" What it was that made me so strangely reluctant to answer, I do not know (certainly not unsureness of how I should reply), but the way he asked me and the expression in his eyes rendered me momentarily without speech. Eventually I murmured 'yes', adding that I did love Ernest very dearly as indeed I do. "You are lonely, are you not?" pursued Stephen. With utter candour I told him that we were both of us, Papa and I, less lonely now that he had become our friend—I said friend to him. "Yes," said Stephen fiercely, "I am your friend and you shall always count on me."

He then proceeded to ask further questions about Ernest but I felt oddly unwilling to give many particulars of him save that he is kind and handsome and clever....

Oh Ernest, Ernest, what is happening to me? Your letter came and I read it once and now I have read it again. I fancy I can hear your voice behind every word and then it suddenly becomes fainter and fainter. I know I love you, I must love you ... And yet, why is it that tonight as I try to conjure up your sweet face in my mind (and why must I *try*?) it grows so dim in my recollection? Why, oh why is it that try as I may, every time I think of you your image becomes pale and vague before my mind's eye and then gives way to the more compelling vision of—Stephen? Why does the figure of Stephen so increasingly interpose itself between that of Ernest and my wandering mind?

Correspondence between Ernest Armstrong and Andrew Fuller

Dear Andrew,

Thank you, old friend, for your invitation. Pressure of work is awful as always but never mind—it will soon be finished. I would say the week after next will be best. After that—well, you know where I'm bound. I wish it were sooner. Elizabeth's father has been far from well, she tells me. The poor old fellow seems to be sleeping badly and gets more tired every day. It would be too awful if anything were to happen to him. I know that he was always a rather sad retiring man since his wife died but he isn't so old and I really don't see any reason why he should sink into a decline at this stage. Anyway, it must be quite a strain for Elizabeth as I can tell from her letters. They aren't as bright as usual and quite frankly I'm worried. From her tone, I can tell she's not quite herself. Oh, she's as loving and devoted as ever—no worry on that score—but there's a funny underlying note of reserve in some of her words. I suppose I'm worrying for no reason—it's just that—well, you know how disappointing it's been putting off my departure. I can't leave a moment too soon. I don't want to find her carted off by some bright young fellow there. If it weren't that I know how passionately loyal she is, I might be half afraid of some local swain paying court to her. You know how damnably handsome those Hungarians are! Anyway, please forgive all this rot. Again, it will be wonderful seeing you and Meg. Why don't we go up to town together. We haven't celebrated your engagement yet, after all. Let's have a jolly supper party shall we?

Yours, as ever, Ernest.

ERNEST ARMSTRONG TO MARGUERITE FENSHAWE, JULY 25TH

My dear Meg,

Will you forgive an old friend for begging you for your advice and help like this—confidentially. The truth is that I am worried—more worried than I can say—about Elizabeth. I haven't said very much to Andrew about this—anyway I haven't seen him lately. You know, I think, that lately Elizabeth hasn't been writing so frequently to me. Well, that's not all—she has probably had her hands full with looking after her father who seems to be taking a turn for the worse but there's been a change in her way of writing that I don't like. No, Meg, I don't like it at all. It's almost as if she was becoming another person. As you know, we lovers are sensitive creatures and the fair sex aren't the only ones to have intuitions. Something tells me that there's been a change in Elizabeth and I just can't rid my mind of horrid suspicions, no matter how ignoble it is of me to have them where she is concerned. The plain fact is that in all her last three letters, there seems to be something forced in her endearments. And there's worse too—first of all she had made vague references to some fellow, a neighbour of theirs I believe, who seems to be coming with increasing frequency to the house. I know he's supposed to be her father's friend (at least that's what she says) but everything in me seems to cry: Danger! And then, after telling her in my last letter of the definitive date of my departure and that of my arrival, she sends me a reply making no mention of it! Can you believe it? What has happened to her? That last letter really was ghastly: everything in it seemed to be forced and constrained—even the most affectionate phrases and to cap it all, at one point where she called me by name, she wrote the capital letter S and then hastily crossed it out with thick pen strokes before writing 'Ernest'. Honestly, I'm not making mountains out of molehills, I know. I could distinctively trace the letter she wrote by mistake as though her thoughts were elsewhere at the time. I am convinced that for an instant, she was thinking of someone whose name begins with an S. Dear Meg, you are her oldest friend and know her better than any other soul alive. Would it be too horribly embarrassing for you if I came down to see you this Sunday with her last two or three letters? I am sure you can help me. I am most horribly perplexed. It's all too sudden. I can't believe that she's weakened in her love for me and yet the way she writes . . . Well, you will see, I just refuse to accept that someone else has stolen her affections and even if they had she would have told me frankly of it. You know how honest and forthright she is. It's not in her character to dissimulate. Oh, if only I could leave now. But I can't and there's an end of it and now I'm half afraid to go for fear of what I might find. Please see me and let us see if you can throw any light on this mystery. You will be surprised, I know, when you see her letters.

Yours, affectionately, Ernest.

Elizabeth Sandor's Diary

A sullen, stormy day that aptly matches with my thoughts. I have been too disconsolate and disturbed to confide much in these pages in the last two days. I really do not know what is happening to me and I feel utterly weary—just as poor Papa did. Stephen's presence here, the insistent way he looks at me, in expectation of an answer he knows must come in the end, my approaching majority, Ernest's absence—all this confuses and dismays me. I feel sure that I should send Stephen (for so I now call him) away or at least (since Papa shows no sign of diminishing pleasure in his company) try to forbid him to speak to me when we are alone but each time I have failed to summon up the necessary resolution and so I am caught yet deeper in the whirlpool of conflicting emotions. A brave, pathetic letter from Ernest today, and a tenderly affectionate one from Meg. She at least has no hesitation in following the course of her life. At times, everything within me urges me to leave here, to fly to Ernest, to marry him at once, anywhere, and to lead a happy, quiet life of domestic bliss and emotional stability which seemed foreordained for me by a kindly Providence but then fiercer emotions such as I have never before experienced possess me. There is a quality in Stephen which calls me irresistibly and it is like a great summons from the lofty heights. Although he says nothing of it, I know that he is challenging and daring me to embark upon a vastly different life—with him. It will be a wild, tumultuous existence, an adventure into some mysterious and remote beyond. I am haunted by the thought that in some manner I already belong to him and by another, even more insidious conviction that in some way this was inevitably destined to be so. A look from him, a chance touch of his hand, the sound of his voice seem to stir strange, half-buried memories in me as though I knew him long ago in some other existence and the way he looks at me shows only too plainly that in my face there is the reflection of some memory that hallucinates him.

I have been alone with him again this afternoon for another promenade. I observed a sudden change in his spirit. By mutual, unspoken consent, we were silent at first. He looked dejected; his eyes were downcast and a sharp frown compressed his lips. Suddenly he looked up at me and said: "You are worried about Ernest, are you not?" No answer was needed—my face told him all. Then, with an abrupt transition in mood which left me perplexed, he began to muse aloud as we sauntered through the woods. His words were wild, poetical and mysterious but although I could not understand the half of his discourse its impassioned tone exalted me. He spoke of immortality and destiny, of man's ambitions and all the earthly limitations that frustrate his nature, of life and death and of how love and ambition, if they be strong enough can exist in a dimension apart from that in which our earthly frames are confined, in a tone of passion and deep conviction which suggested a cognizance of matters well beyond the ken of ordinary mortals. And even while he spoke, even though he kept his gaze fixed on the great mountains before us in the distance, I *knew* that every word concerned me directly. My mind was in a turmoil as we returned. Something will have to be resolved soon. Ernest has told me of the date of his departure. What shall I do?

JULY 29TH

All is settled. Yesterday Stephen came in the afternoon. After a brief but pleasant conversation with Papa who has relapsed slightly again and can only receive visitors for a limited time, we had the horses saddled and rode out together. The fine weather has broken. All day long the skies were wild and leaden-hued and dark clouds presaged an approaching storm. Little passed between us and each was left with his own thoughts, I thinking of Ernest's impending arrival with more of melancholy than of happy anticipation, he musing—on I know not what . . . When we returned, Papa showed signs of his past high spirits again. The repose of the afternoon had done him much good and despite Stephen's demurrings he insisted that he should stay to dinner. It is strange, but Papa no longer speaks of Ernest. He seems to have entirely forgotten his existence and to be absorbed in Stephen. Never the most conventional of men, he has never shown the slightest disapproval of our rides together, unescorted by any chaperone, and I cannot help feeling that what he would question in any other man, he accepts unhesitatingly in Stephen. Let me be frank

129

with myself: Stephen has taken possession of us all here. But let me not digress. This is the most important confidence that I have ever penned in my faithful old companion of mine—this diary in which I seem to speak to myself and to which I confide my innermost thoughts . . . As the day waned, the weather rapidly worsened. A fierce wind had risen then died away as suddenly as it had come, leaving thick storm clouds piled up low in the heavens. Nature was still, the birds fell silent, there was an oppressive hush. Then, as Stephen was about to take his leave, there broke a storm of unusual intensity, with the rain falling in such torrents that visibility outside was restricted to a few yards. Papa urged Stephen to stay until the fury of the elements had somewhat abated but the rain continued to pour down relentlessly while the house seemed to shake with each new crash of thunder as the lightning tore the skies apart with increasing fury. At length, after more brandy had been brought and it had become plain that there was little prospect of the storm diminishing, Papa insisted that Stephen should spend the night under our roof and sent word to Katia to prepare a room for our guest. After seeing that the elements made it quite impossible to ride with any assurance of safety, Stephen graciously assented. I bade him and Papa good-night and retired upstairs, a prey to gloomy thoughts of the most direful nature and at the same time filled by a curious conviction that I was on the verge of some great discovery that would change the course of my entire existence. While the storm blasted outside, sleep would not come to me. For hours I lay awake and restless while conflicting emotions wrestled furiously for dominion of my fevered soul. I was longing with a fierceness that brooded no denial for *him*—for Stephen. All thoughts of Ernest faded in my mind—they are hardly there now. I have but a pleasant recollection of some happy days spent in his company and that is all . . . I longed for Stephen with a passion made all the more imperious by knowledge of Stephen's close proximity—in our house! I had—I *have*—no sense of shame. I was and I am overwhelmed too completely for that. They say that we Sandors were renowned in the past for their tumultuous passions and their impetuosity and I knew it to be true as I lay, a prey to desires such as I had never known before and to atavistic stirrings deep within me that proclaimed that I too come from a stock as wild and uncontrollable as the tempest that raged outside. Yes, Stephen and I are alike—I know this! It is only fitting that destiny should have decreed our meeting before it was too late. It is *he* and no one else that I have always loved. I am sure that I loved him in some former life and that he loved me likewise. I am his for ever and not even death can shatter the bond between us. I dismissed every lingering doubt as it intruded in my mind and troubled my exultation. I had taken my decision and as I wondered at the dramatic and unexpected change that had overtaken me in such a short space of time, the storm gradually died away until eventually there were only a few distant grumblings of thunder to be heard over the mountains. I arose from my bed and crept to the window, opening it slightly and looked out, entranced by the play of lightning over the distant peaks. The sky above had cleared and the stars reappeared, as serene and unchanging as the new emotion that had claimed my heart. After watching thus, for several minutes, a figure moved forward out of the deep shadows of the wall. It was Stephen. Like myself, he had been unable to sleep and had left his room, doubtless to seek the fresh, purified air and to admire the majesty of the night. Impelled by a sudden impulse I hastily slipped into my night-robe and made my way downstairs and so out into the night. Oh what an extent of passion there blazed behind his pallid countenance as he gazed at me, held out his arms, and drew me to him! "I knew you would come to me," he said gravely. Yes, henceforth there can be no drawing back. I have taken the decision, I have made my choice, the responsibility is mine and I am glad. We are betrothed.

JULY 31ST

Papa has been taken ill. The strange weakness that had been assailing him has returned. Yet debilitated as he is, he has divined the secrets of my heart. I told him gently that I loved Stephen and henceforth considered myself engaged. He sighed slightly and asked me if I were happy. I assured him I was. For a moment his eyes betrayed a momentary disquiet—there was almost *fear* in them and then he softly said: "I thought as much. It was inevitable. You see, Stephen has already spoken to me about his intentions." I must now write to Ernest. He must not come here. I cannot see him—it is for his own good that I prohibit him to come. In this resolve I am unyielding. He was to have been here in a week—my birthday, as papa reminded me. Then I shall attain the full age of womanhood.

LETTER: MARGUERITE FENSHAWE TO ANDREW FULLER

My darling,

Poor Ernest has just been to see me. He is quite distraught. Never did I see anyone more dejected, more despairing. It really made my heart bleed to see him. He is such a good, noble, great-hearted fellow and grief and amazement have broken his spirit, I fear. After her last few, dreadfully puzzling letters, now Elizabeth has written him a short letter to tell him that there can now be no question of their projected engagement, that she cannot ever see him again, that her heart is given to another, that there is no point in his arguing with her for her resolve is unshakeable, and that on no account must he endeavour to go near her. It is all quite incredible. It cannot be her! I know her too well to suppose her capable of such fickleness. Oh Andrew, I can't tell you how long and earnestly we talked and how many times we read and re-read her last letters. There is something very disturbing about them. It is almost as though they were being written by someone else although the hand is undeniably the same. Later: the mail bag has just arrived, bearing a letter to me from Elizabeth. It is the strangest letter I have ever received from her. She tells me that she cannot expect me to understand and adds that even if I cannot forgive her for her treatment of Ernest, it is of no account to her. She is possessed, Andrew, possessed. I begin to believe in old wives' tales of enchantment. What else can explain the way she has changed in her affections? There is an exulting, wild tone in her letter that I do not like in the least. But to return to last night: I was utterly unable to give poor Ernest any explanation for her conduct. I know (or should I say knew?) her so well that I am at a complete loss to account for it all. What can we do? Ernest is frantic. Both of us are filled by sinister suspicions of this man who has come between Elizabeth and him. What is he? His name is Stephen Morheim. Do you know any Morheims from your time in Hungary? I think you once spoke to me of such a family, did you not? Anyway, the fact that Elizabeth is so reticent about him makes me only the more suspicious. Do you think he can be some unscrupulous fortune-hunter? In a few days Elizabeth will be twenty-one and an heiress—although far from a wealthy one—and can dispose of her property as she chooses. It will be his of course. Her father is far from well and has been much worse lately. She speaks of marrying this Stephen shortly—her father has consented—I cannot understand him either. They are both utterly bewitched or deranged. And this haste to marry! Why, they will marry even over the grave of her father, I am sure, and the grave of Ernest's hopes. It is too horrible to contemplate. I feel like leaving now but Elizabeth tells me that she will soon be gone, and that she wishes to see nobody from England. Andrew dearest, I am terribly worried about Ernest. He speaks wildly, he will do something dreadful if he is not stopped in time. You must see him and try to talk to him. Perhaps it is not too late to do something. I believe we should leave at once for Torberg, don't you and insist upon seeing her. An old and once close friend has certain privileges, hasn't she? But what shall we do about Ernest?

Your ever loving and very worried

Meg

P.S. I have of course written to Elizabeth.

Andrew Fuller's Diary

Morheim—Stephen Morheim! Colonel Tekely's young ward —my pupil! I find it unbelievable. Worse—it is frightening. I have every reason to believe Meg when she says that this behaviour of Elizabeth's is unnatural for her. She has been persuaded almost supernaturally by him. I remember how disquieting he could be at times. He is unusually ambitious, and quite ruthless in attaining his aims, I am sure. But why Elizabeth? Is she that rich—does he desire her that much? From the little I have heard of his subsequent career after leaving for university, I gathered that zealous study and prolonged investigations into recondite subjects (some rather sinister to my mind) with a special emphasis on the genealogy of certain families constituted the sole passion of his life. I don't know what it is about him, but after this shattering news some formless suspicion keeps invading my mind. Meg tells me that Elizabeth indignantly refutes the suggestion that any unworthy motive could be imputed to Stephen. I only hope that my fears will turn out to be illusory. Ernest is full of the most direful forebodings and insists that Elizabeth's will has been enslaved. Neither he nor Meg can understand the workings of her heart. Amazing that in a short space of time she should have cast Ernest aside for a man who must in some respects be a complete and utter stranger to her! Could material advantage be his chief object in the matter? I must confess that the way he has so rapidly and stealthily invaded the citadel of Elizabeth's heart encourages the wildest speculations. Ernest insists that he is utterly unscrupulous and that Elizabeth has fallen victim to his unreasoning desire through means that imply some sort of hypnotic fascination rather than courtship in the usual manner. And then—the curious weariness and decline of her father and his compliance in her astounding change of plans! They seem to have gone completely mad and Ernest too will be heading in the same direction if no explanation of all this is forthcoming. From what I have seen of Elizabeth and know of her she is assuredly one of the most lovable persons on earth but even so I find it hardly possible that Stephen could so suddenly harbour passionate sentiments of love in his heart. But he has obviously succeeded in completely engaging her emotions and in ousting Ernest from her heart with bewildering efficiency. This is no caprice of a young girl's unstable sentiments. She has been subjugated in some manner. The answer to this mystery is to be found in Stephen, not in her—of this I am sure. I recall how strangely he used to affect me at times even though he was only a boy. That curious weakness, that sense of being *drained*—it all tallies. There is some quality in him that makes others pliant to his will. It is domination that he is after—not love. I must do some detective work. Old Arminius may help me there. The sooner we know more about Stephen the better. In the meantime, it will take some persuading to prevent Ernest from rushing off at once. That would be the worst possible thing in the circumstances.

AUGUST 22ND

Today a despatch arrived from Professor Arminius. He has been exceedingly helpful but there is little of comfort in his disclosures.

*   *   *

AN EXACT COPY OF A LETTER RECEIVED FROM PROFESSOR JOHANNES ARMINIUS OF THE FACULTY OF LETTERS, BUDAPESTH UNIVERSITY, DATED AUGUST 8TH

Dear Friend, former colleague and Colleague-again-to-be, I hope,

What pleasure to hear from you after so long silence. You will be coming soon here, yes? You have still so much useful and good work to do here. Indeed, I was to write you soon for I have a job for you, I think. The Imperial Commission require some such ethnological experts such as yourself for the Siebenburgen province. You know how it is: each of these ethnic minorities is jealous so of its own culture and traditions and with the so complicated political and other arrangements here, we scholars have much to offer in helping them. There: now you must come and bring your bride with you. Why not? Your other matter, concerning the Stephen Morheim, so soon to marry the Sandor daughter who so strangely gives up fiancé number One. I shall try to tell you what I can of him. *Primo*: yes, I did know him if one could say that one knows such a strange and disturbing young man. Let us say I know him for his studying and some of his researches. I have heard it said that he is studying things even stranger now: much of the occult. Why I do not know. *Secundo*: I have heard it that some people of his country speak of his parents' unhappy death and some superstitious peoples will say that his poor mother was bewitched and made crazy but I think that all this is much nonsense. *Tertio*: It has not been so long ago that your Stephen was here at the library to ask me for help in a certain line of investigation. I could not help him but sent him with a letter to my friend, Doctor Karel, who is keeper of manuscripts and old records of the region in the Archives of the Saxon Nation which, as you will remember, are in the Rathaus at Hermannstadt. Now this is curious and interesting perhaps to you: yesterday by chance the good Doctor Karel was here and I asked him did he help our young friend? Yes, he has helped him. Stephen Morheim did want to find the ownership of a very old, ruined and, I think, abandoned castle to the north, in the high mountains. As you know well, with so many old castles, ruins and houses that fill every acre of our fascinating country, it is often not easy to find out who own what. People appoint custodians of a place—they go there little—they die, their children inherit, the custodians continue and the children forget unless they have occasion to deal with problems of the estate. A tumbled down ruin—what is that to a family with other more rich possessions? Anyway, Stephen must know to whom this ruin belongs? Dr. Karel tells him after much looking in records: it has long been in the possession of the house of Sandor. There is too a little story: it came to the Sandors two centuries or so ago when an ancestor married a girl of noble birth and who later is believed to have left her husband, or to have been taken from him by a jealous lover, and who died. Also with this so interesting castle comes a tradition that on no account must a Sandor ever part with the castle or evil will befall and the land will be accursed. So they keep it always and obey their forbears' injunction. Is this not the answer and the key to the mystery that you and your unhappy friend seek? The Sandors keep the castle. It will belong to the young and beautiful Elizabeth whom Stephen will marry so strangely and Stephen will have the castle with his bride. It is odd, no, that he should be so interested in it? Perhaps, since I do not know all the circumstances of the affair, his interest in it is purely coincidental and the fair eyes of the beautiful Elizabeth make

136

him fall in love with her and speak such sweet words that she forgets number one lover? More about this castle only Doctor Karel can tell you. Write him if you wish. He remember you from your visit last and will be happy to help you so. Now good wishes to you and your Marguerite. Let me see you both soon, yes? I keep a very fine bottle of Tokay for you but if you do not come quick, I shall not keep myself from drinking it. Such is temptation! Yours so ever, Arminius.

AUGUST 23RD

I hardly know how to tell Ernest that Stephen has somehow succeeded in stealing the affections of Elizabeth in order to marry her for some old Carpathian ruin? The only possible explanation is that it must contain a buried treasure somewhere. So Stephen is a vulgar fortune-hunter after all? May it serve him right if the treasure is a hypothetical one. Saw Ernest this morning and we lunched together. His gloom and bewilderment are pitiful to see. What could I say? If I tell him what Arminius has told me, then I only make Elizabeth look more fickle in succumbing to whatever blandishments this hypocritical Stephen has employed. *Memo*: must write to Hermannstadt, as Arminius suggests. I really would like to know more about this castle that Stephen seems so set on acquiring.

AUGUST 25TH

Yesterday was Elizabeth's birthday, so Ernest told me. Now she is free to do whatever she likes. Ernest, and Meg, even more insistently, hold that she is not free and that the more they read her last letters they feel that something devilish is afoot and that Stephen is exerting an unnatural power over her. I think it true. Ernest wants desperately to go there at once. How can we stop him? He will only do harm to himself, I am sure.

AUGUST 30TH

Saw Ernest. The doctor says he must stay in bed for a few more days. He looked completely exhausted but then—he has not eaten or slept for days. At least this will keep him from his wild plan for the time being. The character and development of Stephen intrigues me more every day. I looked at the book he once asked me to find in the British Museum when I was there today. A horrifying story about a Countess said to be descended from gypsies and to have inherited certain fearful occult knowledge which she tried to use with the aid of blood sacrifices. A macabre business but then Stephen always does seem to have been interested in tales of blood and sorcery.

SEPTEMBER 7TH

A long reply from Doctor Karel. He has been most kind and helpful for he has sent me a copy several pages long of a story as strange as it is picturesque. Rather than make a laborious translation of it in its entirety, I shall résumé it in my own words here.

This castle which Elizabeth will inherit comes to her after being handed down by several generations of Sandors who, in their turn, received it as part of the dowry of a shadowy, little-known noblewoman called Myrea or Mirea. Although she herself remains a vague personality in this account, the chronicle has much to say about her ancestors. She seems to have been the last surviving descendant of a family who seem to have enjoyed a pretty horrific reputation during the Middle Ages and who continued to distinguish themselves by being more than averagely savage and bloodthirsty, even in that turbulent country. The founder of the line was the infamous Voivode of Wallachia, Vlad V, surnamed "Dracul" or the Devil by his awestruck contemporaries who saw him as Satan incarnate, come to plague the earth, and mentioned in the history books as a ruler who combined insatiable cruelty with the utmost valour and who, more than any warrior, struck terror into the hearts of the Turks during the blood-baths of the fifteenth century. Nearly all his life was spent fighting them after he had sworn allegiance to the king of Hungary, his overlord. All the old chronicles speak of how he refused the Turks' demand for tribute, how he had been entrusted with the defence of the empire's frontier, how he beat back wave after wave of invaders, and how he crossed the Danube to defeat them in their own territory in battles so bloody that it was said that the sun was obscured by reddish clouds exhaled by the countless dead for days afterwards, how he withstood siege after siege in his great ancestral castle that commanded one of the passes into his nation, how he boasted of his origins, being a Szekely by race and therefore one of those who descended from the Huns, and was held by many to be the reincarnation of Attila himself. History knows of no more terrible episode than that of his impalement of twenty thousand Turkish prisoners in an orgy of cruelty unknown even in ancient Rome. What is interesting in this account is that the chronicler speaks of another side of his atrocious character. Not only, apparently, was he a great and fearless warrior and the founder of a line that for generations afterwards cast their gigantic shadow across the course of Transylvanian history and who went down fighting like lions in the battle of Mohacs, but also a man of considerable scholarly attainment, and intellectual powers. The account speaks of how he was rumoured to have the secrets of life and death, of a supposed pact with the Evil One, of strange, lengthy journeys to remote places peopled by witches and alien tribes, and of how he visited alchemists, astrologers and necromancers in his quest for occult knowledge. He seems to have commanded the allegiance and loyalty of the mountain people, the Szgany gypsies who are unlike any other Romany tribe in those parts and who still speak their own dialect that so interests modern scholars, and the Szekelys who recognised him as their *boyar*. His power over these people made his neighbours and even the king himself uneasy and there were many who said that his followers were all the servants of the Evil One whom Vlad worshipped and served in his turn. After an obscure period in his life in which he spent some years in prison by the king's orders, on account of his crimes and some transgressions unknown, we find him retiring from the field and, considerably quietened down, taking as wife the daughter of a neighbouring nobleman and building a new palatial castle in which he dwelt with her and reared their children, while continuing to pursue studies rumoured to be devoted to the secret of the Philosopher's Stone and the attainment of immortality, so that he might rule for ever over his faithful. As the years passed and he grew old, his wife died, his sons continued the martial tradition and he lived the life of a recluse, amid his books and manuscripts, as much as the turbulence of the times would allow. Then one day, so says the chronicle, as he was returning from some minor rebellion he had put down, he was riding through a village near his castle when he found the people leading a struggling and screaming young girl to a pyre, to be burnt alive. As he enquired the reason for the sentence, the village elders and the priest told him that the girl was a gypsy and a witch whose spells and dealings with the powers of darkness had been proved beyond doubt. Struck by the singular beauty of the girl, Vlad ordered her captors to bring her to him upon which the girl flung herself at his feet and cried: "Save me and thou wilt live for ever, my Lord," adding a few words in a language no one present could understand but Vlad himself. Strangely impressed by the girl and, in particular, by her mysterious utterances, Vlad commanded that she should be taken to the castle so that he might question her himself, in private. The protests of the villagers and the priest were roughly rejected, and in a moment the cortège moved on with the girl, flanked by men-at-arms. Several weeks passed without any news of the captive and then, to the great consternation of the people, it was announced that Lord Vlad had decided to take her as his second, lawful wife, summoning the priest to perform the marriage ceremony on pain of death. Thereafter, as the chronicler writes, "a black fear fell over the countryside. Far and wide the people muttered and though they did not speak openly, yet in their hearts they feared that their Lord had been bewitched by a she-devil and the emissary of the Evil One". There were rumours that fearsome deeds of sorcery and unnameable rites were being performed within the castle, that children had been missing in the neighbourhood, and that as long as the gypsy girl remained mistress of the castle and commanded Vlad's love, the Devil would reign in the stronghold and the Vlad would never die thanks to his agency.

The people's fears seemed to be corroborated every time they saw the Lord Vlad himself, during his rare appearances outside the castle. Although he was now well past his seventieth year, his tall body was as erect as ever, his eyes still burned with the fierce fire of youth, and his cragged countenance still expressed an iron determination that seemed to defy both time and death. So they would see him ride past them, at the head of his troops and fierce Szekely followers, and, after he had receded into the distance, look up with fear in their eyes at the great castle that crowned the eminence above the village and go home with unspoken fears gnawing at their hearts. Meanwhile, the marriage had been received with dismay and resentment by Vlad's brothers and sons. In vain protests were made and petitions presented at the king's court. The danger was grave, for once again the Turks were massing on the frontier and the king was far more concerned that the old warrior should once again return to his frontier post, where his ancestral castle lay, and defy the Turks who feared him more than any other warrior, than by his marriage to an alleged sorceress. Word was accordingly sent to him but even as the messenger departed, a rumour spread that the gypsy had borne Vlad a child and that its father had decreed that it should be sole heir. With treachery in their hearts, the brothers plotted and even sent word to the Turks. A diversion was arranged, several thousand Turks invaded and were allowed to pass unheeded into the kingdom, and Vlad rode towards them lest they outflanked the entire army. At the same time, a brother arrived in the village below the castle, to find the population in a panic at reports of yet another child missing and of sacrifices to the Evil One. There were terrible tales that with the witch's help, Vlad had raised the shades of his long-dead ancestors and conversed with them, and that through the evil enchantments of the gypsy, he had become enslaved in the service of Satan. Encouraged by the absence of their Lord, the villagers and peasants from the surrounding district were ready to revolt under the leadership of Vlad's brothers. As the castle was too strong to be stormed the brothers decided on treachery. While the hastily armed villagers and a body of well-equipped soldiers stealthily made their way up the hill after night had fallen, the brothers rode to the main gate, declared their kinship with the master, and requested entry. As the great doors opened, they struck down the sentries and were followed by the waiting rebels. A fearful slaughter then ensued inside the castle with no mercy being shown to man, woman or child. Vlad's wife was seized and held while peasants and soldiers combed every inch of the edifice for her child and when no sign of it could be found, save a cradle, its mother was put to the most fearsome tortures to make her reveal its whereabouts. For the whole of that dreadful night, made hideous by the indiscriminate butchery of the occupants, the castle was made yet more hideous still by the screams and curses of Vlad's wife while her tormentors tried every fearsome expedient known to man to wrest her secret from her before a swift sword-stroke put an end to her sufferings. Her body was burnt and then the whole castle set ablaze so that no trace might remain of the fearful rites allegedly practised in it but even as the brothers rode away, a conviction spread among the now terrified villagers that the child had been smuggled to safety, probably by some faithful Szekely retainer.

After news of the appalling massacre and his brothers'
treachery was brought to Lord Vlad in the field, he shut
himself in his tent for two whole days and when he emerged,
all who saw him spoke long afterwards of how "even death was
preferable than to gaze into that visage". The country was in a
turmoil as the Turks rampaged across the frontier, destroying
everything in their path. In a quick series of battles, always
moving with lightning-like rapidity, Vlad counter-attacked
time and time again until at length he was severely wounded in
an ambush, plotted by his brothers with the Turks. Stricken
unto death, he returned to the village to behold the ruins of
his once proud castle, and there, almost with his last breath,
commanded his troops to exact fearful retribution for the
rebellion of his subjects. Of that vengeance, the chronicler prefers to say little. Let it suffice, that in those last days of his
blood-stained life, the grim Lord Vlad saw his men commit
deeds by his orders that even he might have flinched from in
the past, and that when he finally expired, not a soul remained
alive in the village. According to an old, pagan custom, his
men lifted his body on to a great shield, and faithful even after
death to his king's orders, Vlad returned to his post in the
mountains, as terrifying in death as he had been in life. The
chronicler speaks with awe of the way the funeral cortège made
its way through the ravaged countryside, along the roads lined
with the rotting bodies of men as they swung from makeshift
gallows, through half-ruined villages and on to the mountains.
There is something Miltonian in his description of how Vlad's
Szekely retainers toiled with their burden up the mountain
pass, through the mists and dark forests past wonderstruck
shepherds and peasants, of how the mysterious Szgany gypsies
came to swell the ranks of the cortège and how eventually, to
the accompaniment of strange chants in a language none could
understand but which filled all who dwelt in that region with
an inexplicable awe and foreboding, his loyal and griefstricken
Szekelys laid his remains in that grim, solitary castle of his
ancestors which had symbolised his proud and steadfast resistance to the invader. Such then was the end of the great Vlad
Dracul. In later years, a tradition spread and was accepted by
the population that one day, a descendant would avenge the
treachery of Vlad's brothers and the murder of his wife and
that *in the end Vlad and his blood would come into their own
again and rule for evermore*. Meanwhile Vlad's brothers and
their descendants, henceforth known as the family of Dracula,

showed an ever-increasing streak of ferocity and blood-mania. No spring of pity ever flowed in their hearts, their ambitions knew no limits and even in those wild days, their coevals were shocked by their lack of scruple. Many fell in battle, some were killed at the battle of Mohacs while others died in bitter struggles with their neighbours and rivals who hunted them down with such zeal that it seemed as though the rest of humanity could no longer tolerate the continued existence of so infamous a line. Of that lineage, Mirea was the last and when she married a Baron Sandor, her only dowry was the great castle in the mountains where the great Vlad lies entombed. Yes, the chronicle is certainly a grim one but why should the castle so interest Stephen? There is no mention of any buried treasure there. And yet, he is determined to acquire it as though prompted by some desperate urge, for reasons well beyond our comprehension.

SEPTEMBER 9TH

Ernest is better, thank God! But he still gives us much cause for worry even if he has regained much of his strength. The wildness has gone from his eyes but he is still fiercely determined to go to Torberg. I read the story of Vlad Dracul again and found it a disquieting one though for what reason I am not sure yet. But I have increasing *fears*—fears for Elizabeth and for what Stephen may bring her in her life. He is no ordinary man and the interest he displays in the bloodstained past and her remotest ancestors is no normal one. There is much that is unhealthy in his obsessive investigations—Arminius feels the same—and his hold over Elizabeth is positively sinister. I talked to Meg about it all. She is delighted by the offer of work that Armenius mentions and urges me to accept. We have told her parents of this although we have decided it best not to say much about Elizabeth lest our forebodings cause them distress. In any event, I now think that it would be a good thing if we went soon and married immediately for there is no impediment here. We are only troubled about Ernest lest it be unbearable for him to see us wed after the anguish of seeing his own prospects being so brutally shattered. When does Elizabeth propose to marry Stephen? Meg has heard nothing from her though she wrote again to Torberg. This silence is disturbing. I wish I did not have to go to Edinburgh tomorrow. Even two days' extra delay may be dangerous.

Dearest,

   *come at once I beg you. I have just received a curt missive
from Elizabeth. Her father has just died—peacefully, she says.
She announces that she will be leaving Torberg after the
funeral, will see the lawyers about the estate and* then marry
Stephen immediately. *I know it sounds incredible. She is in the
toils, Andrew, in the toils. He is a* fiend. *We must move quickly
or it will be too late. That man has made her his slave. She
cannot even observe the minimal decent period of mourning
for her parent—he is in too much of a hurry to allow her that
even. But she is still my dearest friend and we must save her*

Your anxious, loving Meg

Elizabeth Sandor's Diary

So Papa is dead and now we have buried him. It is strange how little emotion I feel at his passing. The news came to me as though I were in a dream. I hardly know any longer whether all this is a dream or a reality of my daily existence. Life and death are either one or meaningless. Yes, Stephen, I believe you. Let us marry at once as you say and leave here. Your will is my will, I am yours and you are mine. Without you I do not live. Whenever you are absent I am filled by terrible anxieties. I doubt myself suddenly, and think of Ernest. Why, Stephen, did I fall in love with you so? It frightens and exalts me at the same time. I have weird forebodings and then I see you and am reassured and transported by the joy and wonder of your presence. Before you I did not know the meaning of true love and now that this tempestuous passion has swept me into your arms I know that it is infinitely more wonderful and mysterious than anything I ever imagined. You possess me utterly and beckon me towards strange new horizons. Anything, Stephen, anything and anywhere with you! It is your will and it shall be done.

Dear friend,

Good. So you come. Lose not a day, Andrew. I congratulate you so much on your wedding. This we will duly celebrate all the together of us here. Now, I have learned strange things, some by chance, some by searching. I put them together and I do not like what I see, although I cannot explain. But I have much to tell you and the Ernest who is so unhappy. Warn him and tell him to be stout in his heart. There is much danger for Elizabeth.

Andrew Fuller's Diary

SEPTEMBER 20TH

By day and night we have travelled. I don't think any of us got a wink of sleep on the train. Ernest has been bearing up surprisingly well. He is so obviously happy that we are married after he had begged us not to postpone the ceremony on his account. What a quiet, dignified affair it was! Brave and noble fellow that he is, he was our best man. We were unutterably touched at his attitude. Neither of us shall ever forget the moving way he looked at us then kissed Meg and said: "I'm so glad for you. Really and truly, I am. If it hadn't been for you two I should have gone quite mad and most probably have blown my brains out or jumped into the river," before turning away for a moment to hide the manly sob that escaped him. His delight at seeing us wed was completely unfeigned. How he still loves Elizabeth! His courage, fortitude and constancy make us feel very humble. What a fine man Elizabeth is losing, unless of course there is still time to bring her back to her senses. What makes it so much worse is that none of us believe for a moment that she ever really stopped loving Ernest or that she would not rush back into his arms if only she could be freed from whatever spell it is that Stephen has cast upon her. I begin to feel a terrible, burning hate for Stephen for the way he is destroying the happiness of two people for whatever devilish purpose he may have conceived with that warped mind of his. At all accounts, we may be certain of one thing: no couple ever embarked upon a stranger honeymoon than this that Meg and I are sharing with Ernest.

BUDAPESTH, SEPTEMBER 21ST

I have never seen the city looking lovelier than now, in the golden light of a September sun. We took a cab at the East Station, drove straight down the wide Kerepesi Ut as they call the great avenue in Hungarian, took rooms in a modest but well-appointed little hotel near the National Theatre, had some breakfast and then went straight to the nearby University where we were greeted with outstretched arms by dear old

Arminius who welcomed me as though I were his long-lost son and then greeted Meg and Ernest with the greatest courtesy and charm. After some coffee, we shut ourselves up in his study. What he has just told us there is amazing, incredible, and yet—I know that his veracity is beyond doubt. What a detective he would make! Ever since my last queries, he has worked indefatigably, corresponding here and there with colleagues, following each intuition as it came to him, enquiring and diligently searching in the most unlikely quarters, and then bringing his great intelligence to bear upon the disjointed elements he has so patiently gathered, and endeavouring to fit them together in a logical and ordered pattern. The final significance of this pattern we still have to discover. Some elements are still missing but with his help we shall find them, I am sure. Now before I forget a single detail, let me set down everything he told us, in my own words rather than the halting and often quaint English he employed for the sake of Meg and Ernest.

*　　　　　*　　　　　*

A short time ago, so Arminius told us, he was approached by an elderly gentleman called Ambrose Lessing who claimed that he had been the friend of Conrad Morheim, Stephen's father, many years ago. The story he had to tell was a strange and terrifying one, and until he had decided to assist Arminius in his investigations into Stephen's past he had refrained from revealing it to any other living soul. Lessing told of how, shortly after his friend's marriage to Adelaide, the daughter of a family called Helsdorff, Conrad had sent him an anguished letter imploring him to come at once, hinting at some dreadful catastrophe that had overtaken his wife. What transpired next was described in Mr Lessing's journal which he was so kind as to lend us. We adjourned our discussion with Arminius to read the journal. When we met again, three hours later, all of us were shaken and horrified by the dreadful account of Adelaide's haunting and how, by haunting Conrad in turn, she had made him help her leave her tomb as a vampire.

"And so, my friends," Arminius asked us as we re-entered his study, "of the story of Stephen's parents you know the all?" We nodded, unable to speak for the moment. Eventually, I broke the silence by asking Arminius: "and did they execute Conrad's last instructions—did they really drive a stake

148

through his heart and cut off his head?"—"Yes," replied Arminius gravely, "they did so." Then seeing a shudder run through us all, he added: "Oh, my friends, you ask what I ask. Can such dreadful things be? Is this not a tale of some writer of gruesome stories? So I ask myself but I know it is not. Instead, I say to myself: but why was the poor Adelaide haunted and made into such a dreadful creature? Yes, she was haunted. The question is—by whom?"

And this is what Arminius told us next: like all scholars and historians of that part of the world—myself included—he was perfectly aware of the dark and bloodcurdling superstition of the vampire. Such beliefs are common in one form or another to most races over the globe. In eastern and central Europe, the vampire is a *revenant*, one doomed after death to rise again from the grave and thereafter continue a ghastly existence in a state that is neither that of death nor of life as we know it. In the daytime, although he may appear, he is weak and subject to the physical limitations of ordinary mortals. At night, between the hours of sunset and sunrise, he may stalk abroad in search of human blood which alone can nourish him and prolong his existence, and so he will prey upon the human race, seducing his victims by means of the hypnotic spells he casts upon them, and then biting their throats with his abnormally pointed teeth and so drawing their life-blood from them. Details of these vampires, as they appear in the many stories relating to them, are too well known to bear repetition here. But what Arminius did stress to us was the fact that such vampires are often reputed to show a particular inclination to prey upon their own kinfolk. In this case, whatever the thing was that had haunted Adelaide and subsequently possessed her, and then transformed her into an 'un-dead' fiend after she had died, it was not a vampire in the usual sense. It seems rather to have been a discarnate spirit that needed the body of a victim before it could achieve corporal shape as a vampire. No cases of vampiric activity had been reported at the time of Adelaide's 'illness' as Arminius had found after carefully looking through local records and newspapers. Convinced then that the *revenant* had once been some long-deceased forbear of Adelaide's, he had begun to make thorough investigations into her family history and after a time, he had made some curious discoveries.

Some time towards the middle of the eighteenth century, according to the records, a young man called Sebastian who was supposedly of noble descent, and who since infancy had been in the care of relatives or foster parents (as in Stephen's case), had changed his family name from that of Bathory to his wife's name of Helsdorff. Even so, he continued to be regarded with deep suspicion if not open hostility by his neighbours until he finally left the country to live abroad for many years before returning to spend his late years in his native land. For some reason, his family soon showed signs of a peculiar mental and physical degeneracy, were prone to illness and seldom lived beyond their thirtieth year. The few collateral branches of the lineage soon died out, until there was only one descendant left, who became a wealthy merchant in Klausenberg, and from whom Adelaide was ultimately descended.

The reason why Sebastian had changed his name was not difficult to find. He came of a house that had acquired an evil reputation for sorcery and bloodthirstiness, almost rivalling that of the Draculas, and which was therefore shunned and ostracised by all the local nobility, and his grandfather was a man of whom the most curious and disquieting things had been said, both in his lifetime and after his death. The grandfather's name was Miklos Bathory and he is a key figure in the complicated skein of family relationships that Arminius had so brilliantly unravelled.

Miklos' great-grandmother was no other than one of the most evil women ever to figure in the annals of Hungarian and Transylvanian history—the infamous Countess Elizabeth Bathory, whose story had so interested Stephen when a student, and whose terrifying career and ultimate end may be found in various histories as well as in the complete transcript of the trial in the archives of Budapesth University. She, in turn, was supposedly of part gypsy origin and indeed, it was said by some that her great-great-great-grandmother had been the gypsy girl who had become Vlad Dracul's second wife but no evidence has ever been produced to support such an assertion which must therefore be treated with reserve. She had married a distinguished nobleman, Count Ferencz Nadasdy, who stood high in the Emperor's favour and who fought valiantly against the Turks, and it was not until her son had grown to manhood and she had become a widow that she retired to her favourite abode, the now ruined castle near Csejthe, and embarked on the series of hideous crimes for which she became famous as 'the Bloody Countess', luring uncounted numbers of young girls into her castle where they were subjected to the most fearful cruelties. According to most accounts, her object in perpetrating these outrages was twofold: one to satisfy some deep-seated, ancestral craving for the sight of blood; secondly, to perpetrate her existence and her matchless beauty by means of occult experiments whose secrets had been handed down to her through generations of gypsy ancestors and which demanded the sacrifice of human lives. At the same time, it was rumoured in certain quarters—notably by men of the church—that although the Countess outwardly professed to subscribe to the Christian faith, she was in reality worshipping the old gods of pagan antiquity. Indeed, one record says that she spoke strangely to a passing scholar, deeply versed in alchemy and occult philosophy, of a 'great Lord who lieth to the East' and whose servant she was. In addition, long after she had passed her fortieth year her beauty showed no signs of diminishing and remained that of a woman in the full bloom of youth. But as tales of her criminal activities circulated ever more frequently and widely, some of the odium attached to her name and the fearful reputation she was acquiring became naturally extended to her own son and later descendants. After dying in solitary confinement in the castle at Csejthe where she had been immured for her crimes for four years, the castle became the centre of a new horror that spread over the countryside like a pestilence. Local inhabitants said that her passion for human blood had been so great that it had persisted beyond the tomb and that not even death could prevent her from plaguing the country with her detestable lusts. Stories that she had been seen by night multiplied and in a short time, the villages nearby were deserted by a panic-stricken populace who spoke wildly of the 'Countess's vengeance' and of the sudden deaths that had been occurring among them.

Her great-grandson Miklos was described by his contemporaries as "a dark-visaged man, saturnine of temperament and little inclined for the customary civilities of society" and although he was a brave soldier in the never-ending wars, he had neither friends nor a wife to lighten the solitude of his secluded life, still overcast by the shadow of his fearful ancestress. From his earliest years, he laboured under the sense that he and his forbears had been the victim of some great injustice and with the help of lawyers he even sent petitions to the Emperor to forward the amazing claim that he was directly descended from the gypsy who had married Vlad Dracul and therefore the legal heir to the original Vlad estates. His argument ran thus: after entering into this ill-fated alliance, Vlad Dracul had willed that all his estate should pass to his second wife and her children by him, and their descendants. They had been cheated of their inheritance by the treachery of Vlad's brothers and sons, who had murdered the wife and then endeavoured with success to blot out all recollection of her, after trying in vain to track down her sole child by the marriage. As each successive effort to retrieve what he claimed was his inheritance failed, Miklos grew increasingly morose and bitter against the line of Draculas who had cheated him thus. Then, in circumstances which remain obscure, he met and passionately fell in love with the last recognised Dracula descendant, the beautiful Lady Mirea. Transported by his wild passion, he professed conciliatory sentiments to her father, even offering to renounce his material claims, and formally requested her hand. His advances were indignantly rejected in terms that were as insulting as they were humiliating. But although Mirea had only seen Miklos once or twice, she had been deeply impressed by him and the ardour of his passion aroused corresponding sentiments in her own heart. Furious when he learned that his daughter was not insensible to Miklos' courtship, her father had her locked away in a distant convent from which she only emerged to marry her father's choice, a Baron Sandor. Shortly after witnessing this forced alliance, Mirea's father died, satisfied and possessed to the end by an unrelenting hatred for Miklos and all his family.

The events that followed were typical of the times when rival families settled their differences by the sword and the only law that prevailed in that ravaged, turbulent country was that of the mightiest. Some three years after Mirea had married Baron Sandor and borne him two children, her husband was absent in the field, having taken most of the garrison with him, thus leaving his home poorly defended. Upon learning the news, Miklos, who was also leading a regiment against the Turks, suddenly withdrew from the hostilities and with a few hired mercenaries and retainers rode by night and day to the Sandor stronghold which they stormed and entered after a brief but bloody fight. Once inside the castle, Miklos made his way to Mirea's chamber and there successfully persuaded her to abandon both husband and children and leave with him. Exactly why she surrendered to his blandishments remained a mystery. Perhaps Miklos possessed some hypnotic power of attraction over her, for he was said, like his ancestors, to know magical secrets and to have been born with strange gifts. In any event, Mirea and Miklos rode away together from the castle like two eloping lovers.

The next two years were both idyllic and turbulent for the pair whose mutual passion knew no bounds. The furious Sandor husband pursued them; the Emperor issued stern decrees; Miklos was declared an outlaw and excommunicated by the Church but profiting from the chaos reigning in the country, he constantly avoided capture and resisted all Sandor's attacks, finally killing him in a skirmish, and then repaired to a strongly defended fortress in the accursed neighbourhood of Csejthe where Mirea gave birth to their child. It was then that Miklos began to find himself haunted by the shade of his evil ancestress who had so terrified the local population many years previously. What happened subsequently we know from a fearful confession in his own hand, later discovered by an Imperial delegation from Belgrade, led by the Bishop of Lobowitz who deposited it in the archives of that town where it was eventually found by the curator after Stephen had come to him with certain enquiries. After he had in his turn corresponded with the curator, Arminius had been told that the document was now missing. It had been brought to Stephen in a box containing other manuscripts and he had been allowed to peruse it alone and undisturbed. When he had finished he had simply handed back the box and departed. Nevertheless, the curator had once read the document and was able to reproduce its main gist from memory.

Miklos wrote that he had seen the apparitions of his dead ancestress with increasing frequency, and that she had been calling to him from outside, begging to be admitted into the fortress. Although he had been curiously tempted to let her in he had managed, by a tremendous effort of the will, to keep silent, adding that in such cases of haunting by a *revenant* (of whose habits he seems to have been singularly well-informed), they can only gain admittance into a dwelling if the inmate responds to their entreaties by inviting them. While a series of murders was reported in the district, Miklos' sleep at night became troubled by terrifying dreams. At length, no longer able to endure these apparitions which threatened to unseat his reason and compel him to submit to the *revenant's* demands, and urged by his terrified subjects who implored him to rid the country of the curse, he traced its source to the castle at Csejthe. Profiting from the security of daybreak, he made his way alone to the castle, taking with him certain instruments to which he vaguely alluded as "being of great power". Hours passed as he searched every nook and cranny of the castle and explored the vaults and when finally he found the chamber containing the tomb wherein the Countess's body lay, he feared that the sun had already begun to sink although he had no means for measuring the passage of time in the vast crypts of the castle. At this point in his statement, he becomes reticent, only saying that he had come to destroy the body and that as he gazed at it, its life-like appearance and dazzling beauty caused his hand to falter. What he said next, the curator cannot remember, save that Miklos claimed by some occult means to have made sure that the vampire (for such it must have been) could never again leave its resting place, and must there remain confined for all eternity. The confession ended with a solemn warning to all Miklos' descendants never, never to go near the castle and seek for the tomb for if they did so, and disturbed the arrangements he had made, the curse would be revived.

After he had returned home, no further incidents came to trouble the peace of the countryside but a marked change was gradually observed in his behaviour and countenance. He began to shun all company and even Mirea and the child, and would stay locked up in a great, high room in a tower for hours and then days at a time. One day, he suddenly disappeared, leaving a letter to Mirea in which he enjoined her never to seek for him. Grief-stricken and inconsolable, Mirea, whose love for Miklos had never waned, began to seek her vanished lover, leaving her child in the care of a nurse and faithful retainers, and riding for months and then years from town to town, castle to castle, village to village, always enquiring among the people if any sign had been seen of her beloved Miklos. Years passed, and her perseverance was finally rewarded. Miklos had retired to a hermit's cell in the mountains, living in the wilderness with only a few half-savage gypsy tribes as his neighbours. They spoke to Mirea with curious reverence of the recluse as though he had become some kind of holy or wise man, with a spiritual authority over them, and added that he had lately been ill and even now was lying in his retreat in a semi-comatose state, close to death. Escorted by the gypsies, Mirea went to his retreat, found him dying, and brought him by slow stages back to the castle. He died a few days later and while his body lay in state, in an open sarcophagus, the Lady Mirea barely left its side, remaining in a kind of trance, wavering between the most abject dejection and exultant hopefulness, saying to the few who wonderingly approached Miklos' remains that she was sure that their love would outlast death itself and that "my master will come to me and I shall follow him". A few days after Mikos had been laid to rest in the chapel, Mirea became ill, languished and died, and was laid in a sepulchre adjoining his own. Within a short time, a new outbreak of vampirism was ravaging the country. This time, the scale of the hauntings and the number of murders and mysterious illnesses reported far exceeded in scale anything that had been known in the days when Countess Bathory had been said to walk abroad, and spread across the confines of the province. One family in particular suffered from ghostly visitations which brought first illness and then lingering death in their train and that was the House of Sandor. Fathers, brothers, sons, sisters and daughters perished and only distance from the region saved the survivors from a similar fate. The tombs of Miklos and Mirea were opened and found to be vacant, while subsequent enquiries brought forward witnesses to say how they had seen a great carriage drawn by gypsies leave the castle bearing a mysterious load, and be driven away at a furious pace to some unknown destination. Entire districts were in a state of the wildest agitation, old women reputed to be witches or seers spoke darkly of a great vengeance and of the returning rule of Pandaemonium, of the Lord of the Flies and the Prince of Gehenna who had reappeared to take possession of the earth. The Church was alarmed, and the gypsies in the mountains were observed to be conducting heathenish rites in their encampments while fires blazed by night in the mountains and weird chants were heard by frightened travellers. This was the beginning of the fearful epidemic of vampirism which spread like the plague throughout Carinthia, Styria, Transylvania, Serbia, the Tyrol, Hungary and Dalmatia. At times, the vigilance of both the Church and the civil authorities was successful in stamping out such outbreaks before they had spread far but while one region became quiet for a time, the epidemic broke out again with renewed virulence in another. Old women accused of witchcraft and of communing with the dead died shrieking in torment in torture chambers and upon blazing fires in market places and town squares, tombs were opened and their occupants destroyed, villages were burned and mighty castles left desolate and still the terror of the Undead stalked the countryside. The people protected their dwellings with painted crosses, bunches of wild garlic flowers and hawthorn branches, and spoke darkly of a superstition that somewhere in the land there dwelt a Lord of the Undead who ruled supreme over the awful fraternity of the resurrected dead and whose commands were obeyed faithfully by the legions of vampires who sought to extend his sway by recruiting yet more victims to swell their ranks. Scholars and churchmen began to write treatises on the vampire and his acolytes in ever increasing numbers and it is from this time that we have the authoritative accounts of such eminent authorities as the Abbé Calmet and Harenburg. The pestilence reached paroxysmic proportions in the last years of the seventeenth century and the first decades of the eighteenth, and was causing considerable alarm even at the Imperial Court.

In the meantime, a curious man who claimed to be Miklos' descendant and who produced papers to prove his assertion, had come to dwell in the small ancestral manor at Torberg, together with a wife and a number of retainers who were noticed to be entirely of Szekely or Szgany stock and who remained aloof and distant in all their dealings with the local folk, when they did not treat them with contempt. Strange things were said about the pair and several more observant spirits declared that they had noticed a disquieting resemblance between the quickly glimpsed features of the mistress and those of Mirea as they remembered her. Another peculiar circumstance that aroused much speculation was that the pair had come to take possession of their castle at night, and that they were seldom seen in the daytime or if they were, they would only leave their abode in a carriage with curtained windows. However, neither the Lord nor his Lady gave the population any cause for complaint. The estate was well-administered, justice was meted out impartially and fairly, and unlike other less fortunate districts, Torberg and the villages surrounding it were free from all vampiric molestations. A few gossips commented on the secluded life led by the couple and on their apparent predilection for gypsies and Szekelys as their sole companions, and their lack of offspring or relatives but this was all. Occasionally, some minor official had occasion to visit the castle, but beyond remarking on the extreme frugality of its tenants' habits and on their courteous manners, had nothing to say except that the castle was oppressively dark and silent inside and that there was something that troubled him in its atmosphere and also in the furtive aspect and behaviour of the taciturn servants, who went about their duties as noiselessly as shadows, and the demeanour of a sullen faced priest who came allegedly to provide to the religious needs of the household and who evil-tongued gossips said had been defrocked in another, far away parish. As time went by it was noticed that never had there been any indication of religious ceremonies being performed in the chapel which had fallen into a sad state of disrepair, and that other churchmen were rigorously dissuaded from ever setting foot in the castle. Then, while the vampire epidemic raged in other parts of the country, the countryfolk spoke of midnight sorties from the castle and of the great carriage thundering through the forest only to return days later after the presumed completion of some mysterious mission. At the same time, reports came in to the authorities of the disappearance of numbers of small children of both sexes in neighbouring provinces—a circumstance which, added to the depredations of vampires, only increased the terror of the afflicted inhabitants.

By Imperial decree a delegation was formed under the leadership of the learned Bishop of Lobowitz and set out from Belgrade to investigate these incidents and to seek out the Undead wherever they lay and destroy them in the most efficacious manner, namely by driving of stakes through their bodies, decapitation and burning, the ashes being cast into running waters. Vigils were kept by night, sentinels were posted in the worst stricken spots, and hundreds of people interrogated, a few being put to the torture and imprisoned on suspicion. Suddenly, a Szekely, whose costume and manner proclaimed him to be a servant of some sort, was apprehended in the act of kidnapping a three-year-old child that had been playing in the fields and strayed away while its mother had fallen asleep in the heat. Torture was applied to the prisoner but he obdurately refused to confess the reasons for his crime. The tortures were intensified and still he would not speak. At length, his questioners then sent to Hermannstadt for a man who combined the melancholy offices of public executioner and torturer and who had gained a reputation for inventing even more fiendish methods of torment, and for having taken lessons in cruelty from the Turks whose prisoner he had once been. The hideous interrogation continued for two days and nights until at last, on the point of death and menaced by eternal hell-fire in the life hereafter, the Szekely confessed that he had taken the child "for his lord and mistress who feed on blood" and then expired in one last convulsion of agony before being able to reveal their names and whereabouts.

Inevitably, suspicion became focused on the inmates of the castle of Torberg. Accompanied by a strong escort of soldiers, the doughty Bishop demanded entrance, after having learned that the staff were of similar stock to the tortured prisoner. The Szekelys replied with surliness that their master and mistress had left on a voyage and would not return for several weeks. Ignoring their protestations, the Bishop had them seized while the castle was searched from top to bottom. The chapel was found to be in a state of utter decay, tombs were opened and their pitiful contents were revealed, every room and cellar was ransacked but the search proved fruitless. The Bishop was about to give the order to depart, with the servants who had been taken into custody, when one soldier, more acute of senses than his companions, reported that he had been seized by a violent sense of nausea in one of the cellars, attributing his malaise to a horribly repellent odour which seemed to emanate from one of the walls. The search was resumed and after a minute scrutiny, it was found that the wall in question contained a cunningly concealed doorway which swung open to disclose a flight of steps leading down yet further into the depths of the earth. Of what the delegation found in this nethermost crypt to which the steps led them, the report gives only a horror-struck summary, adding that the stench was so terrible that several soldiers were overcome and that several visits were needed before the atmosphere could be endured for more than a few minutes at a time. The walls were piled high with the rotting, pathetic remains of countless children, and in the midst of their decaying corpses, there lay two open tombs, one that of the intact body of the lord of the castle, the other, that of his wife, each apparently sleeping and resting in several inches of human blood.

After the two vampires were despatched by the usual means, uttering terrible shrieks as the stakes were driven through their carcasses, they crumbled to dust before the horrified eyes of the Bishop and his men. A few days later, while reading through the correspondence and private documents that had been taken from the castle, the Bishop discovered Miklos' confession and, led by a sudden impulse, compared its handwriting with those of the last tenant whose undead existence had so fortuitously been discovered after the kidnapping incident. There was no doubt in the Bishop's mind as he reached this solemn conclusion: in each case, and despite the lapse of many years, the handwriting was identical. Miklos Bathory and his alleged descendant had been one and the same person! Similarly, it was entirely feasible that the woman's body in the tomb had been that of Mirea. Nearly fifty years after their death, they had continued to haunt their countrymen as vampires, and had caused the most terrible plague of vampirism that history has ever recorded. After their destruction, a few more graves were opened, a few more undead corpses destroyed and at last people could breathe again. The land had been rid of the curse and as the years passed the memories of those frightful times passed away into legend and what had once made all Europe shudder became dismissed by other nations as part of the quaint folklore of Eastern Europe.

* * *

None of us dared speak for some time after Arminius had concluded his revelations. At length, I managed to ask: "So Stephen then is the descendant of a vampire?" Arminius nodded: "Yes, through his mother he comes of the Bathory and the Miklos who, by not destroying the thing that had been his ancestress, himself became a vampire and brought so much suffering upon humanity. It is not surprising, no, that this Sebastian change his name after all this?"

"But then, Elizabeth must be related to Stephen through their common ancestress—Mirea?" cried Meg in alarm. "Yes, he is a kind of half-brother if you like. Mirea leave a child by her husband, and Elizabeth come from them; Miklos he leave children, and from them there is Stephen." Ernest leaped up from his chair and began to pace up and down the room wildly. "What does it mean?" he cried, "are you telling me that Stephen is a vampire? Is my poor Elizabeth menaced by such a blasphemous monstrosity? Oh, my God!" He closed his eyes and shuddered while Arminius gently took his arm and made him sit again. "Courage, my friend," he said softly, "that he is a vampire I do not believe. Why should he be? He be not dead or haunted, I think. Only he know much of his past and his cursed ancestry and maybe this affect him too strangely. No, he is not the vampire but still I do not like this. I am afraid— I cannot say of what, but I am afraid. Yes, we must act quickly, my dear friends, this marriage should not be. For Elizabeth, he will bring no good."

"And the castle?" I asked.

"The castle? Ah yes, the castle of the Vlad Dracul that belong to Elizabeth. The reason of all this must lie in the castle."

We leave at once. Our first destination is Torberg.

Elizabeth Sandor's Diary

SEPTEMBER 19TH

Why is Stephen in such haste and why do the lawyers look at me so strangely when I speak with them? There have been legal formalities to be fulfilled, papers to be signed. Dear Stephen has drawn up some documents himself which I have signed. Yes, he is right. Let us marry at once. Stephen has arranged everything. I do not care what they say for all that is mine is Stephen's. Enough of their silly quibbles! What has love to do with such trifles? I wish that Katia would cease her endless whining and moaning, and stop looking at me so distractedly as though I were going to some dreadful fate. Why does she fear Stephen so? Are we not to be united in the eyes of the law (we are already united irrevocably in our hearts and souls). Why must I hurry, she asks? Fool—why should we wait? Fate has decreed that we should meet and love, no matter what Meg may say in her uncomprehending letters. They only irritate me and as for Ernest—I no longer wish to remember him. I was a sentimental fool then and knew not my own nature. Let them deem me mad if they like. If this be madness then it is a glorious madness and I exult in it. We can afford to scorn the vulgar prejudices of the multitude. I should like his detractors to face Stephen if they dare—oh, that wonderful wisdom and the power in his vivid eyes! He is a king among men. We leave tomorrow.

Andrew Fuller's Diary

SEPTEMBER 23RD

They have disappeared. Yesterday, we arrived at Elizabeth's home only to be met by a distraught housekeeper, an elderly, motherly soul called Katia who has not ceased wringing her hands and lamenting ever since Stephen first called here. Not only does she attribute Elizabeth's father's quick decline and death to Stephen's malefic influence but assures us that Elizabeth had been behaving like a person demented. Where she has now gone she does not know. They left unexpectedly, leaving no forwarding address, merely saying that they would be getting wed in the immediate future, would be travelling and eventually communicate with her. Well, so they are not in castle Torberg at least. Even if they were, I doubt if we could gain admittance. Aftey they marry, there is no reason why they should not disappear for a whole year if they wish it. All we can do is pray that we may find them and essay a confrontation of Elizabeth and Ernest. I am sure that not even Stephen can prevent a man paying his respects to his wife to be on the pretext of 'congratulating' her. However, we are desperate and must do something, for Arminius' warnings still resound direfully in my mind.

SEPTEMBER 24TH

They have been heading north, it was reported to us. The main road in that direction will take them to Karlsbùrg, where the road then forks, leading to Hermannstadt in the southeast, and Klausenburg in the north.

LATER:

I think—nay, I am sure—I have the explanation. My theory is as follows: for many years now, Stephen has been mentally deranged and haunted by an overwhelming obsession. His early years were clouded by a strange blankness and mental deficiency as we already know. Later, the discovery of his family history, his mother's dreadful fate and her reported apparition to him have preyed on his mind, poised dangerously between sanity and madness. He has become convinced tha *he is Miklos and that Elizabeth is Mirea* and in his lunacy is re-enacting past events. It all tallies. Did he not practically storm his way into her house and lure her away, just as Miklos seduced Mirea away from her home, husband and children? Like Miklos, he too is obsessed by some fancied inheritance which has been unjustly denied him and which he can only gain by marriage to she who ultimately benefits by it? He is no longer living in this century. His studies of the past have upset his brain. There is tainted blood in his veins, he comes of a race that was shunned and cursed, and his mania will increase until he may commit some dreadful action. Elizabeth has married a madman though she knows it not. But she will soon discover it. Heaven help her if Stephen sees that she has learned the awful truth. She may resist him, attempt to flee or call for help and then, as has so often happened in similar circumstances, the lunatic may murder her rather than risk losing her!

SEPTEMBER 25TH

We came to the pretty little town of Karlsburg, once the residence of the princes of Transylvania and near the site of the great battle that Hunyady Janos won over the Turks in the shadow of the rocky Erzgebirge. Our enquiries have established that they did pass here and were seen to take the road to Klausenburg. We may be gaining on them.

SEPTEMBER 26TH

A day of terrible gloom for all three of us. It is done. They are married. There is nothing more we can do. Ernest has seen Elizabeth for the last time. We took the train to Klausenberg, and immediately started to tour the town by cab as soon as we arrived at the station. We first went straight to the town hall and after asking the clerk were told that the marriage ceremony between a Stephen Morheim and an Elizabeth Sandor had indeed been solemnised both civilly and by the church a few hours previously. We were thunderstruck by the news and I even thought that Ernest would faint under the shock. What occurred next only increased his bitter anguish and disappointment. As we dejectedly passed the Königin von England hotel, we saw a large closed carriage drawn up by the entrance. A young woman, attired for travelling came out a moment later and made her way to the carriage. As soon as he caught sight of her Ernest let out a terrible cry and dashed forward before we could restrain him. "Elizabeth!" he shouted, oblivious of the many curious looks his wild behaviour drew from the passers-by. The young woman paused—it was her. For a moment she faltered, she grew deathly pale, stared wildly at him and then, when he was barely ten paces distant from her, averted her face and quickly climbed in the carriage. There was a sharp command, the driver cracked his whip and the carriage lurched forward while from the depths of the carriage I saw peering the pale, intense face of Stephen, who fixed me with one quick glance from his burning eyes before drawing back again. As we stood there helplessly and rooted to the spot, the carriage gathered speed and was lost to sight as it raced down the main avenue towards the outskirts of the town. There was nothing more we could do. Henceforth Elizabeth belongs to Stephen. After we had managed to speak again, Ernest came up to me and squeezed my arm, saying: "well, old friend, we have done our best. I can never thank you and Meg enough for all you have been to me. *He* has got her after all. But did you see her face?" I will not record the rest of that miserable day, except to note down that we finally dissuaded Ernest from instantly returning to London. He is a broken man and cannot be allowed to go back alone in this state. We shall write to London for him. He is to stay with us in some quiet spot for some days until the worst of his anguish has passed. Have sent a telegram to Arminius, apprising him of the dreadful news.

Elizabeth Morheim's Diary

So we are wed. I can scarcely believe it. It all happened so quicky and for what I can remember of the ceremony, I might have been in a trance. I am still upset—terribly upset—by the sight of Ernest. What was *he* doing there? He was like a spectre from the past. Even worse, although I cannot confess it to Stephen, for one frightful moment I felt that all I have done has been a frightful mistake and was tempted to run towards him. Then the feeling passed, and with Stephen's tender attentions, I was once again radiantly happy. How strong and confident his presence makes me! Now, I want to note down exactly every incident, every deed of mine in this new life of mine which promises such wonderful bliss.

All day we rode in the misty, autumnal sunshine through beautiful countryside which became progressively wilder. I noticed how the appearance of the people we met on our way changed. They are swarthier, smaller, more unkempt and often rougher in manner. Many of them are Szekelys or gypsies, Stephen told me. At one halt, an aged gypsy woman came up to the carriage and spoke fiercely to me in words I could not understand. I gave her a coin or two, but even then she continued fixing me with her basilisk stare, and attempted to take my hand until Stephen returned and roughly repulsed her. She backed away, still fixing me with her glittering eyes, mumbling something until at a sharp word of command from Stephen, she turned her back and was gone. But even as she did so, I could not help noticing something in her attitude and wrinkled countenance that betrayed fear—and besides fear, a kind of awestruck respect. Stephen has some strange power over these people. I noticed it again later. They incline their heads as we pass or else proffer signs of respect as though he was their acknowledged overlord. He might be a king returning to his country and I—their queen.

It is evening and we have arrived at what shall be our home for the time being: a pretty little estate set amidst rolling hills, forests and vineyards. The house is in the style of a fortified manor as is usual in these parts but furnished with every comfort conceivable. The servants too seem to be of gypsy stock and among them was Vihar who welcomed me with great courtesy even though I could not repress a momentary shudder as I beheld his sinister countenance again. I really do not like him and only wish I had the courage to ask Stephen to assign him to some other duties so that I need no longer see him. Tomorrow there is a wine harvest celebration. Already, I can hear the deep-throated chanting of the men in the distance, and the plaintive, high-pitched singing of the women. It is more like a keening than a song of celebration and I wonder that so dejecting a sound can be meant to express rejoicing at so pleasant an annual event. Let me finish penning these lines on this eventful day. I await my lord and lover. Strange though —it is strange how little I really know of him. What a mystery and a wonder life is! Yes, Stephen, I am your bride.

Andrew Fuller's Diary

OCTOBER 22ND

Yet another blow—a shock, a terrible shock that has quite un-
done all the good that our two weeks in the heart of nature
might have done poor Ernest. Stephen has deserted Elizabeth.
He has gained his object and disappeared. Elizabeth is alone.

We learned the news as soon as we returned to Budapesth
this afternoon. A letter was waiting for Meg written in Elizabeth's hand. She had sent it to London whence it was forwarded
to the address we gave here and has just arrived. It was written
just twenty days ago—less than a week after the marriage. I
shall reproduce it here without comment:

My dearest Meg,

*Can you ever forgive me? Can any of you ever forgive me
and can I turn to you again in my distress? I have been mad,
Meg. What came over me these last few weeks is utterly inexplicable and can only be defined as some excess of folly which
has deprived me of all reason, perverted my judgement, and
inflamed my emotions. By what magic did Stephen ever steal
my affections and so enchant me until I was possessed by the
wildest love that any woman has ever known and in my frenzy
rejected all that was noblest and dearest to me? I say 'love' for
this is what the madness signified to me at the time but now I
know I have been the victim of some cruel spell. Now Stephen
has left me and the spell is broken. Yes, Meg, he has left me!
This morning he was not there. From what I could gather
from the sullen servants, he had left before the break of day,
with Vihar, and without informing anyone of his destination.
There was a letter from him waiting for me. I have read it
again and again until my eyes blurred. Here it is:*

"Elizabeth.

*I shall forgo the usual endearments since in this case they
would only seem hypocritical. When you read this, I shall be
gone and you shall never see me again. Deem me mad or
wicked if you like. It is of no account to me. I have a duty
to perform and certain things to accomplish alone, I do not
know what destiny will eventually bring me, but I do know*

that in my future there can never be any place for you. There is something I have to work out; there is an assignation awaiting me which was decreed many long years ago. Fate is inflexible and so is determination. You have had to be the innocent instrument of my purpose. I regret it but it was inevitable. Only let me say this: the feelings for you which I displayed may have been feigned at first but later, by slow degrees, they became real. That is all that I shall say about that subject. Soon, you will be free again: this desertion will make it easy for the lawyers to decree an annulment of the marriage. I shall vanish from the face of the earth and men may consider me as dead. I shall exist no more as far as you are concerned. On no account must you seek for me or endeavour to discover my whereabouts. I repeat, on no account must you try to find me if you value your life and soul. Furthermore, I entreat you to leave this place. Go away—to Budapesth or Vienna but preferably overseas—to England if you like. The farther you go, the better. Do not linger here lest I repent of what I have done for then you would be lost. Go now. I do not expect you to understand or forgive. I can only hope that you will see fit to do as I urge you. Stephen."

Oh Meg, what does it mean? My mind is filled with the wildest speculations. For hours after reading this dreadful letter I was too agitated and overwhelmed to apprehend its import. Only now, as I read it again, do I realize the terrible finality of its tone. What a fool I have been! In the rapture of the unnatural passion that Stephen aroused in me, I thought I had found heaven upon earth with him, and scorned every restraint and every instinct that warned me against him. I stifled every sane and decent impulse and destroyed poor Ernest's happiness. Oh, the way he looked at me that day in Klausenburg as though he foresaw the disaster that has ensued! Please speak to him of my letter and remorse. I am too terrified and abject to communicate directly with him. I have wronged him as deeply as any woman has ever wronged a man and can only pray that one day he may find it in his heart to forgive me. What have I done, Meg? What has Stephen's object been? At least, he has shown what a weak and miserable creature I am and how unworthy of Ernest's love. I shall live with the shame of what I have done for the rest of my life. I shall not leave here yet, no matter what Stephen wrote. I am still his lawful wife, and here I shall stay until some further

*word from him or news of his whereabouts. I must stay. I shall
not be inconstant twice, no matter what may come. Please
send me news of yourself, if you can bear to write to me. I
love you always, Elizabeth."*

There is only one thing for us to do and that is go to Elizabeth directly. This time, I am sure, she *will* see Ernest. We
leave at dawn.

OCTOBER 23RD

No railways in this part of the country. We shall be there
tomorrow. I don't like the region much. It's all very grandiose
and beautiful but there is something sinister in the way the
grey rocks and jagged mountains tower over us, and the people
are suspicious and unfriendly. I suppose I'm prejudiced by all
the horrible Oriental savagery of its inhabitants. Some of the
gypsies hereabouts are reported to be excited and restive.
Several bands have left their encampments and headed for the
mountains in the last few days.

Ernest calm and resolute. Meg full of loving forgiveness
for Elizabeth. I have a feeling that this parody of a marriage
should be easy to annul if Stephen really has disappeared for
good. Perhaps after all this agony, there is hope for Ernest after
all.

OCTOBER 24TH

She has gone. The house was shut and deserted when we
arrived. We found one of the workers on the estate who simply
told us that the staff had been dismissed and that the mistress
had left two days ago. We have contacted the authorities but
there is little that they can do as yet. No reports of any woman
travelling alone.

OCTOBER 28TH

Apparently a woman was seen passing through the village of
Tihucza, high in the mountains, near the Borgo Pass. No
description. Nevertheless we shall go there at once.

Elizabeth Morheim's Diary

OCTOBER 3RD

Another dreadful, forlorn day drags to its end. How silent the
house is. I hate the way the servants whisper. They know I am
deserted and observe my humiliation with covert glances and
secretive whispers. The skies have clouded over and promise
snow. What a desolate region this is when the sun is gone—
as desolate as my wounded heart. No news. I am completely
abandoned among these unprepossessing, alien people. I had
them drive me to the village where I sent word to the authorities that my husband has disappeared. They too will know
of my humiliation. What can they do? And what else can I
do, except stay here and await the oncoming of winter? I
shall not move. Here as everywhere else is hateful to me but
still I will not leave.

OCTOBER 7TH

He was calling to me last night. I heard him in my dreams. He
was calling my name as though from a great distance and I
responded joyfully. I know that he is alive and that he wants
me. As I heard his voice, all the passion that I had felt for
him blazed up in me again. Today I have been feeling strangely
comforted. My earlier doubts and remorse are weakening. I
still belong to Stephen.

OCTOBER 9TH

Such a strange dream. I was wandering in an alien landscape,
peopled by great, towering, shadowy figures, amid mountain
peaks and vast lakes that gleamed spectrally under the silver
moon, my arms outstretched to greet my lover, while his words
"come to me! You shall come to me!" echoed in my brain.
I have been sitting bemused most of the day. I am waiting,
waiting, waiting.

OCTOBER 10TH

I saw the dark mass of some gigantic castle towering over my head from a rocky eminence in my dream. Like a wraith, I was slowly ascending a rugged path, passing through a great portal and then into the cavernous recesses where torches blazed and dim figures moved amid the shadows. Hands reached out for me from every side but I did not falter. Through a succession of lofty chambers and corridors I moved until at length one door opened and there, stern and majestic as an ancient god, he stood, waiting for me, the glow of love illuminating his features. I moved forward and there was a blank. I awoke, shivering uncontrollably. All my yearning for him has returned. Even though I do not hear his voice in my waking hours I know that he is waiting for me, that his great mind is sending forth its insistent summons, and that very soon he will send for me. I long for the darkness and mystery of night, for until he holds me again in his arms, it is the only way we can commune. I looked at that terrible letter he wrote me when he departed and although I was uneasy for a moment, I tore it to pieces and watched the scraps as they burned to ashes in the fireplace. That was not my *real* Stephen who wrote such dreadful words. He is himself again and I am again his true wife and lover. Stephen, Stephen, Stephen!

OCTOBER 11TH

Another agitated night. First he called to me again and then an indescribable terror and coldness seized me. I felt that for a fleeting second I was on the verge of discovering a truth so terrible and awesome that no mortal brain could bear it. I awoke, my heart beating furiously and moved by a sudden impulse went to the window and looked at the distant mountains under the star-strewn heavens, longing that I might be a bird and so fly to them, for I know that he is somewhere amidst those great peaks and that it is there that I shall have to go. Another day of waiting and silence.

OCTOBER 12TH

It has come. One of the servants brought it to me. The note is short but there is no doubting that it is in his handwriting. It says: "It is time for you to come. Vihar will drive you. Go with him and have every confidence. Speak to no one on the way. This is imperative if you love me." I *do* love you, Stephen. I go to you with joy and trust in my heart.

OCTOBER 13TH

The strangest journey and an even stranger arrival. We left before the first light of dawn, after I had gathered together the few barest necessities for the journey. Vihar had provided rugs for he told me that it would be cold in the mountains. No sooner did I enter the coach that he cracked his whip and started off at a furious pace through the darkness. I must have dozed off fitfully for every now and again some sudden jolt aroused me and then, when I opened my eyes again, I could see the grey light of early morning. We had penetrated deep into the region of rolling foothills that herald the Carpathians and where villages and farms begin to grow scarce and the only souls to be seen are a few peasants with their carts and roving bands of gypsies as they come down from the mountains to seek sustenance in the great plains during the harsh winter. After several hours had passed, we came to a halt and while the horses were changed I was glad to descend and stretch my legs a little. By now, the day was bright with autumnal sunshine although the looming mountains were veiled by thick mists and leaden cloud and my tiredness could not prevent my spirits rising with the thought of my early reunion with Stephen. Only one thing disturbed me and that was the sinister presence of Vihar and the sullen looks I received from the peasants as they clustered around the carriage and muttered curiously behind my back in their uncouth dialect. We resumed the journey at a slower pace for by now the road had become rougher on its surface and was rising sharply as it wound serpent-like between a succession of steep hills, forested slopes, tumbling and roaring waterfalls, wooden huts, the occasional wayside shrine and piles of boulders. From either window, I caught glimpses of great castles, whose remains spoke of the turbulent past when every acre of the land was fiercely disputed between Christian and Turk and every lord was a law unto himself. Sometimes, they arose in in all their former majesty, like great ships amid the sea of firs that surrounded them, and sometimes all that remained to testify to their vanished glories was an untidy heap of stones, flung here and there as though by a giant's hand on a

barren eminence or a crumbling wall and half-ruined tower
where only birds now find a refuge. It was well past midday
when we drove into a picturesque little village that consisted
of no more than a chapel, a primitive store, a huddle of wooden
cabins and a rough-looking hostelry. As we alighted and went
to the inn that I might refresh myself, Vihar quietly but firmly
reminded me of his master's injunction that I should speak no
word of our destination to anyone. In addition to some slight
feeling of perturbation at this, my oscillating spirits were
further depressed by the way the peasants and gypsies stared
at me as I went in, and by the sudden silence that fell over the
company within. However, the landlord greeted me with a
great show of obsequious servility and ceremoniously ushered
me to a vacant table where some meats and wine were brought
to me while Vihar went outside to attend to the horses. A few
minutes passed and then there was a sudden commotion outside, the sound of raucous laughter and a violently uttered
imprecation. An instant later, to the accompaniment of what
I presumed to be jeers and coarse jests from my neighbours,
there entered a peculiarly misshapen little man with short,
bandy legs, a hunched back, a long and shaggy sheepskin
jacket too large for his dwarfish frame, and a tall furry hat
such as many gipsies wear, and clutching a tambourine in
one hand and a sheepskin bag in the other. From the wild
way he spoke, having difficulty in uttering each syllable, and
the fact that he was the butt of the customers' cruel humour,
it was evident to me that the poor fellow was not only physically
deformed but mentally deficient as are so many who dwell in
primitive mountain regions. After he had turned away from
the bar, a curious look of ferret-like cunning came over his
wizened features and his close-set little eyes gleamed with the
light of sudden intelligence, after he had espied me. To my
consternation, the poor fellow approached me and began to
mouth disjointed words in bad German. "No good here!" he
finally managed to stammer, "no good here for you. You go
away. He no good", pointing at Vihar who had just returned
as he spoke. There was a rush from behind the bar, and the
landlord brutally seized him by the collar and thrust him out
of the door before making profuse apologies to me for the
way I had been disturbed.

After this distressing incident, we returned to the coach
and drove steadily uphill for a few miles, towards what must
be a mountain pass. It had become cold and I withdrew into

the recesses of the seat, covered with rugs and lulled to sleep again by the ship-like lurching of the coach. An hour or so later, the descending motion of the coach told me that we were now on the far side of the Pass, descending rapidly and then turning at an angle. I looked out and saw that we had turned down a side road that ran along a narrow valley hemmed in with trees. The whip cracked again, the horses gained speed and soon we had begun to mount a steep hill, after passing through magnificent beech forests, succeeded by sparser firs. A mile or so beyond, all was wilderness: beyond us and beside us were torn, rocky embankments, monumental fallen boulders, uprooted trees and jagged rocks that spoke eloquently of the havoc and desolation wrought by the fury of the elements in these heights. The sky was leaden grey, mists swirled below us and above but every now and again the swiftly rising wind tore a sudden gap in them so that I could look down into deep, ravined valleys to catch glimpses of winding streams and tiny hamlets at the foot of steep hills. Fiercer grew the wind, dispelling the clouds until at last the snow-capped summits of the mountains rose straight before us in a glorious blaze of sudden light against a turquoise-blue sky, illumined by the cloud-hidden sun. A moment later, the majestic sight had disappeared again under a mantle of thick cloud. Mists seemed to rise from the ground and swirl about us, the wind roared, the air seemed to grow thinner, yet another mighty peak towered into the sky, huge hanging rocks either side of the road threatened to overwhelm us and depressed my spirits, the mists grew thicker again then thinned and at last, looming through them I saw the soaring, dark walls of a gigantic castle with jagged, broken battlements and massive towers, on a mighty rock rising at a point where the mountains on each side came sloping down. Then the mist hid all again from my sight until we had reached a huge doorway and pulled up in a vast, stone-flagged courtyard where two servants ran forward and solemnly saluted me. We had arrived. Before I had time to take stock of my surroundings, the servants, whose tongue I could not comprehend, had taken the baggage and led me to a comfortably furnished chamber made welcoming by a cheery log fire that blazed in a great chimney-place. There I was brought supper and a note from Stephen. He bids me be patient: he has unavoidably had to be absent. He will return soon. Every necessity will be provided for me. I pen these lines before I retire for the night.

I am sick. Sick or insane—perhaps both. The atmosphere of this great place must be depressing me for never did I have such dreams as I did last night. Let me try to recall what I can of them: I remember the dismal howling of wolves that persisted uninterrupted until I lost consciousness and which then continued to provide an eerie accompaniment to my fitful dreams. Something was oppressing me, I felt a sensation of stifling, I could neither breathe nor move, some mysterious force whose source I could not apprehend was holding me fast, a prisoner in its grasp. Strange, weird words in an alien tongue that yet held some dim significance for me echoed in my fevered mind. I was lost in a cloud of ebon darkness and then, two points of light suddenly glowed before me like will o' wisps, I felt a sharp stinging pain followed by a deliciously languorous drowsiness. Later as my mind struggled back to wakefulness and as the crying of distant wolves and the moaning of the wind mingled in a wild symphony that reached a crescendo, my eyes fluttered open to behold the bluish rays of moonlight penetrating the diamond-paned window and a gigantic, formless shadow on the wall opposite. As I stared as one hypnotised, the shadow seemed to dance on the wall and then dissolve, I heard muttered words as from a great distance, my eyelids drooped again and I sank into sweet oblivion. I woke long past my usual hour to see that the clouds had gone and the sun was high in the heavens. Silent-footed servitors had brought me coffee and bread and sweet cakes, and on my silver tray there lay another note from Stephen, in an envelope bearing no postmark so that it must have been delivered by hand. It merely said: "Be patient, my beloved. I shall be coming soon. Until then have no fear: you are in good hands".

The long coach ride must have greatly fatigued me for at first I hardly had the strength to walk and had to spend another two hours resting. Then, after some meats were brought and a couple of glasses of good red wine, I was sufficiently recovered and fortified to embark on a short exploration of this great pile, which would appear to be my new home. Only about four or five male servants seem to live here and they are all extremely uncommunicative for as I approached them and endeavoured to obtain information from them—mainly by using signs for they understood no civilised tongue—they looked blankly at me and then turned their backs with oafish insolence. Seeing that no help was forthcoming from that source, I began to reconnoitre the building, wandering through great corridors and vaulted rooms. After climbing a winding staircase that took me to a little vantage point where a lookout must once have been posted, I realized as I surveyed the majestic view that I commanded, that the castle was built at the extremity of a mighty rock, with three sides falling away hundreds of feet in a sheer drop into great gorges and chasms with silvery rivers gleaming in their depths. Seen from such a terrifying height, the expanse of wild scenery was even more impressive than when I had seen it from the coach and it was not hard for me to fancy that the former tenants must have felt like eagles, perched high and inaccessible in their mountain eyrie, safe from any assault that their enemies might devise. Descending again, I could not but be struck by the general air of desolation that reigns almost everywhere, with the signal exception of my own quarters. The courtyard, with the grass and weeds growing between the broken flagstones, speaks of centuries of neglect and most of the windows facing on to it, like sightless eyes, are unpaned unlike some others where the glazing seems to have been of more recent date. I turned away from this forlorn scene and made my way into a great hall whence a palatial stone staircase led to an upper suite of apartments, and marvelled at the carvings above a massive fireplace. After musing thus a few moments, a singular circumstance came to my notice. Half-effaced as it was, there was something familiar in the armorial device sculpted in the stone: in every detail that I could see, there was a complete similarity with the great signet ring that Stephen wears so proudly on his right index finger. The arms were the same! But this has not been the only strange thing I have seen today and which increases my nervousness and my vague suspicions a hundred fold.

After this curious discovery, I proceeded to inspect the upper apartments. Long corridors, galleries, yet more staircases and chambers of palatial proportions stretched before me, silent and dust-laden. Few contained any evidence of former occupation and in most, it was easy to see that the dust that lay everywhere so thickly had been disturbed by no human footprint for centuries. Finding it difficult to gauge the exact extent of the castle, I wandered aimlessly for a full hour, always noting the constant air of decay and abandon, until

I came to a smaller chamber where a small, iron-studded door attracted my notice. After a few moments' pushing it yielded, to reveal a small spiral staircase which I followed until it brought me into the only other chamber which seemed at all adapted for human occupation. There was a heavy oaken desk, a high-backed chair, a case full of venerable volumes, writing implements, and a small heap of ancient gold and silver coins, and on another smaller desk, in a corner, a kind of *escritoire*, a number of ancient books and a pile of manuscripts, some written in large, cryptic characters such as I had never seen before and which looked more like symbols to my untrained eye than letters of any known alphabet. But it was not this that so mystified me or increased the perturbation that grew within me with every step I took into this great, gloomy edifice. It was a small, gilt-framed portrait of a lady in a dark dress and high, lacy ruff—a lady of past times whose features might have been my own. Scarcely able to believe the evidence of my senses, I picked it up and brought it over to the light that I might scrutinise it the better. No, there is no doubt at all about it—further study of the lady's countenance only confirmed me in the impression that I was the living original of the portrait. What does it mean? Have I then found the likeness of some unknown ancestress? Why is it there in that isolated chamber? And where is Stephen? Night is falling and I grow nervous. My heart beats faster at every sound, as the wolves lament, and the winds whistles through the broken battlements and gaping windows. The melancholy state of desertion and disrepair into which the castle has fallen, my loneliness and the sullen, secretive aspect of the servants all alarm me. I hear a door banging somewhere in the depths of the building. The wind is growing fiercer and it is with dismay that I prepare myself to face the mysteries of the night, alone and virtually a prisoner.

OCTOBER 15TH

Another strange night. I awoke with heavy limbs and a prey to a terrible faintness as though I had been drugged. I can hardly drag myself about the chamber. Only by a supreme effort of the will was I able to muster the forces necessary to take me downstairs. The sky is still leaden hued and storm swept. The wind is like the mournful dirge of the dying year and everywhere I look the white vapours of the autumnal day veil the scenery from my eyes. I return to my room and there sit until food is brought to me. Listlessly I eat and drink and unable to endure the solitude and silence any longer, I endeavour to distract myself by penning these few lines and in particular to recording my dream of last night which, if repeated, will unhinge my reason, I fear.

After I had retired to bed, some presentiment of approaching evil warned me to resist the overpowering sleepiness that came over me. For at least an hour I struggled to keep my eyes open while the storm outside grew in intensity. I could well imagine the old tales of pagan spirits borne on the wind as it shrieked overhead and tugged violently at the trees and casements, while the great castle answered its violence with a multitude of shakings and rattlings and sinister creakings. Just as I was closing my eyes, there was the distant sound of horses' hooves and the passage of a heavy carriage over a rocky path and then the groaning of a heavy door as it swung open, followed by a thunderous clang that resounded through the castle like a death-knell as it was shut again. I sat up in bed, secure in my conviction that Stephen had returned. There was no sound in the castle, save those made by the elements. I waited an hour and then sleep claimed me. This time, I felt borne away in a whiteish mist through which I could occasionally glimpse dark shadows as they flitted to and fro. I was descending, descending, all grew dark again. Someone whose voice I half recognised was whispering devilish words which filled me with unutterable alarm even though their precise import escaped me. Then the whispers died away and I was left in the dark and silence of the tomb, unable to move my limbs, unable to speak or breathe while some great weight bore down upon me relentlessly as though it would crush my chest. Sparks of fire danced before my eyes, there were more sharp, stinging pains, there was a flash of lightning, a peal of thunder, and I awoke. Another flash of lightning illumined the room and in that one terror-filled instant, I saw over me a face with two gleaming eyes . . . Oh that wolfish snarl and that expression of hellish exultation! I cannot bring myself to describe it. It cannot have been real—it must have been a part of my terrible nightmare. But why am I so weak and drawn today? I barely recognise myself in the mirror. I can write no more.

OCTOBER 18TH

Dull and apathetic all day. The nightmare again.

OCTOBER 21ST

I am dying and only this knowledge gives me strength to record
my last hours. It is he—it is the Master and he gives me joy.
Yes, in serving him I serve Stephen. I am at peace. In love
there is sacrifice. In death there shall be love. He beckons me
into dark regions. It is well.

OCTOBER 22ND

The Master spoke to me. Tonight I go to him. But these last
words and all is done . . . He is near, he is hard by the door.
My great lord . . .

Andrew Fuller's Journal

OCTOBER 26TH

We rode fast, with few halts through the savage landscape towards Tihucza and the mountain pass of the Borgo. The man who spoke of seeing a strange woman alight there was an idiot, a kind of half-breed with inherited mental deficiency. None the less, he was sufficiently lucid to tell us that the lady was young and beautiful and journeying with a "bad man". It must be Elizabeth. After we had asked the man if he had any idea where she was bound, he grinned dementedly, then after a long pause in which he stared at the ground, muttered vaguely something about a "master's castle". It can only be that which Elizabeth has inherited and which Stephen is so anxious to possess. But which castle? There are several ruined and less-ruined castles in these parts and the particulars we have of the one in question are vague although everything points to its proximity in this region. We spend the night here and resume the search tomorrow. It must be one of the several fortresses indicated on the map and which were built in medieval times to command the road leading to the Pass.

OCTOBER 27TH

A day of hope and then frustration. We arose early and were about to depart when we saw our feeble-minded friend, grinning and gesticulating insanely at us. We would have ignored him if he had not suddenly come running over to us and seizing my arm, pointed at a great wagon drawn by a team of horses and driven by two dark-faced gypsies which was rumbling through the village on the way towards the Pass. As I asked him what he meant he nodded vehemently and pointed fiercely again as the wagon receded into the distance. Surmising that he meant to tell us that whither the wagon was bound was also our destination, we set off after it, although keeping a respectable distance behind so as not to arouse any suspicion that we were following it. In any case, there was no reason why we should not be driving behind it, since the road connects with the Bukowina and is used by quite a few travellers until made impassable by the snows. We passed through Tihucza, whence our friend had come, and ascended ever higher into a region of increasing wildness and desolation with the snowy peaks of the Carpathians soaring before us, until we had come to the Pass and begun to descend again on its far side. No sooner had we done so, than we saw the great wagon suddenly turn off the road, on to some side track, and lose itself from our sight behind a line of firs. We increased our pace and followed the track through a narrow valley, up a hill past beeches and firs, and thence onwards through a wilderness that would provide an apt setting for Dante's inferno, until at last, through the gathering mists which greatly restricted visibility, there appeared to us the towering mass and jagged battlements of one of the largest, most impressive castles I had ever seen in that part of the country. We were debating how to proceed once we had come to its entrance, when another carriage drawn by gypsies came along in the opposite direction, towards us. As it drew near, one of the drivers waved his whip at us and began to shout furiously. Unperturbed, Ernest bravely stepped into the middle of the track and waved at it until it came to a halt. "Let us ask these fellows who is in the castle," he said grimly, ignoring the hostile attitude of the drivers who, with knives in their belts and long rifles slung behind their backs, were the perfect image of bandits or outlaws.

After attempting several words I knew in various local dialects, I eventually managed to communicate with them in a primitive version of Ruthenian which they understood fairly well. I said we were English travellers and that we were seeking a friend who dwelt in these parts. Could they tell us whether a young lady and her husband, a tall and distinguished looking young man were there? The gypsies shook their heads for reply. In that case, I persisted, who was the tenant of the castle? The two men looked at each other before replying, and then said it belonged to some great lord. I took out some gold coins and offered it to them in exchange for further information. The eldest of the two drivers leaped down from the seat, snatched the coins from me, sniffed and fingered them suspiciously, and finally reassured that they were genuine, smiled craftily and said "yes, there had been a young man but no woman. But now he has sold the castle to another, old man, and is no longer there. A very old man, and a great lord, lives there alone and no one else except a few servants".

Our mystification knew no bounds on receiving this depressing information. Ernest was insistent that we should continue and question this new proprietor, but the gypsy said that he was a strict old man who did not wish to be disturbed and I pointed out that there was no proof that the previous occupant had been Stephen or that this was indeed our destination. But nothing could alter Ernest's determination to remain in the area, in order to keep a watch upon the castle and to search the surrounding district. Finally, we reached a compromise: near the top of the Pass there were two or three of the mountain refuges the government has built for the convenience of travellers in recent years. Ernest would take a horse and stay in one of them while Meg and I continued downhill towards Bukowina and then—if no one in the villages that lay beyond us could tell of any lady who had passed that way, we would return to the Pass and all together we would go down again to Bistritz and there begin investigations, to see whether any local lawyer or land agent in the town (the most important for the region) had recorded any transaction by Stephen in the last two weeks or so, and whether he had left an address. Tonight, Meg and I are staying at the little village of Pojana Stampi on the frontier, in a snug though primitive inn. Tomorrow we resume our enquiries. I wonder how Ernest is faring in his refuge. We found a guardian there who promised he should be comfortable.

OCTOBER 28TH

It has begun to snow. We pressed on towards the valley of the Golden Bistritz. I fear we have been led astray. We overtook a gypsy who smiled cunningly at our enquiry and then with exaggerated emphasis told us that a young woman in a carriage had indeed gone that way recently. I did not like the way he grinned when he pocketed the coin I gave him as reward and our subsequent failure to find any trace of the carriage have convinced us that he deliberately misled us or lied, either through cupidity or for some darker purpose. We are utterly worn out and terribly depressed. The roads are bad, winter will be here any moment and all track of Elizabeth is lost. Tomorrow we shall go back.

Rode the long way back. It had already begun to snow though only lightly. Ernest was in the refuge, looking horribly pale and drawn. Poor fellow—I am sure he has had hardly any sleep! He must have spent every minute of daylight hunting for some clue. He is convinced that Elizabeth is nearby although why he will not say. He was, in fact, strangely secretive and said that the guardian of the pass was going to help him, and refused to come back with us despite our implorings. We argued in vain: he insists on staying there a few days longer and then promises to rejoin us at Bistritz. What could we do? We could not drag him forcibly down the pass with us. We shall have to leave him there for at least two days. Meg is very anxious and says that she does not like the look in his eyes or his pallor. He is wearing himself away and must soon give up this search. I do not like the way he insisted on staying and urged us to leave him. I cannot sleep yet. I am uneasy for him.

An extremely helpful clerk at the town hall gave us the name and address of the lawyer who, with a colleague, attends to most of the land purchases and property transactions in the mountains. We went straight to their office and what we learned there is both baffling and highly alarming.

The castle we saw *was* Stephen's and he has sold it to a buyer whose identity must remain a secret to us. We beseeched the lawyer, a crabbish fellow as dry and heartless as the old files that littered his office, to tell us to whom the castle had been sold but he maintained that the purchaser and Stephen had insisted that the identity of the new owner must be kept from all curious enquirers. But what right did Stephen have to sell the property? Surely he owned it jointly with Elizabeth? Was his wife not a party to the transaction? After tut-tutting a while the lawyer eventually relented somewhat and informed us that everything had been in order and perfectly legal since his client, Stephen, had a signed authorisation from his wife empowering him to dispose of the castle as he chose. The sale had been effected upon his written instructions. Only the anonymous gentleman had appeared in person in the office where the documents legalising the transaction were duly signed, and payment had been made to Stephen's account. As for Stephen's whereabouts, he had not the slightest idea. I fear we have sad news for Ernest when he joins us tomorrow.

NOVEMBER 2ND

Not a sign of Ernest all day. We are terribly worried. Tomorrow morning I go alone, back up the pass. Meg must stay here. I have insisted.

NOVEMBER 4TH

Ernest is no more. He died in my arms late this afternoon. The driver who brought me here returned to Borgo Prund to fetch a priest and a doctor a little while previously, and will have a note sent down at once to Bistritz telling Meg to remain in the hotel until further notice. On no account will I have her here. There are certain things I have to do after our dearest, faithful friend is laid to rest. When I reached the cabin that serves as a refuge, the guardian had fled. I found Ernest lying, deathly pale, his eyes closed, on a rough bed, too weak to move, his sunken lips in his emaciated face barely able to utter a whisper. At length, after I had ministered to him as best I could and sent the driver off for a doctor, his eyes fluttered open and he smiled weakly and then, with a strange gleam in his eyes, said: "I am so glad you have come, old friend. I have been waiting for you and so has Elizabeth. She was here, you know. She will be with us soon." Apart from his condition, some horrible change had come over his countenance. With a sinking in my heart, I observed the way his gums had drawn back, the peculiar sharpness of the teeth, the mesmerised, voluptuous way he smiled and gazed at me and the change in his tone, and, in an extremity of horror, as he moved his head slightly I observed two small marks in his neck, like the punctures of an insect or some tiny rodent, *gradually disappearing under my very eyes*! There was a long, soft sigh and all was over. Ernest was dead and I know that the vampire is no old superstition but a deadly reality for although Ernest had managed to tell me that Elizabeth had been with him in that hut, *I also knew by an undeniable intuition, that she too had died some time before*. And so I remain alone with his body as the night wears on and thick snow flakes begin to fall. I have made a cross with a piece of wood. She shall not come here tonight.

NOVEMBER 8TH

And so we have buried Ernest, a thousand miles from his native land. The doctor's report was acute amnesia and general debilitation due to insomnia and excessive exertion leading to a failure of the heart. At least, this is what he said in his official report but privately, he agreed with me that the body had almost entirely been drained of blood and given the mysterious absence of wounds, and two similar cases reported not long ago in the same region, he must inevitably be led to the same conclusion: that the vampire again walks by night in this haunted land no matter how incredible it might seem to a scientific, materialistic mind. I have done my best to shield Meg from the full, frightful truth but I know that she has guessed all. Bless her for the brave way she has borne all! Despite her objections and premonitions, I have at last persuaded her to return to Budapesth and there wait me. The doctor and the consul will accompany her. Now, with the priest I have taken into my confidence, I have a terrible duty to perform here. Then I go back to the Borgo Pass and there execute the most dreadful task of all. God give me the strength to succeed!

NOVEMBER 10TH

I spend the night alone in the fear-ridden country. My return has obviously aroused much comment among the local population who have been looking at me with deep suspicion and not a little hostility. They draw away and shun me as I pass, as they draw away and cross themselves as increasing numbers of gypsies pass through the village and as great carriages rumble through the ill-paved streets at night. But I am not afraid for I go armed and resolute. At dawn I shall go forth and destroy that which *was* Elizabeth and *he* that made her the instrument of Ernest's death and laid the curse of the Undead on her. It is not a pleasant nor an easy thing to disinter by stealth one's dearest friend, to see on his countenance the frightful hue of unnatural life that knows no physical decay, and to drive a wooden stake through his breast and then cut off his head. There is a heavy debt of vengeance to be paid. Before nightfall tomorrow I intend to close the account.

NOVEMBER 11TH

This may well be the last time that I shall ever write in this journal. I only can pray that when it is time for me to put it away that it may one day fall into some friendly hand. With the other papers, I shall make a packet, address it and place it somewhere in this hut. *They* shall not find it.

Of how I made my way to the castle, unobserved by the gypsies who have been so active there lately, I have not the time to relate, nor of how I avoided their vigilance and made my entry. Let it suffice that although I found the castle in a general state of abandon and disrepair, the number of large packing cases and crates suggested that its tenants are in the process of furnishing it and again making it fit for habitation after centuries of neglect. After traversing a multitude of deserted, cobweb-festooned rooms, occasionally shrinking into the darkest recesses of labyrinthine corridors and crypts as some sudden footfall and muttered words told me of the proximity of the gypsies, I was able to ascend the great staircase that led from the entrance hall to the upper regions of the castle. There I continued my explorations with less fear of discovery, the workman and gypsies confining their activities to the lower parts of the edifice for the time being. At length, I came to a richly furnished room containing a fine four-poster bed, much antique furniture and sumptuous hangings, a *secretaire* of massive mahogany, and signs of recent occupation by a female tenant. With a palpitating heart I approached the *secretaire* and in a drawer found a little notebook bound in red velvet and stamped in silver with the arms of the House of Sandor— it was Elizabeth's journal. Her last entries and in particular, her account of the castle, told me all that I needed to know and had already surmised respecting her fate. After this, it only remained for me to seek her body and that of the vampire that had taken possession of her soul. For hours I searched in that cavernous castle, while the sun sunk even lower over the mountains. When I had almost abandoned hope I came to a room with a heavy door, swung it open and made my way down a stone passageway that led to a circular stairway that descended steeply to yet another darker passage and beyond that another door and beyond that, a ruined chapel of immeasurable antiquity, its darkness only broken by the last feeble light of evening that filtered through the broken roof. There, I found yet more steps leading down into the vaults of vast dimensions and still another door leading yet deeper into the rock but no longer did I need to pursue my investigations for there, in an open stone tomb, lying as though she were asleep, in the full flush of her maiden's beauty, her eyes open and glazed, her ruby lips slightly parted to reveal two exquisitely pointed teeth, was the unnaturally living body of Elizabeth Morheim, *née* Sandor. As I beheld her form, there was the roaring as of some great wind in my ears, my eyes blurred, my limbs were weighed down as though by sleep, a curious numbness stole over me and I felt a sudden imperious longing to kiss those voluptuous lips which seemed to promise unimaginable bliss. Confronted by such a vision of radiant beauty, my soul was assailed by such longings and temptations as only Saint Antony himself must have known. I would have succumbed there and then had not the distant sound of horses' hooves and the wheels of a heavy coach over the flag-stones of the courtyard brought me back to my senses before my every faculty was completely paralysed. With a final desperate effort of my will, I shut my eyes, moved my head away from the tomb, brought out my implements and then, uttering a prayer as I did so, placed the stake against her bosom and struck it with one mighty blow of my mallet. There was a terrible screech, a last convulsive writhing of her body, a foaming and a sudden jet of blood and then merciful silence as my keen knife sheared through her white throat and severed the head. But there was more to be done before night fell. I had to find another tomb and that without a moment's delay. After lighting my lantern, I hurriedly passed into an adjoining chamber, vacant but with certain footprints that seemed to lead straight to the wall. Some long minutes later, after I had frantically explored every inch of the wall, my efforts were rewarded and a concealed door swung open. There, in another vault, lay a monumental catafalque, its massive lid bearing carved armorial bearings and strange medieval inscriptions. My efforts to prise away the lid were unavailing. I dashed back to the castle to search for some tool with which to open the tomb and had found a heavy crowbar left by a workman when I heard a footfall resound through the gigantic hall. The sun had sunk below the mountain peaks and the castle was steeped in darkness as night and its powers held the earth in their thrall. Louder and louder became the footsteps. I raised my lantern high, and there, on the lower steps of the great staircase, there stood a tall and elderly man, clad from head to foot in black, his lean and aquiline features contorted with a terrible hatred as his eyes blazed at me from under massive white eyebrows. Thank Heaven for the crucifix I had brought with me! It may save

me yet. As the old man advanced towards me, I raised it instinctively rather than by any conscious volition of mine. With
a terrible hiss, the old man retreated a few steps. For several
long minutes—an eternity to my mind—we stood stock still,
contemplating the one the other. Neither of us spoke. No words
were needed to underline the fearsome malignancy in the old
man's features. At length, prompted by desperation and an
urge to bring matters to their inevitable climax, I began to
ascend the great stone steps while he retreated before me. With
a snarl, he raised his hand as though to ward off the crucifix.
As my eyes lit upon *the great ring he wore upon his right hand*,
a titanic suspicion seared my mind and then blazed into terrible
certainty. My vision blurred, my head swam, my mind reeled
and I stood as one turned to stone. There was another long
silence and then, following the direction of my horrorstruck
gaze, the old man spoke in a sepulchral voice tinged with unholy triumph:

"And now you know all, my friend."

Fighting to retain what little I retained of sanity, I backed
away. The old man descended another step as I lowered my
arm and in a hellish whisper, scarcely louder than the sighing
of the wind outside, spoke the terrible words:

"YOU ARE RIGHT, MY FRIEND. I *WAS* STEPHEN!"

*   *   *

They had begun to close in on me. I must finish quickly.
Two shots from my revolver have granted me another temporary respite. Let the world find this journal and rid mankind
of the monster. He must be destroyed. Only the Cross has
saved me but against his Szgany followers, it can do little.
They mean to kill me.

I have five bullets left. Good-bye Meg! At least I shall die
like a man. God bless you darling and protect you! He will be
merciful. Good-bye, my beloved darling!

His name—the name the lawyer in Bistritz would not reveal—DRACULA!

*   *   *

LETTER: MARGUERITE FULLER TO PROFESSOR JOHANNES
ARMINIUS

Dear Professor Arminius,
    *Thank you so much for your kind letter. No words can
express how happy I am at Andrew's safe deliverance. They*

say that it was a miracle that they found him at all in that storm. The delirium has at least abated although what effect the shattering experience he must have undergone may still have on his mind is to be seen. I can only pray for him. There seems to be some merciful blank in his memory. All he will say is that all is now well and that beyond reaching the Pass again, he remembers nothing. Again, I showed him that calm, reassuring letter I received from Elizabeth just after he left, begging us not to go to the castle since she and Stephen were leaving the country to travel abroad, Stephen having sold the castle in their best interests. So they were not there after all: who then is there save this old man? Andrew merely sighed gently after a brief moment of unease in which he seemed to be making a desperate effort to recall something. Whatever it may be, I think it better that it is erased from his mind. There was something there that caused poor Ernest's death and Andrew must have destroyed it—but at what a cost to himself. He is exhausted and must have peace and quiet. We return to England next week and shall call upon you on our way.

Affectionately and gratefully,

Marguerite

Several Years Later

LETTER FROM JOHANNES ARMINIUS OF BUDAPESTH UNIVERSITY
TO ABRAHAM VAN HELSING, M.D. OF AMSTERDAM
SEPTEMBER 16TH, 1890

Good friend,
  *of he of whom you wish to know, there is much I have to tell.
This news that the Dracula still exist, it comes to me like a
thunderclap. I have believed that this curse was no more. Alas
that it was not so! I send you many notes under another
cover ...*

Johannes Arminius

*   *   *

TELEGRAM FROM ABRAHAM VAN HELSING AT BISTRITZ, NOVEM-
BER 7TH, 1890 TO PROFESSOR JOHANNES ARMINIUS, BUDA-
PESTH UNIVERSITY

ALL IS WELL, WE HAVE DESTROYED HIM. HELSING.

By the Same Unknown Hand

So Van Helsing and his companions destroyed the Dracula that lay in that coffin and so they thought that the story had ended. I have read the last pages of Stoker's book again and again. Van Helsing spoke of the tombs in the chapel and of that great sarcophagus 'more lordly than all the rest' but of that other tomb, that 'monumental catafalque' in the hidden vault that Fuller found years previously, they knew nothing. How could they? But if they had found those diaries that were taken from Fuller as he lay unconsicous, the memory of what he had discovered blasted from his recollection for the rest of his life by the Count who refrained from slaying him lest his disappearance bring still others to the castle, then they would have known that another greater secret remained to be unveiled. That 'monumental catafalque'—it has haunted my thoughts constantly. Now that I have found Fuller's journal and with it, that of Elizabeth's, its whereabouts will soon be found, its secrets will become mine and at the same time I shall know the answer to that other riddle: *what happened to Stephen's own body?* When I shall have known that, shall I not have mastered the mysteries of the tomb and is it not my right that I do so? Fools that they were—did they not know that the line did not come to an end? *Did they never discover that Elizabeth Bathory had another descendant who came to England in the eighteenth century?* Miklos and Stephen only acquired the hideous immortality and murderous powers of the vampire. Where they failed, I shall succeed. The destiny of the House of Dracula has yet to be completely fulfilled. The honour is mine and if I fail—then I too shall reign as a lord in that kingdom of darkness. Did the poet not say that it is better to reign in Hell than serve in Heaven?

From the *Daily Post*, July 18th; 19—

Unconfirmed reports from Reuter's office in Bucharest state that an unidentified English traveller has been reported missing during a walking expedition in the Carpathian mountains near the Bukowina. Police enquiries in the neighbourhood have so far been unsuccessful. It is also reported that the gypsy population inhabiting the area has been subject to great agitation lately and that a number of superstitious rumours have been terrifying inhabitants of outlying mountain villages. The region is one of the most primitive in the Transylvania and a number of other mysterious disappearances have been mentioned there in past years.